Just One Kiss
(Very Irresistible Bachelors, Book 2)

LAYLA HAGEN

Dear Reader,
If you want to receive news about my upcoming books and sales, you can sign up for my newsletter HERE: http://laylahagen.com/mailing-list-sign-up/

Copyright © 2020 Layla Hagen
All rights reserved.

Chapter One
Ryker

"Congrats. I'm proud of you," I said. I clinked my glass of champagne to my sisters'. Tess and Skye just quit their jobs to focus on their business full-time. They'd been running an online lingerie shop for a few years, but now they were preparing to open a brick-and-mortar store. The official opening was in three weeks.

"Thanks, brother," Tess answered. I could see she was truly pleased with my praise. But it was the truth; I was damn proud of them both.

"I'm so glad we finally took the leap," Skye said, stretching on the couch that had just been delivered to the shop. Tess and I sat on the armrests.

"And because we're all about setting goals, let's hope we'll nab an investor soon," Tess added. Although they'd made a lot of money on their own, they could expand faster with an investor.

"You know I can help," I offered for the millionth time. I was director at a venture capital firm and knew many investors.

The fund I worked for couldn't invest directly—that would be a conflict of interest—but I could pull *some* strings.

Tess shook her head. "We already told you we don't want you to put your skin in the game for us. What if this doesn't work out? Your reputation on Wall Street will suffer."

I didn't care about my reputation when it came to my family. I just wanted to ease their way as much as possible. The business world was ruthless, and I was convinced the best way to succeed was to approach it the way we'd done everything else: by sticking together.

"Besides, you're already helping." Tess was batting her eyelashes. I knew something was up.

"What do you need me to do?"

"Don't phrase that so open-ended, because our list is a mile long," Skye warned. We'd already hung curtains before the couch was delivered.

"I know. I saw the list. There are still a million things to check off." That was the reason our family took turns coming to the store after work. They'd gotten the keys to this place two weeks ago, and we'd divided the weekdays among ourselves. Until the store opened, our brother, Cole, came Thursdays, I did Monday, and our cousin, Hunter, and his wife, Josie, stopped by on Wednesday. Mom and her husband came Tuesday and Friday.

Skye winked, sitting upright again. "Nah, you did enough for tonight. Thanks for helping us hang the curtains. Tess and I have to pack some new online orders."

"Is that why we drank only the small champagne bottle?" I pointed to the floor, where there was a large one next to a pile of boxes.

"Oh, no. We're keeping the large Dom Perignon for the actual opening, when the whole gang will be here," Tess said. "Minus Josie and Hunter."

"Why aren't they coming?" I asked.

"They might come. They're taking a trip and aren't sure if they'll come back in time. Those two are using every free moment to travel," Skye said with a grin.

Sometimes I still couldn't believe that our cousin was married to his best friend, but I didn't say it out loud. My sisters picked up on it anyway.

"Still haven't recovered from Hunter breaking out of the bachelor pack, huh?" Tess teased.

"Something like that," I admitted. Even though Hunter was our cousin, we considered him a brother. After our parents' divorce, Mom moved us all to New York, and Hunter had practically grown up with us. Josie had been a family friend for a long time, and she was one of my favorite people. I just never imagined she and Hunter would marry. I'd always thought Cole, Hunter, and I would be eternal bachelors. At least Cole was still in the same camp as me.

Skye clinked her empty glass against mine, grinning from ear to ear. "Fearing things might change for you too, *Flirt*?"

"Absolutely not."

Josie had been the one who'd nicknamed me back when we were teenagers. I was proud of my nickname and did it justice on a regular basis.

"I definitely detected a sliver of fear," Tess said on a chuckle.

Skye nodded, pointing a finger at me. "Yeah, look. He has that expression when his pupils widen and his eyebrows sort of go down."

"What about it?" I asked, confused.

"It's how you look when you're semi-afraid," Skye informed me. I groaned.

"I don't *get* afraid. It's one of the reasons I'm in venture capitalism." I loved the fast pace, the risk, the unpredictable nature of the market even after analyzing all performance indicators.

"Ha! I definitely remember a few incidents that contradict that statement," Tess said.

Skye snapped her fingers, as if she'd just remembered something vital. "Like that one time you partied so hard before Christmas that you didn't think you'd make it to family dinner. I believe the words 'save my ass' were said in a pleading tone."

I groaned, rising from the couch and placing my glass on the large box we were using as a makeshift counter. Since they were a few years older than me, they remembered stuff I didn't... and didn't let me forget things I'd rather overlook.

"Girls, if you don't need me, I'll get going."

"Wait! Let's not forget the daily selfie," Tess asked. "Let's move further away, so the couch is in our backdrop."

"Why are you taking these?" I inquired.

"So we can keep track of our progress. Helps

when we think we'll never get through the to-do list."

"Hey, this is the last time we come here in our office clothes," Skye said. "It's going to be sweatpants-palooza in here until we actually open up for customers and need to look professional again."

"Come on. Squeeze in for a Winchester selfie," Tess said. I laughed as the two of them stood at my sides. I held the phone so the three of us and the couch were in the same frame. Skye adjusted the lighting, mentioning something about how the fact that I had dark blond hair and theirs was light brown made it difficult to find a filter that fit us all.

Afterward, I picked up my guitar case, strapping it to my shoulder.

"Performing tonight?" Tess asked.

"No, just taking my new guitar to the bar."

"Have fun," Skye said.

I loved playing the guitar, and performing was the best way to unwind and put the day behind me. I hadn't scheduled anything for this evening because I didn't know how long I'd be here. I walked out of the store, looking around and taking in the surroundings through the lens of an analyst: the location was excellent. It had decent foot traffic and attracted both locals and tourists. My sisters had experience in the industry. They had a great shot at making this work. It was early March, so they'd missed out on Valentine's Day sales, which was huge in their industry, but if they managed to open by April, as planned, they could still make a killing with Easter sales.

I headed straight to the Northern Lights, the bar where I performed from time to time. It was crowded tonight. Happy hour had started a while ago, and a bunch of suits had come in right off Wall Street. When I was on stage, watching the crowd relaxed me. When I had to make my way through it, not so much.

"Rose, I have something for you," I called to the bartender on shift. She was also the manager. I placed the guitar on the counter.

"Oh, brought your new toy for safekeeping. Can I take a look at it?"

"Sure."

She opened the case, gasping. Yeah, I was proud of it too. Some people collected cars. I had a weakness for guitars. This one was a brand-new electric model. The sound was sleek, with a smooth undertone.

"Ryker Winchester, you're always full of surprises. Love how you always change things up. You've never brought an electric one before," she murmured. I liked challenging myself—it gave me something to look forward to.

"I'll play on it this week."

"Want to take the old one back?"

"No, leave it here too. I'll just switch things up from time to time."

"Want a beer?"

"Sure!"

She filled a pint glass with draft beer, sliding it

to me. Before I took the first sip, a raised voice reached me.

"For fuck's sake, you're not my wife. You're not even my girlfriend anymore, so none of that is my responsibility."

I looked around for the source. What douchebag spoke like that to anyone? I located him a few feet away, and the woman he was talking to. She had round eyes and dark brown hair. Damn, she was beautiful. Her shoulders were hunched, and her gaze darted to the nearby patrons apologetically.

I left my beer on the counter and marched toward them.

"Apologize to the lady," I said, voice calm and collected.

"What the fuck is your problem?" the guy asked.

"My problem is that you're a douchebag. Apologize to her."

Up close, she was even more beautiful—full lips, wide, green eyes. She opened her mouth to say something, but next thing I knew, Douchebag pushed me into the crowd behind us that was waiting to order a drink.

They moved out of my way but someone's shoulder brushed my cheek in the process. My elbow hit the pint, sending it flying over my brand-new guitar. Beer spilled all over it. Rose threw napkins at me, and I wiped the liquid off immediately, but I knew some of it had reached the electric circuits. *Fuck.*

I inspected the strings, but it was impossible to tell the extent of the damage. When I finally lifted my head, I realized Douchebag wasn't in his spot anymore.

"Gil threw him out," Rose explained. Gil was the security guy. I looked around, trying to locate the woman who'd been with him, but she was nowhere to be found. Damn. I really wanted to make sure she was alright.

"That thing still working?" Rose asked, pointing to the guitar. The surface was sticky from the beer.

"I don't know. I'll take it to my repair guy, see what he has to say."

"This sucks. Brand-new and all. Are you hurt?"

"I'm okay. Do you know them? The couple?"

"No."

"So they're not regulars?"

What I really wanted to ask was if *she* wasn't a regular, even though I already knew the answer. I would've remembered seeing her before if she was.

"No. I have a good memory. They haven't been here before. Want some ice for that cheek? You'll have a bruise tomorrow."

I groaned. She was right. I could feel the skin around it pulsing. "Ice sounds good. Thanks."

At thirty, I was already one of the youngest investment directors in the company, and my youth usually worked against me. I balanced it out with an all-encompassing knowledge of the market and an enviable track record. A bruised cheek would earn me no favors with the clients who trusted me to handle their million-dollar portfolios.

Grabbing the bucket Rose handed me and placing the damaged guitar back in the case, I headed to one of the couches in the corner. Even though I knew it was pointless, I looked around the bar again. She hadn't left with him, had she? It had sounded as if he was ditching her. *In public.* I detested men who had no sense of responsibility or respect.

I held ice to my cheek for the rest of the evening… and made plans to find this mystery woman I couldn't stop thinking about.

Chapter Two
Heather

"Mommy, it says on the box number thirty-eight?" My seven-year-old pointed her tiny finger to the numbers I'd scribbled on the box with silver marker.

"Yes."

"Does that mean we're done?"

I grinned. I'd told her that we'd stop after unpacking the thirty-eighth box, and she'd been paying attention.

"Yeah, we are."

Avery squealed. I lowered myself to my haunches, and she threw her arms around my neck. I couldn't explain it, but Avery simply *smelled* like love. My little girl was like my own personal sunshine. Blonde and blue-eyed, she looked like a little angel.

"Can we have a bubble bath now?" she asked.

"Sure, little bug."

Our apartment had two bedrooms and a tiny living room. It was in a converted refurbished warehouse. I loved the huge windows. They allowed in plenty of light on sunny days. We'd moved here a week ago, hence all the unpacked boxes. We opened six boxes every night, and we still had a pile in the kitchen, which was also my office. As a reporter, I worked from home a lot, only traveling to my office in Manhattan if I had a meeting.

We headed to the bathroom, and while the water level rose in the tub, we had fun pouring all the almost-empty shampoo and shower gels in it, and a package of glittery goo with a unicorn on it. I had no idea how easy it was to scrub off, but my girl needed some glitter in her life, and honestly, so did I.

After Gerald dropped the bomb on me, I took Avery shopping and explained that our apartment would be an all-girl zone. That led to us buying all manner of glittery items such as nail polish, bath salts, lip gloss, and bedsheets. Since it was March, we got everything at an end-of-winter sale. I loved our purchases just as much as Avery.

The second I turned off the faucet, Avery jumped inside, splashing water everywhere. Laughing, I slipped inside too.

"We have our own small pool," Avery exclaimed. We'd only had a shower at the old apartment. "Can we have a glitter bath every night?"

Ah, my girl had many talents. As much as I liked to say she was an angel, she could also be a little devil. She knew exactly when to ask for things, but I'd learned how to say no.

"Not every evening, but once in a while, we can do this."

She perked up, her eyes wide. "YES!" After a few beats of silence, she added, "Mommy, Gerald isn't coming back, is he?"

My heart sank. Did Avery miss him?

"No, baby. He's not."

"I like it when it's just the two of us, Mommy."

I barely resisted the urge to hug the living daylights out of her.

"I like it too, little bug. I like it too. It's just the two of us now, baby."

And I'd keep it that way.

After putting Avery to bed, I headed to the kitchen, microwaving popcorn and pouring myself a glass of wine. Dinner of champions. I sat at the round kitchen table, glancing around our new home.

Seven days ago, Gerald called, saying he needed to talk to me about something important. I was in the middle of coordinating movers and ordering furniture and hadn't stopped to think about what that might be. Honestly, I'd just been happy that he was finally going to be in New York for longer than a few days. He was a tour guide and led groups around the world.

Two days ago, we'd met at the Northern Lights and he'd told me that he wasn't moving in with us. That he'd met someone on one of his trips. I'd felt as if my brain had short-circuited and I'd forgotten how to breathe.

In retrospect, I should have known he wasn't going to stick around. He'd never warmed up to the idea of *the three of us,* but I'd been in love and I'd wanted to offer Avery stability, especially since she didn't even know her dad. We broke up shortly after

I found out I was pregnant. He signed away all rights, because he wasn't interested in being a parent. Fresh out of college, that had been a very difficult time for me, especially since my parents lived in Arizona. When Gerald had come along two years ago, I'd had stars in my eyes and fallen hook, line, and sinker for him. I'd jumped into the relationship with both feet. From now on, I'd do things differently.

My limbs felt a little lighter after I finished my glass of wine. It was the first break in two days. I hadn't had time to process anything, because I'd still had to coordinate the rest of the movers and take our things out of the boxes. Mostly, though, I just wanted to block that awful evening out of my brain. Now that I wasn't elbow-deep in boxes, I couldn't help rewinding the details. When security had showed up, I'd used the opportunity to dart out of the bar. I'd wanted to do that as soon as I realized Gerald had asked me there to break up. Everyone within earshot had looked at me with pity, and I'd just been so blindsided that I hadn't even known how to react. *What about Avery? The apartment?* I'd asked.
None of that is my responsibility.
I couldn't believe he was just brushing us off like that. I pressed a palm on my stomach to stop feeling the knot in it. I remembered the guy who'd stepped in. A complete stranger had cared enough to ask Gerald to apologize. The longer I rewound the scene in my mind, the antsier I became. Gerald had

pushed him. Crap! Was the guy okay? Why hadn't I thought about this before?

I googled the name of the bar and called them, clasping my phone tightly.

"Northern Lights. How can I help you?" a female voice asked.

"I was wondering... I was at your bar two evenings ago. My ex-boyfriend caused a ruckus. Security stepped in."

"I remember."

"A man tried to intervene. My ex pushed him. Do you know if he's okay?"

"Oh, that was Ryker. He performs here sometimes. He was okay. Nothing some ice couldn't solve. Beer spilled all over his guitar though."

Shit. That didn't sound like he was okay at all.

"I'm so sorry about that. The guitar still works?"

"It was electric, so I'm not sure. He took it to a repair shop."

Damn, I had to make it up to him. If the guitar needed replacement or repairs, I had to pay for it.

"When is he performing next?"

"Tomorrow. His set starts at eight."

"Thank you." I placed the phone back on the table, poured myself another glass of wine. I vaguely remembered the guy: dark blond hair, absolutely gorgeous blue eyes. Hmmm... maybe I was building him up in my mind, with a little creative help from Mr. Sauvignon Blanc here. Oh well, I'd find out

tomorrow.
I twirled the glass between my fingers, looking around with a smile. I was determined to focus on all the amazing things in my life: I had an adorable girl I loved to the moon and back, a great job, and a brand-new apartment.

Welcome to the new chapter in my life!

Chapter Three
Ryker

It was Thursday, and I couldn't wait to get on stage. The pressure on Wall Street was relentless. Having a way to let off steam was crucial, and for me, it was this. Performing for a crowd gave me the release I needed. And as an added bonus, it also gave me a chance to get out of a suit. I'd never been a fan of the financial district's uniform. I took my guitar, stepping on stage with the other guys I usually played with: a vocalist, Josh, and a drummer, Steve.

The second my fingers strummed over the cords, my muscles loosened, the strain leaving my body. All thoughts of Wall Street drifted to the back of my mind. The company was in hot water because one of the other investment directors had just been fired for screwing over a client to maximize his own bonus. Everyone was worried about the company's image. I was too, but I was also pissed that the client was now in financial trouble because of a greedy moron. As I'd predicted, the bruised cheek earned me glares from colleagues and clients alike.

Tension was high, but now it was just me and the guitar, the music. The crowd was thinner than usual tonight. I scanned the room, soaking in the energy of the place, of the patrons dancing to our beat. My gaze rested on a petite woman leaning against the bar.

Were my eyes playing tricks because I'd wanted to find her so badly, or was my mystery woman in the crowd? No, there she was: brown hair pulled back in a ponytail, smiling and drumming her fingers on the counter. I scanned those around her quickly. Douchebag wasn't anywhere in sight. Fuck, yes.

I loved being on stage, but I'd never wanted to leave it more than I wanted to now. I didn't want to lose her again. I kept my eyes trained on her, ready to follow her if she left.

When the set was over, I practically jumped off the stage, making a beeline for her. She didn't move. Instead, her smile widened.

"Mystery girl," I exclaimed when I reached her. Damn, she was even more beautiful than I remembered. I hadn't looked close enough before to notice her sexy curves. She was wearing a tight dress that teased enough of her cleavage to tempt me to look more, but I fought to maintain eye contact.

She laughed softly. "What?"

"I don't know your name."

"Heather."

"I'm Ryker."

"I know."

"Oh?"

"I asked the manager about you."

"Music to my ears."

"I feel guilty about that. Is it the one the beer spilled over?" She pointed to my guitar.

"No, that's in a repair shop."

"I'm sorry."

"Don't worry. My guy says he can fix it."

"Well, I feel guilty anyway."

"Not your fault. It's that douchebag's."

She lowered her gaze, shrinking into herself right before my eyes. I wasn't going to allow it.

"I'll pay for the repairs," she said.

"Thanks, but it's not necessary."

"I insist." She held her chin high, pressing her lips together.

"Not negotiating."

"Let me at least buy you a drink, then."

"A lady never pays." I tilted toward her. Her eyes widened in surprise. She smelled like flowers and cinnamon, and I barely refrained from inching even closer, invading her personal space.

"Even if she is indirectly responsible for your guitar being in the repair shop?"

"Even then."

She played with a strand of her hair, giving me a guarded smile. I wanted a real one.

"So how am I supposed to assuage my conscience, then?"

I leaned in, whispering conspiratorially, "We can work that out. *I* will buy *you* a drink."

"What's in it for you?" She tilted her head lightly to one side. Her hair drifted from her shoulder down to her back. One single strand got caught on the shell of her ear. My fingers itched to push it away, to touch her.

"We'll see."

She laughed, and I detected a light blush in her cheeks. I just couldn't keep myself from flirting with her. I wasn't *the Flirt* for nothing. She was beautiful and newly single. I only interrupted our eye contact to drop my gaze to her mouth. She licked her lips, exhaling sharply. I could feel her about to give in.

"You win," she whispered. I smiled triumphantly. Her voice bordered on disbelief, but that brilliant smile was a sure sign that she liked my balls-to-the-walls approach to... everything.

We climbed on barstools, looking at the cocktail list. The beauty of not being able to drive in Manhattan was that you didn't have to worry about drinking and driving.

I was close enough to smell that intoxicating mix of flowers and cinnamon again. Perfumes weren't something I usually noticed, but hers was messing with my senses. *She* was messing with my senses. Everything from her unassuming beauty to her showing up here to buy me a drink surprised me.

"What are we drinking?"

"You're trusting me to pick your drink?" I teased.

"You *do* know this place better than I do. Plus, I think you're trustworthy."

I laughed, shaking my head. "Half my family would disagree with you."

"And the other half?"

"Would probably tell you to wait until the end of the evening to decide if I'm trustworthy or not."

"Oh, crap. I'm in big trouble, huh?"

I wiggled my eyebrows.

"Huge."

She shook her head but didn't say anything.

We ended up ordering Mojitos—the Northern Lights made the best one in the city.

"So how large is your family?" Heather asked after a few drinks. The crowd in the bar thinned even more, but honestly, I was barely aware of what was going on around us. She was just too captivating.

"Two sisters, two brothers. Well, three. We have a cousin here too, but I consider him like a brother."

"I see. So three versus two, huh? And you don't think the balance would tip in your favor?"

"That should tell you something."

She whistled loudly. "I don't know, Ryker. I think this is more than I can handle."

"Oh, you're handling me just fine." I tapped my temple. "Ah, forgot to add Mom to the mix. She'd definitely be on the team warning you off."

"Ouch. So not even your folks think you're trustworthy?"

"Unfortunately not."

She held her drink up and we clinked glasses.

"Do you have another set tonight?" she asked.

"Yes, but later on."

"I like to hear you play. You're very talented."

"Thank you."

"How long have you been doing this?"

"All in all, about eight years, but I've taken breaks."

"That's a commitment."

I liked Heather. It was so easy to talk to her. I realized she probably thought I was some artist living on tips, and I couldn't rectify that right now. Working my occupation as a venture capitalist in the conversation would make me sound like a douchebag bragging about his job.

When her glass was empty, she looked at it regretfully. "I need to go."

"I disagree."

"Ryker...."

"You said you like to hear me play. I still have that one set coming up."

"I know, but it's late."

It was barely nine.

"What's your favorite song? I'll convince the guys to play it."

Her mouth formed an O. "Are you trying to trick me into staying?"

"Yes. I'd try to do it with food, but they only serve burgers around here, and they're nothing to brag about. Don't tell anyone I said that, or they'll kick me out of here."

"I'll keep your secret."

"So. Favorite song." I slid off my chair too, stepping right in front of her. I needed to win her over. No way was I ready for my time with her to end.

"I really can't. I'm sorry."

For the first time ever, I was tempted to ditch the guys, just to spend time with her, walk her home, whatever. But I couldn't let the guys down, and I had the feeling that Heather wouldn't want me to. This was New York City. Letting a stranger walk you home could be dangerous.

"How guilty do you feel?" I asked.

She frowned. "Huh?"

"Guilty enough to give me your phone number?"

Her frown melted, giving way to a smile. She rattled off her number, and I immediately typed it on my phone. The guys called me on the stage.

"When are you picking up your guitar from the repair shop?" she asked.

"On Monday at seven. Why?"

"I'll come with you. I'm paying for that."

"Not what we agreed on earlier."

She shrugged, smiling. "I was just pretending to agree. Thought you'd be more willing to play along after a drink."

"See you on Monday, then. I'll text you the name and address of the repair shop," I said, walking backward toward the stage. Laughing, I realized she was just as good at getting her way as I was. I still wasn't going to let her pay for it, but she'd just given me the perfect excuse to see her again.

Chapter Four
Heather

I swooned all the way home. On the train, I tipped a busker generously when she sang one of my favorites from Whitney Houston. It made me think about Ryker and wonder what they'd played after I left the bar. I hadn't built him up in my mind; quite the contrary. Some delicious details about him hadn't registered that first night, but there was no forgetting them now.

I hurried from the station to my building. Even though it was March, the wind was still cold and cutting, seeping into my flesh and bones. I had a thick jacket over my dress, but I wished I'd had on an extra layer of clothes. Brrr. If I could, I'd hibernate from November to April.

When I reached my apartment, Natasha, my neighbor, gave me the rundown of how the evening went before going back to her apartment. She was a friend from my spin class, and she was the one who'd told me this unit was free. A single woman who loved kids, she was the perfect resident babysitter for the occasions when I needed someone.

Avery was sleeping already, so I was on my own for the rest of the evening. Of course I couldn't stop thinking about Ryker. Just remembering the way his eyes had glinted when he'd asked for my number was enough to make me shiver—as if he was silently making me promises. *Sinful* promises. Nope. Won't go there. And I was supposed to see him on Monday? That just spelled danger... of the hot and sizzling variety.

Before going to bed, I riffled through my mail, and my heart nearly stopped when I discovered an envelope from my landlord. With shaky hands, I opened the letter.

Please don't let this be what I think. Please, please, please.

It was exactly what I'd feared. My landlord was asking for proof that I can afford the apartment on my own.

The rent contract had been in both mine and Gerald's name. I'd texted Gerald yesterday, asking him to hold off on contacting the landlord until I could find a solution. He'd done the exact opposite.

I crumpled the paper in my fist, before taking my anger out on it, ripping it into tiny, tiny little pieces. *That piece of shit.*

Finding a new place to live in the size I wanted would be difficult. Most landlords find it too risky to rent a large apartment to a single-income household. What if one gets fired?

As a reporter for a national newspaper, I made excellent money. The problem was that half of my income came in the form of a bonus paid at the end of the year, so the actual salary wasn't the least bit attractive for a landlord. The other problem was that the living costs in New York were ridiculous.

Tendrils of panic crawled up my throat at the prospect of apartment hunting all over again. Sighing, I dropped onto my couch.

This was a setback, all right, but I only needed a minute to regroup. Just one minute, and then I'd kick ass, as usual. I closed my eyes, leaning against the headrest. An image of Ryker popped in my mind.

No, sexy-as-hell guitar player. You can absolutely not hijack my thoughts. I need to focus.

Aha, that didn't help. Not one bit. That wicked smile, the dangerous allure surrounding him were just branded in my mind. Every time he'd leaned closer to me tonight, he'd looked as if he'd had every intention of kissing me.

A shiver ran through me. I pressed my thighs together, trying to gather my wits. I blinked my eyes open. Yup. Much better. I couldn't daydream about Ryker if I stared at my TV console. Clearing my throat, I grabbed my laptop. I could get us through this! I'd done it before, when the odds had been stacked against me: finding out I was pregnant had been a surprise, as had been Avery's father bailing on me... I'd gotten through that, and I would get us through this too. I wouldn't lie to myself though, I was daydreaming about a future where I wasn't one bonus away from financial disaster. At twenty-eight, I still wasn't quite there, but I knew I'd reach that point one day.

Opening my laptop, I sent an email to my

editor, Danielle, right away, pitching her ten ideas. I was assigned stories, but initiative was encouraged. I finished the email by explaining my situation and that I needed at least half the bonus paid now. *Her* bosses had promised they'd raise my base salary this year, make it less dependent on the bonus. They'd been dangling that carrot in front of my nose for a while.

I was still so wired up from the letter that I couldn't go to bed, couldn't wind down. What my landlord needed was the certainty that I could cover my rent.

Thoughts of what could happen wouldn't quit... the big one being, what if my boss said no?

Getting a second job seemed impossible, but so was sharing the apartment with someone else. I didn't want a stranger around my daughter. A second job would mean that I'd spend even less time with Avery.

Tears threatened my composure. Why couldn't things just work out easily, just this once? I dreamed about a more relaxed life... perhaps sharing that future with someone. But that was just wishful thinking. Right now, I had to find a solution to our predicament.

What if I managed to get a job later at night, after putting Avery to bed? And maybe I could pay Natasha to just stay in the apartment with her until I returned?

A bartending job, perhaps? The Northern Lights came to mind. I'd done that until three years ago, when I'd been promoted from junior to senior reporter. But I could do it again—a second contract would prove to any potential landlord that I had a safety net. I was grasping at straws, but I just had to exhaust every possibility.

Breathe in, breathe out, Heather. Maybe it wouldn't come to that. But I hadn't gotten to where I was by waiting. I liked to be one step ahead, make contingency plans. I grabbed the phone, intending to call the manager of the Northern Lights. I'd saved her number when I'd called to ask when Ryker was performing.

When I unlocked the screen, I discovered a message.

Ryker: I had a great time tonight. I can't wait to see you again.

A shiver ran through me, followed by a wave of heat. I held my breath, thumbs hovering above my screen. Was it wrong to indulge in a little flirting?

Heather: Who is this?

Ryker: Ouch. You have so many dates in one evening?

I grinned. I should just ask him to tell me the address of the repair shop, which was the reason I'd given him my number in the first place, but instead, I typed something else.

Heather: I didn't know that was a date.

Ryker: You're right. A date ends with a kiss. Dirty and deep, making you long for more.

Holy hell! I could practically feel his lips on mine. I was on fire. On freaking fire. My skin was sizzling, the tips of my breasts turned sensitive. The brush of my bra was torture. This was getting out of hand. I had no idea what to write back.

Next thing I knew, I had an incoming call from Ryker. I seriously considered *not* answering. Surely, the sound of his voice wasn't going to improve... anything. But it would be rude to ignore the call. Plus... I wanted to hear his voice. It was just a call.

The second I answered, I knew I was in deep trouble.

"Hi, Heather."

"Hello, possible stranger," I teased. I had no idea why I kept up the charade. Well, it was fun.

"You need a reminder about our evening. Let's see. You came to look for me under the pretense of making it up to me for the other night."

My jaw dropped. "It wasn't pretend. I absolutely meant it."

"You also used that excuse to invite me to a drink," he went on as if I hadn't interrupted.

"Again, not an excuse." I was grinning. By the tone of his voice, I was sure that so did he.

"So my good looks and talent didn't have anything to do with your invitation?"

Yes, they totally did, but I couldn't admit that and not talk myself into a corner. Of course I would have offered to pay repairs to anyone, but inviting them for a drink? When I didn't reply, he simply went on.

"We had drinks. Then you had to leave, and I tried to trick you into staying. I almost convinced you—"

"You didn't."

"Really?"

Eh... what could I say? He'd gotten an excellent read on me.

"You know, even though your interpretation of the events is a little imaginative, it does ring a bell, *Ryker*."

I was fully aware that I'd avoided answering every time he'd put me on the spot.

"Imaginative?" he asked.

"Very," I emphasized. "Are you still at the Northern Lights?"

I wondered if any woman in the audience had caught his eye... if he was leaving the bar alone. What on earth? It wasn't any of my business if he was with a woman. Except... I was really hoping he wasn't.

"Nah, I'm home already. Set was short, and I left right after. I have an early call tomorrow," he said.

"Oh. I assumed you slept in, since you work in the evenings."

"Guitar playing is just something I do for fun. My day job requires me to wake up early, unfortunately."

"What is your day job?"

"Venture capitalism."

"You work in finance?" Holy hell.

"Yep."

His leather jacket flashed in my memory. I'd

gotten an eyeful of his jeans too. They screamed nonconformity and all-around bad boy.

I whistled. "You had me all fooled. Thought you're an artist through and through. You sure rock that leather jacket and scruffy jeans."

His laughter was so unexpected that I couldn't help but laugh with him. "I assure you I rock a suit just as well."

Come to think of it, I had no idea what he'd been wearing that first night.

"Full of yourself, are you?"

"You can say that. I called to ask if you want to come to another set next week. I can lure you here with music, drinks, and a few other things I won't mention, or you'll call me imaginative again."

Something in the way he said those last two words made my skin sizzle. I couldn't go, though. It meant missing out on an evening with Avery again. I wanted to say yes but knew I shouldn't. I wanted to talk to the manager anyway about a job, but I could do that over the phone.

"Let's talk about that on Monday." Apparently, I couldn't bring myself to say no either.

"Music to my ears."

"And why is that?"

"Because I'm even better at... *being imaginative* in person."

Chapter Five
Heather

On Monday, I was a little giddy as I headed to the address Ryker had texted me. Did I have an actual reason to be happy? I did not. Was I determined to stay positive? Yes, I was.

My editor had told me the chances of my bonus being paid out early were slim, but if I brought in a great story and the response to it was enthusiastic, it was possible. The ten ideas I'd pitched weren't what they were looking for, so I was back to the drawing board.

Just in case I could not come up with a story idea to their liking, I checked into plan B. Unfortunately, the manager of the Northern Lights said they didn't need any additional personnel at this time. So although I could look for other waitress jobs, I'd decided my time was better used coming up with a good story.

I stepped out of the subway at the corner of 57th Street and Seventh Avenue. The second week of March was already much warmer than the first one. Somehow, through the exhaust and leftover garbage on the sidewalk the air smelled fresh, as if the city was preparing itself to go from gray to green any day now. My fellow New Yorkers seemed to share my opinion; I noticed a few more joggers than usual coming out of Central Park. I preferred the gym, where I was safe from the whims of the weather.

When I stepped inside the guitar shop, I told myself that my giddiness had nothing to do with the fact that I was seeing Ryker again. Except, my heartbeat intensified when I saw him at the far end of the room, talking to the green-haired guy behind the counter. My breath caught when our gazes locked. The intensity in his eyes made me burn.

He smiled at me, wiggling his eyebrows. Laughing, I made my way to them.

"How much are the repairs?" I asked.

"Zero," said Ryker.

I glanced at green-haired guy. "He already paid, didn't he?"

"He did."

Placing my hands on my hips, I shook my head at Ryker. "What am I going to do with you?"

"Give me shit?"

"I'll let you get on with that while I pack the guitar away. I'm Arlo, by the way."

Arlo disappeared behind a curtain, leaving me alone with Ryker.

"I came a few minutes earlier, thinking you might do this," I said.

"That's why I came even earlier." He grinned, and I took stock of his appearance. He must be coming straight from work. He was wearing a fancy black coat, and I could see the bottoms of his suit pants beneath.

"So, Rose said you asked if she has any openings at the bar," he said.

I nodded. "My landlord wants proof that I can afford the apartment on my own. My base salary is low and most of my money comes from a bonus. But I want my daughter to have her own room."

Oh… I hadn't told Ryker about Avery until now. I hadn't meant to keep it a secret… I'd just got so caught up in our flirting that I didn't get a chance to mention her.

"You have a kid?" Ryker asked.

I nodded, my stomach tightening in a knot. "A seven-year-old girl. Avery."

"And that asshole is her dad?"

"No. Her dad was an even bigger asshole. But Gerald was supposed to move in with us, and the lease was in both our names. Anyway… I asked him to hold off telling the new landlord he'd changed his mind, so I could have time to get my ducks in a row. Instead, he informed him right away."

"He had to know you'd have a huge problem on your hands. This is New York. It's hard finding apartments even in normal circumstances."

Ryker's eyes were feral.

"I know."

"Why don't we grab some burgers and you tell me more?" He flashed a smile that revealed sexy as hell dimples. Wow. I'd noticed them on Thursday too, but in the dim lighting of the bar they didn't make an impact. Now, under the neon flash, things were different.

"I only have forty minutes."

"I know a small bistro a few blocks away. They serve excellent burgers, and they're quick."

I was sold. What harm could forty minutes in a bistro do?

"Okay."

Arlo returned with the guitar, and after Ryker strapped it to his shoulder, we left the store.

"It's a ten-minute walk. We can grab a cab if you like," Ryker offered.

"No, it's fine. I want to stretch my legs a little."

We walked side by side, with him occasionally placing a hand on my lower back to steer me into a side street. Every time he touched me, my body temperature seemed to rise.

The bistro wasn't what I expected. I felt as if I'd walked into a tiny vacation cabin. Everything was wood paneled, and the seating area consisted of long tables with padded benches. They were so crowded that I couldn't find a single spot to sit.

The woman manning the counter seemed to be in her late seventies. She lit up when she saw us.

"Ryker, finally decided to share your secret eatery with others?"

He'd brought me to his secret place?

"No, Mary. Promised I won't bring Wall Street in here, and I'm sticking to it. Heather is...

special. We need to take good care of her, or I risk her not wanting to see my face again."

"Pretty face like yours? Tut-tut. I don't think so. Besides, those dimples are to die for, aren't they?" She directed the last question to me.

Ah, his dimples were a national treasure, clearly. Ryker looked at me as if expecting me to actually answer. Instead, I proceeded to order the house specialty: garden burger and chili fries. He ordered the same... and watched me even after Mary started preparing our food. I became hyperaware of every breath I took. When I couldn't stand the tension anymore, I glanced at him. He wasn't just watching me. He was studying me.

"What?" I whispered.

"You didn't contradict her."

"About what?"

"The dimples."

"It's rude to contradict someone older than you."

"Are you sure it's the only reason?"

I rolled my eyes but was giddy inside. I felt as if we were engaging in a foreplay of sorts.

To my astonishment, after we ordered, Ryker didn't lead me to one of the long, crammed tables. Instead, we went to the back, up a tiny spiral staircase I hadn't noticed before. My heartbeat intensified with every step, as if warning me that I was going to get more than I bargained for.

I sighed when we reached the upper floor. It was small and intimate. There were only a few other people here, and I knew I was absolutely in trouble.

"You call this a bistro?" I teased.

"Mary does. I'm just following her lead."

Uh-uh... as if. Ryker wasn't the type to follow anyone's lead but his own. There were small round tables set around the room.

We sat at the one near a fake fireplace at the back. Ryker put his guitar against the wall. When he took off his coat, I couldn't help but stare. He was wearing a navy suit and platinum cuff links—he was every bit a respectable venture capitalist. That half smile didn't quite fit; too charming, too seductive.

"And? What's the verdict?" he asked. "Like the scruffy look or the suit better?"

I blushed. "Can't decide."

"You need more occasions to decide? I can make that happen."

I laughed, just as our food was delivered. I bit into my burger right away. I didn't even know what to say.

"So, Mr. Venture Capitalist, care to tell me how you went into finance?" I asked.

"I've always been good with numbers, and I got an internship when I was a college freshman. They said I could have a bright future, so I threw everything I had at it. Worked part-time at the fund after the internship."

I had the feeling that was his motto in life. He worked with dedication, played the guitar with passion. I was certain that passion would carry on between the sheets too. I felt my face heat up at the mere thought.

"What's that?" he asked.

"Hmm?"

"That blush."

"Nothing."

He didn't believe me, I was sure of it.

"Did you ever think about doing something with your music professionally?"

"Honestly, no. Family finances were precarious. I wanted to contribute. I did odd jobs in high school too. We all did what we could. It was so weird, there were a few years when absolutely everyone in the family was just trying to make ends meet. And then we all sort of started to do well at once. Hunter and Cole suddenly hit it big in real estate, my sisters got great jobs right out of college...."

"What are they doing?"

"They've just left their jobs to focus on their own business, a lingerie store. They've been working twelve hours a day for years, juggling their online shop and jobs. Now they're also opening a physical store. I don't think their workload will decrease at all. I have a feeling they're going to have a tough time in the following months."

He frowned, clearly worried about his sisters. I had the sudden urge to reach out and comfort him.

"But tell me about your living issue."

"Well, I really don't want to move Avery somewhere else. It's our new home, you know? And she's already had to change schools once. She loves her room. We've just finished decorating, and I don't want her to feel disheartened if I just drag her somewhere else now."

"I'm sure she doesn't feel that," he said softly.

"I don't know, I just want to give her the best there is.... Anyway, I either need a second job or to convince my current employer to pay part of my bonus earlier, not all of it at the end of the year."

"What do you do?"

"I'm a reporter for the *New York Reports*. Pitched a few ideas I could work on along with my current articles, but none were of interest to them."

Ryker drummed his fingers over the counter, deep in thought. Even with a table between us, his sexual energy was inescapable. It wrapped around me, pulling me to him like a magnet.

"Would writing about the Pearman Fund make the cut?"

I blinked. Sitting up straighter. "That's the fund you work for?"

It had received a lot of bad press in industry journals as of late; maybe I could write something to help improve their image.

"Yes. The HR and marketing departments are trying to come up with ways to improve the company's reputation."

"I'd focus on the people, not the company per se. Letting the workers behind the numbers shine. Do you think I could interview some of the employees?" My brain was already spinning a story.

The more I thought of it, the clearer I saw the angle. This actually could work, and I'd enjoy piecing it together.

"I'll talk to my team—I think the timing is right, and it's something we really need now," he said.

"Why are you willing to do this?" Honestly, after my last two relationships I was feeling a little raw. I couldn't believe someone would want to help me.

"You scratch my back, I'll scratch yours?" He smiled, wiggling his eyebrows but then became more serious, saying, "You need a good article, and we need something positive written about us."

"It's not the only reason though, is it?"

"I was raised by a single mother. I know how much work it takes; how hard it is. Mom struggled a lot raising the four of us and Hunter, our cousin. I don't want that for you."

Oh my God. I couldn't believe he cared so much, when the man I'd spent two years with didn't give a damn that Avery and I would be evicted. Ryker seemed so sincere.

"Thank you," I said. I wished I could find the right words to tell him how much this meant to me.

"I'll talk to my team and let you know. And now, no more talking about stressful things. Tell me about Avery."

Of course I beamed, I couldn't help it—my baby and I were tight. "She's smart and likes to collect coloring books. She's just the best kid in the world."

Ryker watched me with a smile as I filled him in on my daughter's accomplishments. But his grin kept growing, and I had to stop and ask him, "What?"

"Nothing, you just... transform when you talk about her."

I blushed, shrugging. "I can go on forever."

"I don't mind."

Checking the time on my phone, I gasped. "Oh, no. I have to leave. I promised Avery we're going to watch a movie."

Ryker pushed back from the table. "I'll walk you out."

"Oh, no, no. You're not done eating."

He held my gaze, smiling shrewdly until I squirmed on my seat. I wasn't ready to spend even more time with him, and he saw right through me.

But my excuse was good—I'd already finished my food, but Ryker still had half a burger and almost all the fries. I rose from the table, smiling when Ryker did the same. Taking my coat, he held it for me. His fingers brushed my shoulders. Even through two layers of clothes, the touch made my whole body sizzle. I tried to pull myself together, but clearly that wasn't possible when I was so close to him. Everything about Ryker was just all-consuming: the way he looked at me, as if he was determined to see right through me; the way he leaned into me, as if he was just barely restraining himself from touching me. I wanted his touch just as much as I feared it.

"The burgers are excellent. Pity it's out of my way." I turned around and licked my lips when I realized we were only inches apart.

"I'll lure you back here," he said confidently.

"How?"

"Do you really want to know, or rather I surprise you?"

"Hmm... now that you mention it, I do like surprises."

"I'll keep that in mind. We'll see each other soon, Heather. One way or another."

I was caught up in his flirting game again. How had that happened? Thursday, I thought a little flirting couldn't do any damage, but now I was wondering if I hadn't started something I couldn't stop.

He smiled, winking at me before I left. My stomach flipped a few times. I pressed my palm against it, but all that accomplished was to make me aware of how erratic my pulse was. Yeah, I'd definitely started something I had no idea how to stop... or if I even wanted to.

Chapter Six
Ryker

I intended to talk to Owen, a fellow fund director, first thing the next morning, but he was out of the office until later in the day. At noon, I met with my siblings and my cousin Hunter for lunch.

We had "working" lunches once or twice a week. It was the perfect opportunity to catch up. All our offices were located in Manhattan. My brother Cole worked with my cousin, Hunter. They ran one of the most successful real estate development companies around.

A few years back, we'd started having work lunches because it was the only time we had to talk about our joint charity project, the Ballroom Galas.

The gala season ran from September to June, and we had events periodically. There wasn't a set number of galas—it depended on how many projects we were donating to and how much each event raised. The March ball was approaching fast.

We called these meetings family councils because the galas were a family affair, and we took great pride in it. Tess, Skye, and I were in charge of the organization, Cole and Hunter brought in the donors. I couldn't invite clients, because that would be a conflict of interest.

In the beginning, it had been a hell of a lot of work setting everything up, but now it ran like a well-oiled machine, which meant that our family councils were actually catching up time.

Cole and Hunter were already in the meeting room we always met in when I arrived, sitting on opposite sides of the rectangular glass table. I decided to sit next to my brother.

"Where is Josie?" I asked Hunter.

"She's got another meeting and couldn't make it."

"Ah, the perils of being a successful lawyer," I said.

My sisters came in just after me, dropping into chairs on either side of Hunter.

"The delivery app says our food will be here in fifteen minutes," Tess said. "In the meantime... who has news?"

"Or even just juicy gossip would do," Skye added. I considered mentioning Heather, then immediately decided not to. I wasn't ready for everyone to chime in with their opinions.

I schooled my features to appear neutral and shrugged. "Nothing on my front."

Skye pouted. "Come on. Tess and I could use some distraction."

My thoughts went to Heather again. Did she have family here? It didn't seem that was the case from the way she spoke.

"Why don't we focus on the upcoming gala?"

I said. It was just one week away.

"Because everything is ready. There's no open issue." Tess grinned. She was onto me.

Cole cocked a brow. "You keeping secrets, Ryker?"

Hunter grimaced. "Don't do that. Didn't work too well for me and Josie."

I had no clue why I thought my subject change would go unnoticed.

Skye was the only one who wasn't pouncing on me.

"You're definitely keeping secrets," she said after a few seconds, flashing me a shit-eating grin.

"Girls, why so mistrusting?" I grinned, looking between the two of them.

"I don't know... something in the way you're trying to shift focus from yourself. You usually do the opposite," Skye said.

Cole nodded. "She has a point."

Our food delivery arrived just then, and we all dug in. We had a mix of the best New York had to offer, at least from what was in a five-block radius: pizza with goat cheese, burgers with onion rings and jalapenos, as well as kale salad and sweet potato fries.

I was suspicious that no one pressed the issue while we ate, but when I rose from the table, about to leave, Tess asked, "See you on Monday?"

"Yes."

We had a no-secrets policy in the family, and this was the first time I wasn't honoring it. I had a hunch that was going to change the upcoming

Monday. I'd missed the last one because I went to the repair shop with Heather.

After lunch, I headed straight back to the fund. Cole called me on the way.

"Forgot to ask, want to go have drinks tonight? I can be your wingman," he said.

"Ha! Name one instance when you were my wingman. More like the other way round."

"Happy to prove you wrong tonight."

I grinned. We always gave each other shit about this. But I wasn't up to going out tonight. The thought of picking up a stranger held zero appeal.

"Nah, not in the mood," I replied.

Cole was silent for a beat. "Damn. I'm having a real déjà vu right now."

"To what?"

"Hunter refusing to go out and then breaking out of the bachelor pack."

I chuckled. "What are you, channeling our sisters right now?"

"I'm a quick learner. Putting two and two together."

"Cole... don't you have a real estate empire to run?"

"I can always find time to annoy you."

"Glad to know, but I've arrived at the fund, and I have no time to be annoyed right now."

"No problem. We'll pick up later."

"I'm sure we will."

Grinning, I disconnected the call before entering the fund building. I'd started as an intern and climbed the ladder ever since. I spent so much time here that it should feel like a second home by now, but I was still not used to the marble floors and granite counters of the reception area, nor the mahogany desks and leather chairs. It was all over-the-top, but our clients were heavy hitters. *They* needed to feel at ease.

In my free time, I was a guy with a guitar, singing for his own amusement. At work, things were different. As an analyst, I'd been one of the most sought-after on Wall Street, which was why I'd shot up the ranks to director before I'd even hit thirty. I brought in heavy-hitting clients, making the company money and earning exorbitant bonuses.

The receptionist told me Owen was back, so I headed straight to his office. He worked closely with the PR team, trying to put out the scandal.

I'd prepared a convincing pitch for Heather, because I wanted her to get this gig. I'd seen the way she'd shrunk into herself when she mentioned the rent issue, and fuck if I'd allow it.

A little voice at the back of my mind told me that Heather should be off-limits. She was a single mom, and I was the opposite of what she needed.

But ignoring that voice was far too easy.

When she'd said that she wanted to give her girl the best, I'd had a flashback to those difficult years after Dad had left, when Mom had worked herself to the bone until late into the night to make ends meet. I'd be damned if I'd let Heather go through that. I wouldn't allow it. No way. No how.

"Owen, do you have a few minutes?" I asked, stepping through the open door.

"Five until my next call. Shoot." He ran a hand over his bald head.

"I've been thinking about the scandal... ways to do some damage control in the press."

"I'm listening."

"How about an in-depth spread about the team? An article that highlights the human side of venture capitalism. Showing that we're not all just greedy bastards."

Owen leaned back in his chair. "That could work. You know anyone willing to do that? Everyone I've talked to just wants a scandalous angle."

"As a matter of fact, I do. I have a contact at the *New York Reports*."

He scoffed. "I was hoping for the *Times*. Or a freelancer with a huge platform."

"As you said... no one's willing to say anything nice about us right now. Beggars can't be choosers. I'll give you her number. She's a good friend."

Owen ran a hand over his bald head again. It was his thing when he was nervous. "A good *female* friend? I hope this isn't one of your hookups."

I straightened up, training my eyes on him.

"My personal life is none of your concern."

"Sure... except your personal life also had you walk in here with a bruised cheek."

"That was one time in eight years."

I leveled him with a stare. Owen and I had

some history. He'd always thought I wouldn't make it, that I didn't have what it took to survive on Wall Street. He'd taken it personally when I was made director, because I was so laid-back about everything. It was just my style, but Owen was among the crowd that thought if you didn't have a stick up your ass all the time, you didn't belong in the building. I never let anyone give me shit, and I wasn't about to start now.

Chapter Seven
Heather

"Who's got interviews for a kick-ass story? Who's going to absolutely nail it? That's right. I will."

I couldn't believe Ryker had moved so fast. We'd only spoken about the article on Monday, and three days later, I already had interviews scheduled.

I was dancing around in my bathroom while fixing my hair in a bun, admiring my classic suit in the mirror. I usually wore jeans and sweaters when I was on field assignments, gathering stories, and pajamas when I was at home, editing articles. I could write everywhere—on the subway, in cabs, in coffee shops, but I needed absolute silence for editing. Writing was more like a stream of consciousness, whereas editing was where I shaped the content into a coherent article. Truthfully, I tried to work from home as often as possible so I could spend time with Avery, who'd learned from an early age that when Momma had her headphones on, she needed quiet.

Typically, Avery would grab her coloring book and just sit next to me, drawing in silence.

Right now, Avery was at school though, so I'd pick her up after my appointment. Pity, I'd wanted to snuggle her a little, share my happiness. If this worked out, we wouldn't have to move. I'd spoken to my landlord this morning, letting him know there was a possibility for my bonus to be paid out early.

"Look, Heather, I'm willing to wait a few months for you to sort out the bonus situation and give me proof you can afford this if you can cover the rent in advance."

I bit my lip. "I can do it for two months."

I didn't want to dip into our emergency fund too much.

"Okay. We'll take it from there." I felt better knowing I didn't have to move us right away, but we weren't out of hot water yet. Sorting out my bonus would take some time. Big corporations moved slowly, but I was happy that at least for now, we didn't have to move.

I left the apartment with a huge grin on my face and was in an even more excellent mood when I reached the building that housed the Pearman Fund offices on floors twenty-seven, eight, and nine. It was a staple in the New York landscape. A behemoth of glass and steel, it towered even over the rest of the buildings surrounding it. The energy on Wall Street was markedly different than the rest of Manhattan. Suits walked everywhere, almost all with headphones on, engaged in continuous conversations.

When I walked through the double doors of the bank, I was so excited that I was practically bursting with energy. Not that my excitement was entirely due to the opportunity at hand... I also couldn't wait to see a certain sexy guitarist in a suit.

I admired the enormous entrance and waiting area with wrought iron chandeliers and white leather couches. The mix of traditional and modern was right on trend. The half a dozen receptionists talked on their headphones while typing even faster than I did—not to brag, but I could type over a hundred words per minute. Combined with the sound of heels clicking on the marble floors, the background noise was infernal.

To my astonishment, it wasn't Ryker who picked me up from the reception, but Owen, the man I'd spoken with on the phone three times already.

"Thank you for coming here on such short notice, Ms. Prescott. We appreciate it. You said that you need at least four or five interviews to pull quotes from, is that correct?" Owen said as we entered one of the nine elevators. He pressed the button to the twenty-seventh floor.

"Yes. The more, the better. That way I can interweave multiple personal stories into the article. I'd say if we can get ten or fifteen, that would be just great. A mix of men and women is also important."

His mouth quirked up. "Wouldn't want all the feminists on our ass for only hiring men, right?"

I disliked Owen instantly based on that comment alone. It sent shivers down my spine. Odd how on the phone calls this tone was not evident.

Disturbing as it was, I forced the corners of my mouth in a smile.

"This is Ryker's floor," Owen announced when the doors opened.

The tips of my fingers instantly tingled. It was as if my entire body was on alert just because Ryker was somewhere close. And when I heard the deep baritone of his voice, my breath caught.

Holy hell. If I reacted like this when he wasn't even in my line of vision, how was I going to fare in his presence?

I didn't have to wait too long to get my answer, because Ryker appeared at the end of the hallway the next second and walked right toward us.

Yum. Hot, hot damn. To be honest, until this very moment, I couldn't imagine Ryker working as a venture capitalist. But that crisp white shirt and the modern cut of his navy suit fit him perfectly. Everything from the way he walked to the way his colleagues greeted him spoke of self-confidence and power.

He stopped right in front of us.

"Heather, you made it. I've got a few colleagues who are more than happy to talk to you about their stories."

Wait, what? I wasn't going to interview *him*? I hadn't expected that.

"Perfect."

"Do you want to begin right away?" he asked.

Something was awry. Ryker lacked his usual charm. He was so serious. He seemed like a different person at work.

"Sure. Let's go," I said. Owen returned to the elevator without so much as a goodbye, which was fine with me. I was here to do a job, get paid, and get out.

I'd expected a change in Ryker's demeanor once Owen left, but he retained the serious manner. I didn't expect him to do anything inappropriate, obviously, but I didn't know what to make of this frostiness between us.

With a pang of disappointment, I wondered if finding out I was a single mom had put him off me romantically. Maybe it had nothing to do with the stuffy office and he just didn't want to get involved with someone with a child. *It's better that way*, I told myself. I didn't have anything to offer him anyway. I'd just gotten through a bad breakup that left me feeling empty and unsure if I wanted a relationship again. I was sure a man like Ryker wasn't interested in a ready-made family, so that was just fine.

Ryker led me through a labyrinth of corridors, and we stopped in a huge room with at least three dozen desks. Wow. If I thought the waiting area was deafening, it was nothing compared to this. Most were on the phone, and *everyone* was loud. The floor-to-ceiling window captured my attention. Up above the street, Manhattan looked different, like a snapshot of a science-fiction movie.

We stopped in front of the desk of a gorgeous brunette. Her curly hair was wild around her face, her dark eyes contoured with light blue eyeliner.

"Ruby, here is the reporter I told you about, Heather Prescott," Ryker said.

"Fantastic. You're just saving me from a boring lunch break, Heather."

"Do you want to do the interview here?" I asked.

"No, no, no. We have meeting rooms. Those are more private. Not gonna spill my secrets in front of everyone. They'll just have to wait and read about them along with the rest of the country."

Ryker grinned. "We can always eavesdrop."

Ruby narrowed her eyes. "You do that, Ryker, and I'll drop salt in your cocktails at the next company party. Accidentally, of course."

Judging by the friendly atmosphere, camaraderie wasn't frowned upon. And yet, Ryker still remained serious with me when Ruby led us to the meeting room. I was so used to him either joking or flirting that it completely threw me off-balance.

As Ryker walked beside me, I realized I had to stop being so aware of him, but it was impossible. The scent of his aftershave mixed with a cologne that smelled like cypress and leather. The result was knee-weakening sex appeal. How come I hadn't noticed it before? Probably because I'd always met him in the evening until now, when the scent dissipated.

I rearranged the strap of my shoulder bag, mentally chastising myself for my wayward thoughts. I couldn't react like this to a man I didn't know, and I shouldn't want to anyway.

When we stopped in the doorway of a small

meeting room, Ryker set his hand at the small of my back. I tried to ignore the jolt coursing through me and was ready to dismiss it as an involuntary touch, when he moved his fingers in small, deliberate circles. They set my skin on fire even through the two layers of clothes.

I tilted my head in Ryker's direction, cocking a brow. His mouth curled in a half smile. He dropped his gaze to my feet, and then raised it slowly. I felt as if he was undressing me and barely bit back the irrational impulse to check if I still had clothes on.

Sheesh, this man was a danger to my senses.

I couldn't get a good read on all the mixed messages he was sending... though my body didn't find anything mixed about them, it was just on fire. Added to the fact that I was still melting because he'd gotten me this opportunity in the first place, and he wasn't a danger just to my senses. He was just a danger all around.

"Here is where I leave you," he said. "If either of you needs anything, just let me know. Ruby, you know where my office is."

Ryker had his own office? I'd assumed he was an analyst, housed in a cube setup like everyone else.

After he left, Ruby pointed at the ten chairs around the table. "Where do you want to sit?"

We ended up sitting opposite each other, my trusty recorder between us.

After writing about the business world for years, I knew the lingo and had even done my homework on this department's activities before coming over, thinking that everyone would be more comfortable if I eased them in by first asking about the business before moving on to more personal questions. But I needn't have worried; all Ruby needed was just a little prompting, and then she couldn't stop talking.

She told me everything. First about what had driven her to take this job in the first place, why Wall Street, why this specific branch, why she would do this even without the bonuses. What the atmosphere was usually like at the office, about their work ethic.

This was going to be epic. Since I was recording everything, I was already mentally editing the article.

"You know, with all the changes in this in industry, I don't think anyone can do it if they don't have a passion for it," she said.

"I know what you mean," I told her. "It's the same in my business."

I was lucky to still have a job, what with the ever-changing landscape in the print world. I'd escaped all three layoff waves at the newspaper, and my boss had assured me more than once that I was a highly valued employee. I wasn't kidding myself, though. The way the news world evolved, I was certain that in a few years, I'd have to pivot and find another career. By then, though, Avery would be older, and I'd have time to breathe and actually consider my options. Maybe I could even venture into a similar industry, like publishing. I'd always been a bookworm... eh, truth be told, I'd always wanted to write a book. But that wasn't for another few years. Until then, I just had to make sure I didn't fall off the hamster wheel.

"Ruby, I think I've got a lot of intel from you."

"Oh, no. You're sure we can't keep on going for another hour? I love my job. But a break now and then doesn't hurt," she said with a wink. I laughed, shaking my head.

"I still have to talk to four other colleagues of yours." She'd given me a list. Ryker's name wasn't on it.

I'd decided not to dwell on that... or on Ryker in general.

By the third interview, I knew I had a winning article on my hands. Maybe it would even get me that entire bonus paid out earlier, but I didn't want to get ahead of myself. I was happy enough if I got half the bonus. Then I wouldn't have to leave my girl in someone else's care three nights a week.

During every interview, I managed to forget about Ryker, but during every break... oh boy, oh boy. He was everywhere. At the coffee machine. At the water cooler. How did he know exactly when I had a break? I felt his gaze on me everywhere I went.

I was exhausted by the time the day was over but so happy that I could jump up and down with joy. My instinct had been right. I had a winning article on my hands. I'd have to come back at least once for more interviews, but my priority right now was editing the material I had.

Ryker was nowhere to be seen as I left his floor. Had my instincts been right about him too? I was just trying to convince myself it was for the best when I stepped out of the building and noticed a certain sexy venture capitalist who doubled as guitarist twice a week waiting for me with a smile the size of Texas.

Chapter Eight
Heather

He was almost one block away, leaning against a lamppost, legs crossed at the ankles. Straightening up, he walked at the same pace with me, and we met at the next crossing. I had no idea how to act. Was I supposed to be mad at him? I wasn't even sure... but I found myself smiling. I'd gotten caught in his charms again without even realizing it. How was that even possible?

When he came close enough, I immediately identified the culprit: those dimples of his. I couldn't be mad at someone who had dimples this gorgeous when he smiled.

"Fancy seeing you here," I said. We'd stopped at a corner where we risked being trampled by passersby, a mix of Wall Streeters leaving work and tourists come to see the glittering glass buildings at sunset.

"I was waiting for you."

"I thought I'd get to interview you today too." My voice sounded mutinous.

"I sense I'm about to get my ass roasted."

I almost melted under the intensity in his eyes

but stayed put.

"You feel like you deserve it?"

"Utterly and completely."

I laughed. What was going on?

"Well, okay, then. Why did you act so... I don't know—not like you?"

"Owen wasn't happy that we know each other. I didn't want anyone giving you a hard time."

"That still doesn't explain why I didn't get to interview you."

Ryker cocked a brow, smiling sardonically, as if the answer was obvious. Well, it wasn't to me.

He stepped closer, bringing a hand to my cheek, pressing the back of his fingers against my jaw. The contact electrified me. For one brief second, it felt as if the traffic had stopped, the passersby vanished into thin air. I was only aware of his skin against mine, his warm breath on the tip of my nose.

"Because I didn't want to push our luck... I don't think I can be in the same room with you for longer than five minutes and not make it clear to everyone what my intentions are."

I was so overwhelmed by him that I didn't know what to do with myself. This close, the leather and cypress in his cologne permeated the air. They were much fainter than at lunch, but strong enough to ensnare my senses.

"Ryker...."

"I haven't handled this too well. Let me make it up to you with dinner."

"Ah... you did say you want to lure me back

to Mary's burgers. But I can't tonight."

"Can't or won't?" His eyes flashed, determined and demanding.

"Avery's chorus lessons finish at seven."

He flashed me a triumphant smile. "That still leaves half an hour."

"The train ride takes twenty minutes."

"I'll walk you to the station, then. I can give you insights about the fund. All unofficial, of course. But you reporters like that, don't you? Insider knowledge and all that."

"How come you're even done with work? There were still lots of people inside."

"The perks of being a director. Hours aren't as long, though when we have a deadline, I have to pull all-nighters occasionally. If you get past the initial years when you have to practically sleep at the office, things get better."

"That makes sense. Where do you live?" I asked as we walked side by side.

"Nearby," he said vaguely.

I grinned. "Let me guess. Penthouse overlooking Central Park?"

He laughed. "Nah. Bachelor pad on Duane."

"Thought you didn't like the noise of downtown."

"I dislike long commutes even more."

"Ah, that makes sense."

I was relieved we were walking. I was hoping that would help diffuse this tension between us, make me less aware of this constant thrum in my body when he was near me.

I took a deep breath when we crossed the street together with a million other pedestrians. The smell of spring was thick in the air. Unfortunately, that thrum hadn't lessened, not one bit. And when Ryker placed an arm around my shoulders as if it were the most natural thing in the world? That thrum turned to an inferno.

"What are you and Avery doing tonight?" he asked as we descended the steps to the station.

"Nothing special. Just painting our nails, ordering pizza."

I felt all warm and fuzzy just because he was asking about her. Ryker was different from anyone I'd met before. What would it feel like to be with him? No, no, no. I couldn't allow myself to even think about that. There was no more room for risks in my life right now.

I searched my brain for a way to change the subject.

"Oh, by the way... I got wind today that your last name is Winchester."

"It is."

"As in the Winchesters behind the Ballroom Galas?"

"Yes."

"Holy shit! That's amazing. Why didn't you say anything?"

"It didn't come up."

"Well, I think the whole thing is just genius. I'd love to go to one." Their galas raised a lot of money for charity. They ran several events every year, and one never knew just how many events would take place in a year—which made invitations even more coveted. The station was semi-empty. I groaned when I looked at the digital display. The train had a five-minute delay.

"I'll wait with you," Ryker said.

"You don't have to."

"And miss out on five more minutes with you? No chance. I'm staying." His voice was determined, final.

I shivered.

"And warm," he added, stepping closer. God, I shouldn't want him, shouldn't want this, but I did. His nearness, his touch… I wanted all of it. When he lifted his hand, I felt fire dancing on my nerve endings in anticipation. Where would he touch me? My waist, my shoulder? He surprised me by cupping my cheek. For a brief second, I thought he'd rest his thumb on my lips, but he pressed it gently on my jaw before he slid his hand to the back of my head. He brought me closer until his mouth was barely touching mine, kissed one corner softly… then captured my lips. His kiss was demanding and determined. A shudder ran through me. I was consumed by his passion—the way his fingers first pressed against my skin, then tugged at my hair. I needed to be closer to him, touch more of him. When I felt him pop open a button of my jacket, sliding his hand around my waist, my knees weakened. I didn't think I could feel that skin on skin contact and not make a fool of myself.

He slid his hand slowly around to my back, bunching the fabric of my sweater in his fist. I felt his fingers hover a fraction of an inch away from my skin. The anticipation was killing me. When he splayed his palm wide on my lower back, I moaned against his mouth.

Far from giving me any reprieve, Ryker intensified the kiss until I felt completely owned. That tiny skin-on-skin contact sent me spiraling. I had no idea how I could react like that.

I lost all sense of time and place... right until the sound of the train snapped me back to reality.

Ryker reacted first, taking his hand away and buttoning my coat again. When I attempted to pull away, he kept me in place, threading his fingers through my hair, resting his thumb just above the shell of my ear.

"No, just a minute. We have one more minute until the train arrives."

"Maximizing every minute, huh?" I teased.

"Every fucking one."

My knees buckled. After that kiss, I had a hunch that anything he'd say would spur such a reaction. I did step out of his arms, though, because the train was pulling in.

"Umm... not sure when I'll see you again," I said quickly.

"But I am."

"Oh, care to share with me?"

"Nah. When it comes to you, the element of

surprise is my best shot."

He watched me board the train. I didn't break eye contact as the doors closed, or even as we lurched forward. I kept eye contact right until he was out of sight.

Only in this case, out of sight wasn't out of mind. Quite the contrary. The second he wasn't in my field of vision anymore, giggles bubbled out of me, and I didn't even try to rein them in despite all the curious looks I got. It wasn't every day that I got so thoroughly kissed. Why make apologies for it?

Chapter Nine
Ryker

My mind was so full of Heather that I couldn't even think straight or focus enough to decide what I wanted to do next. I could still taste her, feel the light tremor in her body, the way she'd opened up, tugging at my hair and demanding more. I'd been on the brink of obliging her. I'd almost forgotten we were in a train station. I never lost my head—not when I was making million-dollar bids, not even when I was playing my guitar at the Northern Lights. I was always in control—of the situation, of myself. I hadn't been in control with Heather, not by a long shot. I'd been driven by an impulse that was completely new to me—to be closer to her in every way possible. I'd needed to touch her more than I'd ever needed anything else. I still needed to.

Turning around, I searched for the schedule of trains, then zeroed in on the one I was interested in. It was arriving in twelve minutes. I could jump on it and catch up with Heather. She'd told me the station where she was getting off.

No, wait. She'd gone to pick up Avery. I couldn't go after her. What was I thinking? I wasn't... not really. I was *still* acting on impulse.

Just to be on the safe side, I rushed out of the station before I gave in to the temptation to take the next train. I couldn't just barge in on Heather's life.

I needed a better plan.

I needed my sisters. Instead of heading to my apartment, I headed to Soho, to their shop. I didn't need to call them to know they'd be there.

Tess and Skye weren't in the front when I arrived, but the light was on.

Stepping inside, I asked, "Anyone here?"

"Yes. We're in the changing rooms," Skye called.

I strode to the back and found the girls propping a ladder in the first changing room. Several things had been delivered since I'd last been here, including the curtains of the changing room and the rods, and boxes of shelves and lamps.

"To what do we owe this surprise?" Skye asked.

I clutched at my heart theatrically. "Surprise? You wound me. I'm your trusty handyman around here."

Tess pointed a finger at me. "Yeah, but today is not your day. It's Cole's."

"Why isn't he here?"

"Oh, he had some stuff to do. So... what gives?"

"Can't believe this. I'm getting shit for trying to be a good brother."

I shouldn't push my luck too much, because

once they caught on that I wasn't here *only* to help, they'd give me hell.

Tess sighed, dropping her chin to her chest. "I'm sorry. We've just got screwed over today with a delivery, so I'm extra jumpy. Forgive me?"

She rose on her toes, giving me a kiss on the cheek. Skye followed suit. Oh, hell... now I was feeling guilty.

"Who screwed you over?" I asked.

"We paid for one thing and received another," Skye said. "They delivered it when I was here alone, and I think they thought I'd just accept it, because they only talked to Tess before. But I roasted their ass."

I bit back a smile. Next to Tess, she always seemed quieter, even shy. But if you pissed her off, you were in for a scare.

"Can I help with anything?" I asked.

Tess smiled like a Cheshire cat. "The answer to that will always be yes."

"We're hanging some lamps in the changing rooms." She pointed to the ceilings.

"Say no more, I'm your guy."

"You need us? Otherwise we're out to sort the merchandise from the new collection," Skye said.

"I'm good. You go do your thing."

Some lamps turned out to be twenty-five spotlights. My arms felt as if they were about to fall off by the time I was done. The changing rooms were enormous. Some even had a black velvet chair inside. I could imagine myself sitting there while

Heather tried on lingerie in front of me. I pressed the heels of my palms against my eyes. It didn't help. If anything, the vision became more vibrant. I just couldn't stop thinking about Heather, could I?

I headed straight to the front, where Tess and Skye stood behind the counter Cole and I had assembled two nights before. The girls were elbow-deep in boxes.

"Girls, do you have any printed invitations left for the March Gala?"

"Yeah, we always have a few spares," Tess said without looking up.

"I need one. Actually, two."

"Just tell us the names and I'll send them tomorrow," Skye murmured.

"They're new guests. Just add plus two to my name."

Skye looked up. "Okay. We still need the names though. For the seating chart."

"They'll sit with us."

Skye's jaw went slack. Tess looked up too, eyes wide.

"Wait a second... you're inviting someone new... and they'll sit with us. We do need to vet them first, though. It's protocol," Tess said.

"I've already vetted her." Big mistake. I tried to correct myself. "Them. I've vetted them."

My sisters' expressions turned from shocked to smug in a fraction of a second.

Tess propped her chin in her palm, studying me before turning to Skye.

"So… what do you think? A couple?" she asked.

"No way. He looks like his tongue is stuck to the roof of his mouth."

"A lady friend who's coming with another friend?"

Jesus, they weren't going to give this a rest.

"A lady friend. And she's bringing her daughter," I said finally. My sisters turned their attention to me at once.

"We're going to need more info," Tess said slowly. I shook my head.

Skye straightened up. "Ryker… we have a no-secrets policy in our family." To be honest, usually I stood by the no-secrets policy. It had been in place ever since Dad left. We had zero dollars for therapy, but Tess decided that we all needed to talk among ourselves at least. For now though, I wasn't sharing anything.

"Besides, we're going to meet them anyway," Tess pointed out. "But I'm putting two and two together. One… you're keeping secrets. Two, you asked for *invitations*, which means you want to impress said lady friend. Am I right?""

"Yes. Give me the invitations, please."

"I'm on it, I'm on it," Skye said. "I have some in the back." She disappeared through the door to the back room. "Aha, you're lucky," she exclaimed a few seconds later, running toward me with two golden envelopes. "These are the only two I have here." She was clutching them to her chest. "I can write the names for you. I have the most calligraphic writing out of all of us."

"Nice try, Skye."

She handed the envelopes over with a pout.

Tess narrowed her eyes. "I can't believe you made us feel guilty for suspecting you have a hidden agenda."

Ah, I was surprised she'd waited so long to play that card.

"Want to have dinner together?" Skye asked.

"Already ate," I said. I'd grabbed a snack before I met up with Heather.

"Second dinner. Or just cake," Skye said.

"Girls, I have a call early tomorrow. I can't stay."

"You're ditching us? Especially after the shitty day we've had?" Skye pouted, leaning into me. I laughed, putting an arm over her shoulders, kissing her temple.

"I'm not ditching you," I assured them. "Just need to be rested for tomorrow."

Skye sighed, stepping away from my half hug. I was grinning as I slid the envelopes in my pocket. After bidding them goodbye, I headed out on the streets with renewed energy. I didn't want our next meeting to be at the fund.

I wanted Heather in *my* domain this time.

Chapter Ten
Heather

I spent the next morning editing the interviews, weaving them into a storyline. I wasn't in the mood to work from home, so after dropping off Avery at school I headed to the coffee shop across the street. It was a great way to escape the solitude of my apartment without going through the hassle of taking the train into Manhattan.

I was pumped about the article, and not just because I'd had three lattes before eleven o'clock. This was going to be epic; I felt it in my gut. I had enough experience as a reporter to know when a story was ho-hum or a home run. Ruby, in particular, had some excellent quotes. I still regretted not interviewing Ryker. He was insightful, saw things in a different light than most. I hadn't met anyone who stood by his family the way he did, who'd made some of the biggest choices in his life by considering others too, not just himself.

I set my laptop on the small coffee table in front of me, and curling in the armchair like a cat, looked out the window. I wasn't really watching anything, though. My mind was too full of Ryker. His smile, that intensity rolling off him in waves, wrapping tight around me. Just remembering the way he'd kissed me made my lips burn. Grinning, I went to the counter, buying my fourth latte—this one was decaf.

I just needed a treat to go with my Ryker daydreaming. Yeah, I'd made the executive decision that I wasn't going to fight thoughts of him. It couldn't hurt to indulge in a little mental daydream, could it?

Oh, yeah. My decaf nonfat latte really was the perfect choice to indulge in a little Ryker break. I held the cup tight, glancing out the window with a huge grin. I loved coming to this coffee shop. It overlooked a small park that was splendid year-round. In winter it looked like a scene straight out of a fairy tale, with the trees covered in a thin coat of snow or ice. The rest of the year it was either vibrant green or a mix of yellow, red, and brown in fall.

Right now, it was in the transitioning phase. I only spotted a few patches of green. The clear blue sky was a pretty sight, as were the New Yorkers milling under it. The rhythm here was a little more relaxed than in Manhattan.

I felt like I could breathe better out here. Over the years, I'd thought about moving away from New York to a city with lower living costs. But newspaper jobs were concentrated in the big hubs anyway, and I loved New York to bits.

After downing the last drop of latte, it was time to get back to typing. I wasn't working only on the Pearman Fund article. I had several others in various stages of editing. Five minutes into rereading what I'd previously written on a global warming article, I caught myself rewinding yesterday's kiss in my mind's eye again.

Heather, get yourself together. The Ryker break is over.

Ah, but there was the problem with allowing myself to indulge. Daydreams worked on their own schedule. I just couldn't shake Ryker off. At least I wasn't going to see him soon, which meant that in a few days, the aftereffects of the kiss would subside. I was still under his spell, that was all.

I hoped.

Shaking my head, I turned the volume on my headphones higher, focusing on my keyboard.

As the afternoon rolled in, I briefly considered buying another latte in one of my breaks, but eh... no. I seemed to be associating the taste with Ryker today.

I bought a boring soda. There, that couldn't lead to any daydreaming.

Nope, wrong again. Ryker was front and center in my mind. I caught myself smiling again. It couldn't be wrong, right? Right? I'd had so few reasons to smile over the past two weeks, and they were all tied to Ryker.

After the soda break, I went on a writing sprint. I'd intended for it to last forty minutes only, but I hit such a great stride that I went on for an hour and a half.

I was just about to gather my things and pick

up Avery when my phone rang. Ryker was calling. My palms became sweaty. My fingers and hands became jittery again, just like after the kiss yesterday.

Holy shit! Apparently, I didn't need to see him in person. Just his name on the screen of my phone made my stomach knot. Squaring my shoulders, I took a deep breath, focusing on the point just above my belly the way I did in Pilates classes. This technique had proved useful in many tough moments.

"Hi," I greeted, still focusing on my breathing.

"Hi, Heather. Is this a good time?"

"Yes."

"Good. I need to talk to you."

"What can I do for you?"

"Say yes to what I'm about to ask."

I'd thought I was on edge before? Ha! I'd been wrong. That was nothing compared to the tension spreading through me like a vise. My pulse ratcheted up. I heard the rhythmic thumping in my ears, felt it against my rib cage. My trusty breathing technique had gotten me through intense conversations with my editor and difficult interviews.

But it was no match for Ryker.

"That would depend on what you're asking."

"You know the March Ballroom Gala is coming up next week."

"Of course. The entire city knows about it."

"I want you and Avery to come."

Wow. I sank lower in the armchair, pressing my palm above that pesky spot on my stomach. It wasn't tight now anymore... just full of butterflies, which was *not* helping.

"Aren't the invitations for donors only?"

"They're for whoever we want there, Heather. And I want you and Avery there."

"I thought the invitations were sent out months ago."

I was buying time. I just didn't know what to say.

I had to say no.

I wanted to say yes.

Avery would love it. Crap, I couldn't use that as an excuse... but I almost did. I'd only known this man for two weeks, and yet, I wanted to be around him every chance I got.

"You told me you'd love to come to one."

"I don't know anyone in the city who wouldn't."

"So why aren't you saying yes?"

I licked my lips. "I'll think about it."

"You'll love it."

"How can you be so sure I'll come?"

"It's still one week away. Plenty of time for me to win you over. And I intend to do just that." Had his purpose been to make me blush and grin at the same time? Because he'd succeeded with flying colors. I'd almost asked how exactly he intended to do that but caught myself in time. I didn't need to know everything. In fact, it was better if I didn't.

***

Avery and I spent that evening pampering ourselves. I loved these quiet evenings at home with her, where we got to dream and just be girly. I'd brought out the nail polish and was currently painting her nails. Next, I did mine, even applying a coat of glitter (having a kid gave me a perfect excuse to let my inner four-year-old come out and play).

Once we were done, we both danced around the house, waving our nails in an exaggerated manner for the polish to dry (I'd learned the hard way that even with a coat of "quick-dry" you were never safe for at least fifteen minutes).

We blasted music through the living room, being silly and just forgetting about the world, right until the doorbell rang. I stilled. Avery frowned as I turned down the volume. Had it been too loud?

"Is someone coming to visit?" she asked.

"No."

I just hoped it wasn't the landlord, coming to tell me that he'd changed his mind and two months of prepaid rent wasn't enough.

"Why don't you go to your room while I see who it is?"

"Okay, Mommy."

In case it was the landlord, I didn't want Avery to hear us. I hadn't told her that we might have to move. We'd painted the walls in her room by ourselves, bought the furniture together. It was the first real home we'd both had. I *wouldn't* lose it.

I gave myself a mental pep talk, trying to

decide on the best course of action in the seconds it took me to reach the door.

It wasn't my landlord. It was a delivery guy holding an envelope.

"Ms. Heather Prescott?"

"Yes."

"I have a delivery for you."

"What is it?"

He cocked a brow. "I don't know. I'm just delivering. Sign here, please."

I signed the sheet of paper he held in front of me.

After he left, I closed the door, leaning against it and inspecting the envelope. It didn't say who the sender was. Everything I'd received from my landlord before had had his contact information scribbled on it.

Come on, Heather. You're not a chicken. Just open it.

I opened the envelope and found two smaller ones inside. They were golden, and I could swear they smelled like lavender. One had my name on it, one Avery's. What on earth? I opened the one addressed to me.

Dear Ms. Heather Prescott,

You are hereby cordially invited to the first spring ball. We are celebrating in style on Friday at the March Ballroom Gala. The party starts at 6:00 pm. We hope you will join us and look forward to your RSVP.

Yours,

The Winchester & Caldwell Families

I reread the invitation about five times before it sank in. Below was an RSVP card with the date of the event on it. Oh, Ryker. I couldn't believe he'd actually done this. I didn't even know they sent out printed invitations. I held it closer to my nose, sniffing. It smelled like lavender. He probably knew my address from the fund's HR. I'd had to tell them my information.

"Mommy, can I come out?" Avery called.

"Yes, yes, of course."

"Who was it?"

"The postman. He brought us something. Here, this is for you."

She snatched the golden envelope I handed her. Her little mouth formed an adorable O when she read her name. I never saw her handle anything with more care than this envelope. She opened it slowly, retrieving the invitation even slower.

"It says here Miss Avery Prescott. I am a miss? Wow."

I went behind her, reading over her shoulder.

Dear Miss Avery Prescott...

Oh, Ryker. He certainly knew how to play his cards. Our names were handwritten. Had he done this himself?

I could read it out loud to her, but since she'd started reading, she loved doing it by herself. It took a while longer, but I loved watching her. I could practically *feel* her light up. The Ballroom Galas were so legendary that even Avery knew about them.

When she turned around, she was smiling from ear to ear. I melted on the spot. I hadn't seen her this happy in a while.

"Mommy," she whispered. "I don't understand. It says here it is for me."

"It is."

"But kids at my school say only important people go."

"I guess you're important, lovebug."

"Can I go without you?"

What?

I waved my own invitation in front of her. "I've got one too."

"So, you're important too?"

I burst out laughing. She looked almost disappointed that she wasn't the only important one here.

"Yes, lovebug."

"And we're going?"

"I have to check my calendar."

I read over the note again, trying to buy myself time. But Avery was watching me with wide, expectant eyes. Then she wrapped her arms around me.

"Please, please, Mommy. I promise I'll be good for a whole month. Go to bed early, not steal cookies."

"You've been stealing cookies?" I feigned surprise.

She winced. "Sometimes. Please don't be

mad."

"I'm not mad. But you have to be careful. They're not good for your teeth."

"Mommy! Please say yes."

I was so torn. I wanted to make Avery happy. I wanted to make Ryker happy too… even though I had a hunch that involved far more than agreeing to the gala. But whatever reservations I still harbored, I just didn't have it in myself to wipe Avery's smile away. Which left me with only one outcome.

"Yes, we're going."

"Yeeeees! Thank you, Mommy."

Avery jumped in my arms, lacing her small arms around her neck in one of those hugs I loved so much.

"Can I stay up late tonight?"

I laughed. Typical Avery. She'd gotten her way with one thing, and automatically pushed the next item on her agenda.

"No, honey. You still have to wake up early tomorrow."

Avery pouted but didn't insist. I was dying to try on a dress I thought would fit, but first had to put Avery to bed.

I shot Ryker a quick message.

Heather: Just received the invitations. Avery is psyched. And so am I.

The next second, the screen lit up with Ryker's name. I debated answering, but instead rejected the call, typing yet another message.

Heather: I'll call you after I put Avery to

bed, okay? About half an hour.

Ryker's reply came almost immediately.

Ryker: Non-PG 13 call? I like the sound of it.

I blushed violently. I finished Avery's routine with ten minutes to spare, took the invitations, and darted to my bedroom. It was small—since I was single, I'd left the bigger bedroom to Avery, and even that wasn't too much space. I'd pushed a small double bed against the wall and had a tiny nightstand next to it. My dresser was just at the foot of the bed.

Instead of calling Ryker right away, I took a dress out of my closet. It had a black lace corset and golden organza skirt that flowed to the floor. I'd worn it at a newspaper event at the Plaza but hadn't had another occasion worthy of this beauty since. I slipped it on, admiring myself in the mirror.

Even my messy hair looked as if it was messy on purpose. Of course, it helped that the room was semidark, hiding any imperfection, giving me a mysterious air. For a brief second, I forgot all my troubles. I wasn't a reporter chasing her bonus or a single mom. I was a woman.

My blood thrummed when Ryker called. Thirty minutes on the dot, as if he didn't want to give me a chance to change my mind.

I picked up the phone, returning in front of the mirror, admiring the dress some more.

"Heather," Ryker greeted in a low, gravelly voice. If I closed my eyes, I could almost imagine he was in the same room with me.

"Hi! I was just about to call you."

"So...."

"You made good on that promise to win me over," I said.

"I did well, didn't I?"

"Yes. She was so happy, feeling like a lady."

"I'm glad to hear it."

"You did it on purpose, didn't you?"

"I'm not going to answer that. So is that a yes?"

"Well, I'm trying on a dress right now, so I guess you have your answer."

"Describe it to me." His voice sounded even more gravelly than before. Dangerous, somehow. I licked my lips.

My voice trembled lightly as I spoke next. "It has a tight corset out of black lace. The skirt is organza."

He said nothing.

"Are you having trouble picturing it?"

"Yes. All I come up with is you wearing absolutely nothing."

Holy shit! A flash of heat lit up my body. I gripped the edge of the mirror with my free hand, leaned my forehead against the cool surface. It was no use.

"Goodnight, Ryker. I'll see you at the gala," I said. "I can't wait."

My breath was still shaky when I hung up. The tips of my breasts turned hard, brushing against the fabric of the bodice. The contact of the dress on my outer thighs made my skin turn to goose bumps, as if Ryker was here, touching me. I wouldn't be able to wear this dress and not remember this exact moment, when he'd made my entire body feel like a live wire.

Chapter Eleven
Heather

On the day of the ball, I received a message from one of Ryker's sisters, Tess, asking me if I wanted to come earlier. I jumped at the opportunity. I was curious to see the famous ballroom, and I knew Avery would enjoy it too.

It was even more magnificent live than in pictures. The second I entered it, I felt as if I'd stepped into another century. Crystal chandeliers and balconies with wrought iron railings surrounded me. I spotted tables on the balconies. In the center was a dance floor with a small stage at the end of the room. There was a bouquet of buttercup winter hazel on every table. I loved that they used seasonal flowers.

"Mommy, are we in a castle?" Avery whispered.

"Something like that."

Two women walked towards us. I could tell they were Ryker's sisters. Something about them instantly reminded me of him. One had dark brown hair, the other light brown—interspersed with highlights. They were both wearing gorgeous evening gowns. I had yet to change into mine. I was carrying it in a plastic cover over my shoulder. Avery was already wearing her dress—she'd asked to change at her school.

"You must be Heather. And this is Avery?" said the one with light brown hair and highlights.

"Yes," I answered.

"I'm Tess," she said.

"And I'm Skye," the other introduced herself. "We have about half an hour before guests will start arriving. Avery, want me to show you the kids' corner?"

She pointed over her shoulder to a corner I hadn't paid attention to, opposite the stage. There was a small slide and a mountain of toys. There were also three women milling around that corner.

"We have certified sitters that will be present at the event the whole time," Skye explained.

"Mommy, can I go?" Avery asked.

"Sure, honey. Let's go together." Tess and her sister led the way. Avery headed straight to the slide while Skye introduced me to the sitters. I spoke with them for a few minutes, and afterward, they headed to Avery. Since she was the first kid to arrive, they didn't have much to do yet.

"Wow. That's going to keep kids occupied for hours," I said.

"That's the plan. From experience, we know kids don't like to sit at the tables. It's boring for them. They usually only interrupt their games long enough to eat or drink, and we've set up the kids' snacks in the corner by the playground. Our sitters have been working our events for a few years now, and we trust them completely."

By the ease with which they interacted with Avery, it was clear they knew what they were doing.

"You're magic. Do you have kids?" I asked.

"No, but we've got Mom to advise us. She's a school principal and raised four of us, so... what she says goes."

"Want me to give you a rundown of everything?" Tess asked.

"Yes, please."

"The funds raised tonight go towards charity. One of us holds an opening speech. Usually Hunter, but this time, it's going to be me. After food is served, the dance raffle begins."

"What's that?"

Tess grinned. "Every dance is raffled off. You want to dance with someone, you have to buy a ticket. We alternate women and men buying tickets throughout the night."

"And that money is also for charity?"

"Yes. I mean, the amount is small—the actual donations are by checks. It's mostly just for fun. We always test new ways to entertain our guests, and this was by far the most popular strategy, so we do it for every event."

"Where did you get the idea?"

"From *Gone with the Wind*."

"Love your taste in movies."

"*Thank you!* Can you please tell that to Ryker too? He forever teases me about it."

I laughed nervously. "Sure."

After I explained to Avery that I need to step away to change, Tess led me to a smaller room on the floor above the ballroom. I laid my dress on the comfy couch at the back of the room.

"Hey, here's an idea! Do you want to participate in the raffle?" she asked.

"I'd love to. Oh, wait, Avery—"

"You won't dance all the time, and Avery will barely even look at you. Trust me, we've thrown plenty of these events."

I pondered this, but knowing my girl, she would barely leave the kids' corner. And I could step away from the dance floor whenever she needed me.

"Okay. I'm in."

"Perfect. I'll tell Skye to add your name to the list. She's in charge of that. Need help with the dress?"

"No, thanks. I'm good."

While I changed behind a lovely golden screen, I asked, "You and Skye have a store for lingerie, right?"

"Exactly. We've only been online until now, but next week is the opening of our brick-and-mortar location. We still have a lot of boxes to unwrap and some last-minute shelves to put up."

"Wow, will you even have time to recover after tonight's event?"

"Not really. Timing isn't great, but it couldn't be helped. We were hoping to open this week already but weren't ready, and we can't afford to stay closed much longer. We're having a hair and makeup party, and everyone who attends gets a discount for the lingerie."

I remembered Ryker being worried that his sisters were taking on more than they could chew, and it sounded like he was spot-on. When I came out, I twirled around a few times.

"Ready?" Tess asked.

"Oh, yeah."

"So, my brother surprised us all when he told us you and Avery were coming."

I grinned. I'd just wondered why she wasn't asking anything about Ryker.

"I've always wanted to come to a Ballroom Gala," I replied, unsure what else to say. It was true after all.

"I see. So you're just here for the gala, not for my brother?"

***

Ryker

One thing I loved about the Ballroom Galas was that the time we put into organizing them also doubled as family time.

I arrived at the venue before the event began to oversee the last preparations. I was just about to shoot Cole a message when I saw Heather and Tess coming out of the changing room. What was Heather doing here so early? She looked stunning. I had to admit, when she'd described her dress, all I could do was picture her out of it. The top was tight, and her cleavage tempted me. All I wanted to do was pull her closer and touch all that soft skin until she blushed just for me. But we were not alone. Yet.

Tess waved at me. "Hey, brother."

"Hi!" Heather said shyly.

"I asked her to come a little earlier so I could explain a few things."

That made sense, except the glimmer in my sister's eyes told me that wasn't the only reason. And how exactly had Tess known Heather's number?

Before I had the chance to ask anything else, Skye joined us too.

"Avery's already all set up," she said. I peeked at the corner we'd set up for kids. It wasn't all that usual to bring kids to high-profile events like these, but we'd set it up this way from the very beginning, and our donors loved it.

"Oh, Skye, Heather agreed to participate in the raffle."

Wait, what? Hell, no. I'd asked Heather here because I wanted to spend time with her. If she danced half the night, we'd barely exchange a few words. Heather wasn't going to dance with anyone but me.

"Perfect. Come with me to our table so I can tell you exactly how it works," Skye said. My sisters exchanged a glance. I bit back a smile. Yeah, I was starting to put two and two together. As was often the case with my family, I could guess the general gist, but not the depth or the intricacy of their plan. Life in the Winchester clan was just one surprise after the other.

"I'll just check on Avery real quick," Heather said. "I'll find you later."

Skye nodded.

As soon Heather was out of earshot, I focused on my sisters.

"You asked Heather here earlier on purpose?" I asked Tess.

She smiled. "Of course. You didn't think I'd wait until the event starts to meet the woman who's got you all tied up in knots, right? I wanted to have enough time to get the right picture of what's happening."

"And?" I asked.

"I only had about ten minutes with her."

"So you didn't get the picture?"

Tess jerked her head back. "I'm offended. I already got all the intel I needed."

"In ten minutes?"

"Yep."

"I've known Heather for three weeks."

"What can I say, I work fast."

"I'm impressed. So?"

Tess smiled saucily. "Who said I'll tell you anything?"

I groaned. Skye elbowed Tess. "Tess! This is a time-sensitive matter. You can tease him another time."

"So good to know that at least one of my sisters loves me unconditionally."

Skye winked. "I can't help it. Have to go,

though. Need to finalize some details. You'll have to fill me in later."

After Skye left, Tess tilted her head, sighing. "I think she's trying to protect Avery and herself from heartbreak and getting their hopes up. It's hard on kids to just see people walk in and out of their lives, you know?"

"I know."

She looked at the kids' corner, wringing her hands. "I understand where Heather is coming from, wanting to protect Avery. The day Mom told us Dad left, I thought she'd just meant he wasn't coming home that evening. I waited on the windowsill for him that entire week. I waited for him to come back for years. Right until he remarried."

Jesus. I had absolutely no comeback. She'd never told me this.

"Tess..."

She waved her hand. "Let's not get into all that. We're talking about Avery and Heather right now."

"She told you everything you've just said?"

"Not in exact words. She just told me her story and I inferred the appropriate conclusions."

"Right...."

"Oh, by the way, Mom and Mick are coming tonight."

"What? They never attend."

"I mentioned you invited a lady friend and her daughter. I think it was a strong incentive."

I barked out a laugh. These things only

happened in my family.

"I need to check on a few last-minute details. See you later?" she asked.

"Sure."

I wanted to say something more on the subject of Dad, but honestly, I didn't know what, and Tess usually folded into herself whenever she spoke about him. I didn't want to spoil her mood.

Looking around, I realized that a few guests had already arrived. Damn! I'd wanted to talk to Heather before it began. She was at the kids' corner, speaking to a little girl.

I stopped right next to them. Heather bit her lower lip when she saw me.

"Avery, this is my friend Ryker."

Avery looked up at me, stretching out her tiny hand. "Hello, Mr. Ryker. I'm Avery."

Heather laughed, ruffling her daughter's curls. I crouched on my haunches until my face was level with Avery's.

"Nice to meet you, Avery. You like it here?"

"Yes. I feel like a princess."

"He's the one who sent us the invitations," Heather clarified.

"They were so pretty. Mine said *Miss Avery*. Mommy, can I go back and play?"

"Sure."

She darted right to the slide the next second. I rose back up, watching Heather intently.

"I'm glad you came," I said. "Hope Tess didn't drive you too crazy."

"Not at all. She explained how everything works. Can't wait for the raffle." Wiggling her eyebrows, she added, "Think you'll get lucky for one dance?"

"Ms. Prescott, are you teasing me?"

"What do you think?"

"I think that you have no idea what you just got yourself into. I'll get my dance." I leaned in, brushing her cheek until someone called my name.

"I need to make the rounds, but I'll find you later," I promised.

"Okay."

I couldn't resist lingering for another beat. I skimmed my hand down to her waist, enjoying the way she shuddered at my touch. It was impossible to be this close to her and not want to be even closer, but we weren't alone.

Yet.

Tearing myself away from Heather, I headed toward the guy who'd called me, the sound technician. After discussing a few details, I headed straight to the organizers' table. Our entire family would sit at it, plus Heather and Avery, but right now, only Skye and Cole were there.

"Skye. I need to talk to you about Heather and the raffle," I said.

She looked up from her iPad. "Shoot."

"Pick me for all of Heather's dances."

"Ryker! We don't cheat. I won't rig the system, not even for you."

What did I expect? Skye was a stickler for

rules. To my knowledge, she'd never cheated in school or in college.

"What if I promise to make it up to you? Whatever you want."

Skye cocked a brow. "Bribery doesn't work with me."

Well... that was debatable. She's been known to soften if presented with the right bribe, but I knew better than to think I stood a chance. I might be overconfident and cocky on occasion, but I wasn't delusional.

"Fine. But pull me out of the raffle."

Up until recently, family members didn't participate in it, but we'd changed that a few events ago, and I'd had a blast. Tonight, I wasn't interested in anyone but Heather.

Cole just looked between us with a grin. "Well, I'll be damned. Didn't think I'd see the day when Ryker voluntarily gave up on the opportunity to dance. That means I win by default."

We competed for who had the most raffle tickets.

"You don't win if there isn't a competition," I pointed out with a grin.

"I'll take you out of the raffle, but I won't be meddling with Heather's tickets."

That meant one thing: I had to apply plan B. One way or another, Heather was all mine tonight.

Chapter Twelve
Heather

While Tess delivered the opening speech, everyone was focused on the stage, but I kept glancing around. Where was Ryker? The skin on my entire body tingled, anticipating the moment he'd walk up to me again.

Once Tess descended from the stage, the emcee walked up to the mic.

"Ladies and gentlemen, the first dance of the evening has been raffled off. Gentlemen bought tickets for this one. We're going to switch after five dances. Gentlemen, you can now approach your dance partners. Ladies, do check the raffle ticket. We've had cheaters in the past."

Everyone laughed, and I even heard a few whispers of "it happened to me." I briefly wondered if Ryker planned to cheat. Honestly, I'd be disappointed if he was.

I waited by the dance floor, as Tess said was tradition. This evening was so out of the norm for me that I was grasping for anything that sounded familiar.

My heart pulsed at a lightning-quick speed when I noticed Ryker. He was walking straight toward me, stopping only half a foot away.

"I believe I'm the lucky winner." He handed me the ticket. When our fingers brushed, an electrifying heat jolted straight through me. He smiled, flashing his dimples. I glanced at the ticket. It simply said *Ryker*. My heart was beating wildly. My fingers shook a little.

"How exactly did you game the system?" I whispered.

"I bought every ticket for this dance."

"Wow."

Those deep blue eyes pinned me with such an intensity that they lit up every cell in my body.

"I told you I'd get my dance, Heather."

"I didn't know you wanted it so badly."

"Now you do." He was half leaning into me, his warm breath landing on my cheek. His gaze dropped to my mouth. I licked my lips, pushing a strand of hair behind my ear. I became aware that everyone else was already in position to dance, so I followed suit.

Ryker expertly led the dance, only I wasn't paying much attention to the music or our steps. I was too wired up, too consumed by our proximity.

"This is a great event. How did it all start?" I asked.

"It was Hunter's idea, but we just wanted to create something together, as a family."

"So you participate in all of them?"

"We try to, but there are instances when we just can't make it. Hunter and his wife are skipping this one."

The rhythm of the song changed lightly, and Ryker's hold on my waist tightened. He kept me close enough that I was certain he could *feel* my heartbeat.

When the song finished, Ryker lowered his hands, taking a step back.

"Pleasure to dance with you. Can't wait to do it again," he said.

"What do you mean?"

"This isn't the only dance I'm bidding on."

And just like that, my heart rate quickened *again*. I couldn't keep my smile under control either.

"On how many, exactly?"

He tilted his head playfully. "Someone's eager."

"Just want to be prepared."

"I'll keep you guessing. Just know that you're not getting rid of me tonight."

"Ryker, you don't have to buy out every single dance. It's expensive."

"It's worth it."

Oh, my. What could I say to that?

The next hour went by in a blur. Whenever he had to go to buy tickets for the next dance, my entire body hummed with the need to be closer to him. No matter what I did—even if it was to sit down for a minute or to check on Avery, I longed for the sound of the gong announcing the next round. With every dance, he kept me closer, his touch became more daring, and I leaned into it every chance I got, because this felt damn good.

To my dismay, the last dance came far too quickly. I wasn't ready to let go, but I had to.

"Forgot to give you the ticket for this last one," Ryker said.

I laughed. "Not necessary."

"What if I cheated?"

"Did you?"

"You won't know until you read it."

I wanted to tell him that weeding out cheaters was always easy. The real dance partner would have popped up. But that mischievous glint in his eyes... hmmm... he had something in mind. He was insisting on me taking the ticket for a reason, so I did.

I glanced down at it, feeling his gaze on me, the tension sizzling in the air.

Ryker: Meet me behind the red curtain after my speech.

I looked up. Oh, God... there was so much heat in his eyes, so much promise. He was expecting an answer, but before I could give him one, we were flanked by Tess and Skye.

"Don't forget you're giving the second speech tonight," Skye said.

"I know. Ten minutes left."

"Heather, do you want to sit?" Tess asked.

"Great idea. My toes feel as if they're about to fall off."

I was even more aware of Ryker than before as we all headed to the organizers' table. I held the note in my fist, the words still playing around in my mind. Where was the red curtain? I glanced around the room slowly, until I noticed it at the far corner. My stomach flipped, especially when I realized Ryker was watching me. I wanted to say yes right away, but I had to think this through, and I honestly couldn't with six-foot-two of sexiness right next to me.

Tess, Skye, and I sat at the table. Ryker stood between his sisters. I took my feet out of my shoes and stretched my toes.

"In our completely unbiased opinion, you lucked out, Heather. Ryker is the best dancer around here," Tess said.

Ryker grinned. "Any chance you can use the time during my speech to sing my praises to Heather?"

"You can count on us," Tess assured him just as a man joined us. He had black hair and deep blue eyes that were eerily similar to Ryker's.

"Our brother, Cole," Ryker said.

"Hi, Cole."

He shook my hand, glancing between Ryker and me. "Couldn't miss meeting the woman who ensures I'll take in the most tickets for the raffle by taking Ryker out of the equation."

"I thought there was a certain number of tickets for each dance and participant?" I asked, laughing.

"That's right, but they aren't sold out usually."

Skye shook her head, smiling. "Will you two ever stop competing against each other?"

Cole shrugged. "Not in the foreseeable future."

Organizing these events was hard work, but they made it all seem like so much fun that I just wanted to be part of it all.

"Besides, you should keep a closer eye on Ryker from now on," Skye told Cole. "He wanted to cheat—make me rig Heather's raffles so he always won."

I placed a hand on my hip, turning to Ryker, who was glaring at his sister.

"Ah, wasn't supposed to say that to Heather, right? But I think it counts in your favor. Shows your commitment to dance with her," Skye said.

"I thought you said it was worth buying all the tickets," I teased.

"Yes, but there's always a risk of someone placing a bid before me and then being picked."

I brought a hand to my mouth but still wasn't able to mask the guffaw escaping my lips. Ryker's siblings were merely smiling or shaking their heads. As soon as Ryker left, they immediately started singing his praises—even Cole.

"He's smart, hardworking. Are we missing something?" Tess asked.

"Loyal," Skye added.

Cole held up a finger. "I have one. Fun."

"You're really giving this praising thing all you've got," I said.

"That's the family motto," Cole informed me.

"Just so you're warned, Mom is here tonight," Skye said. "Don't know where she is now, but she and Avery talked a lot during the dances."

"Oh, really?"

"Yeah. She'll find you eventually," Tess said.

They were such a delight that I wanted to linger with them during the entire break, but I needed to check on Avery. I almost left the table barefoot before remembering that I'd taken off my shoes. Damn, I'd only spent a few dances with Ryker and was already losing my head? How was I going to fare at the end of the evening?

Avery paid exactly zero attention to me. She was already sweaty from playing so much, but there was nothing I could do about that. I hadn't thought about bringing a second dress for her. She was grinning and jumping up and down in excitement, along with two other girls. I felt about as old as her right now. It occurred to me that I hadn't felt this childish joy in such a long time. I'd missed it, and I had Ryker to thank for making me feel that way again.

I was lost in thoughts, watching her, until a woman walked up to me. Her gray hair was pulled up into a high bun. Her smile was warm and vaguely familiar.

"Heather, I'm Amelia, Ryker's mother."

"Amelia! It's great to meet you."

Her smile widened as she looked between me and Avery.

"I've already had the pleasure of meeting your daughter. She's lovely."

"Thank you."

"I miss the time when they were all little," she murmured, looking at the playground.

"Wasn't it hard though?"

She shrugged. "It was... especially once I was on my own, but there were so many good memories."

"How did you do it?" I asked suddenly. Crap, this was too personal.

"Honestly, I don't know. It somehow all worked out, though it often seemed like it wouldn't. I was stubborn though, not wanting to let anyone get too close to me. Poor Mick had to fight his way to me, and we lost precious years because of that."

Hmmm... that was a pretty heavy-handed hint. Had Tess told her about our conversation? All signs pointed to yes.

"You're happy now, that's what matters," I said.

"True. My boys gave Mick such a hard time when he first asked me out. But they were just protecting me."

She launched into story after story about her kids, painting a picture so vivid that I felt right there in the moment with them. Damn, she was even better at praising Ryker than the rest. I wasn't certain if she was doing it on purpose, but it worked like a charm.

When Ryker went on stage to deliver his

speech, Amelia headed to her table to sit down, but I stood where I was, leaning against the wall.

Ryker commanded the attention of the room effortlessly. He spoke with passion and conviction, and he exuded this *je ne sais quoi* that made you look his way no matter how crowded a space was. In my case, it was also impossible to look away. I was rooted to the spot, eyes on stage. Ryker shifted his focus through the room during his speech. Every time our gazes crossed, I involuntarily looked at the red curtain, then at my girl, who was currently laughing at something one of the sitters was telling her.

Once the speech was over, Ryker moved off the stage. He stopped to chat with some guests. I headed to the playground, catching up with my daughter just as she was about to climb on the slide again.

"Avery, I'm going out of the room for a while. I need some air, but then I'll be back, okay?"

"Sure, Mommy."

I laughed as she just plowed down the slide. *Guess she won't miss me.*

I turned to one of the sitters next. "I'm stepping out of the room for a beat, but I'll be back. I'll have my phone with me, so you can call if Avery needs anything."

"Of course. We'll be here," she said, handing me her phone. I typed my number in it.

"Okay, then."

After picking up my small bag from the table,

I headed toward the red curtain before I could talk myself out of it, aware of the heat in my cheeks, the wild beat of my heart.

Holy shit, how could I be so nervous?

Oh, Heather. You're looking for trouble.

Past the red curtain was a door. My palms were a little sweaty when I pushed it open. I felt as if I was at a clandestine meeting.

Chapter Thirteen
Heather

There was a long corridor behind the curtain and then a staircase leading to the next level. I came face-to-face with a door. I opened it, stepping into what seemed to be yet another changing room, but larger. There was a leather couch, as well as a huge mirror with a counter on one wall. I set my bag on it, checking my phone to set the ringtone to loud, not just vibrate. The second I shoved the phone back in the bag, the door opened. My stomach tightened. Ryker stepped in, closing the door behind him, hovering in front of it for a few seconds before striding toward me. He stopped right behind me. Our gazes were locked in the mirror.

"That was an excellent speech," I said.

"Thanks."

"This whole evening is amazing."

"I'm glad you're having fun."

"It's all so surreal. The ballroom, the music, the whole vibe."

"So I'm not contributing at all?"

"Maybe. Not sure yet. I'll let you know at the end of the evening."

His eyes flashed. "I'll make sure the balance tilts in my favor, Heather."

I smelled his cologne for the first time tonight—wood and citrus. Had he tilted closer? I didn't think so, but it was as if now that I'd been close enough once, I could smell it no matter how faint it was.

"What are we doing here?" I asked.

"I wanted a few moments alone with you. Out there, there's always a guest chatting me up."

I felt his fingers against the bare skin on my upper back. I shuddered lightly, the contact zinging me. He snapped his gaze up the next second, locking it with mine in the mirror again. God, how he looked at me. He was still touching my upper back, trailing his fingers from one shoulder blade to the other. I shivered again, biting my lower lip.

"Want me to kiss you here?" he asked in a low, dangerous voice.

I nodded slowly, unable to reason or think. I just needed his mouth. Needed him. When his lips made contact with my skin, I gripped the counter for support. When I felt the tip of his tongue, my knees buckled.

He brought one hand to my right hip, possibly attempting to steady me. His touch had just the opposite effect. I was now so jittery that I could barely stand.

"Where else do you want me to kiss you, Heather?"

"Everywhere." I couldn't reason, couldn't

think past how much I wanted him—needed him. I'd thought for sure Ryker would whirl me around, kiss me. Instead, he brought his arm around my waist, stepping so close that I could feel his hard-on pressing against my ass cheek. His mouth explored my neck, and he was bunching the fabric of my dress, lifting it higher and higher... I moaned when his fingers brushed the bare skin of my thigh.

"Ryker, the door...."

"I locked it."

Those three words unleashed an inferno inside me. I was so aroused I couldn't even breathe. He'd locked the door... because he'd come here for this. For me.

"You're so beautiful, Heather, so fucking perfect." He brought his hand higher until he reached the rim of my panties... and then he rubbed two fingers right along the center, pressing the damp fabric against my sensitive skin. On reflex, I buckled forward, gripping the counter even tighter when I felt him rub his erection against me. Tiny needles speared me *everywhere*.

"Fuck, baby. You're already wet."

With every rub of his fingers, I came apart more. *OhGod, OhGod.* "Ryker. Ryker!"

Abruptly, he stopped touching me. I moaned in protest. He turned me around, capturing my mouth. I fisted his hair with both hands, demanding all he had, but Ryker kissed me slowly. So damn slowly.

I tugged at his shirt and managed to undo one

button before he captured both wrists in one hand, smiling against my mouth.

"Why the rush?" he murmured.

"I want you."

His eyes flashed. He pulled me closer until his erection pressed against my belly. "You feel this? It's all for you. I want to savor you, Heather. Everything about you. The way you look at me. The way you feel against me. I've wanted you since that first evening I saw you."

I lost my trail of thought when he captured my mouth again. He pinned me to the wall with his hips. I parted my legs, wanting him closer, needing him closer. His erection pressed right between my thighs. The tip nudged against my clit with every lash of his tongue. When we paused the kiss to breathe, we both laughed. He looked at me with heat and unexpected tenderness.

"I don't know what you're doing to me, Heather, but I want more of it. Of you."

He skimmed his hands down my face, the sides of my neck, and then my shoulders, as if he wanted to memorize my body.

When I felt his hand on the zipper, waiting, silently asking for permission, I drew in a sharp breath before nodding.

Ryker lowered the zipper the next second, pushing the dress off my shoulders, letting it drop to the floor. The dress had sewn-in cups, so I wore no bra, just panties. Ryker's eyes were hooded with lust. Hooking an arm around my waist, he lifted me onto the counter, bringing my breasts level with his mouth.

I wasn't sure how it was possible to affect me so much just by *looking* at me.

He cupped one breast, teasing the nipple with his thumb until it was so hard and sensitive that every stroke was pure torture. I moaned, pushing my hips forward, gripping the counter tightly. Pushing my thighs wide, Ryker kissed a path downward until he reached my panties. His mouth teased at the hem, setting me on fire.

"Lift up your ass a bit." His voice was low, rich, and so commanding that I instantly became even more aroused. I focused my weight on my palms, lifting my ass just enough so he could lower my panties. He watched me hungrily, drawing one finger along my center before putting his mouth on me. He sucked my clit between his lips until my vision faded... and then he slid one finger inside me.

"Oh, fuck." I swallowed hard, leaning against the mirror, hoping to cool off. It had just the opposite effect. Feeling Ryker's hot mouth and the cold surface of the mirror at the same time overwhelmed me.

The rhythm of his fingers and his mouth was maddening. It was too much. I could barely breathe past so much pleasure. My orgasm formed in slow motion. I felt every pull, every cell wiring to my center. When my inner muscles clenched, Ryker came up, pressing his fingers on my sensitive spot, claiming my mouth while I gave in to my climax. I squirmed and moaned and even though I was still light-headed from the aftershocks of the orgasm, I reached for Ryker's belt, desperately needing him.

He watched me with hooded eyes as I unclasped it, lowering his zipper. He tugged at his buttons, removing his shirt. My hands trembled a little as I pushed down his pants, then his boxers. He was just beautiful. Every part of his body was defined and so damn sexy. I cupped his erection, flattening the heel of my palm on the tip.

Ryker buckled forward, slamming his hands on the mirror behind me. His mouth was in the crook of my neck. His hot breath tickled my skin.

He pressed his fingers into my waist. "Heather! I want to fuck you tonight."

"Yes, please. Please."

I'd just climaxed, but I was so hungry for all the sensations he spurred, everything he made me feel. I was so desperate for him that I couldn't even see straight.

"Fuck. Have to bring a condom," he said.

"I'm on birth control and healthy," I whispered.

"I'm clean."

He swallowed hard, lifting me off the counter the next second. I hung onto his neck, awkwardly pressed my knees into his sides. He sat on the couch. I was on top of him, pressing his erection between us.

He teased my clit with his tip in little circles. He was driving me crazy! I was still so sensitive from before that my inner muscles pulsed. I couldn't wait any longer.

I lowered myself onto him slowly. This felt delicious. Our gazes clashed, and I smiled, not feeling self-conscious in any way. How could I, when he looked at me like that?

Bracing my palms on his shoulders, I moved my hips back and forth, drinking in every sensation. When Ryker pressed his thumb on my clit, I cried out, unprepared for the flash of heat coursing through me.

The next second, Ryker took control. He lifted me off him, placing me on my back on the couch. I cried out in protest, feeling empty and cold until he slammed inside me. I lifted my legs a little higher, taking him in as deeply as possible, loving the pressure of his pelvis on my clit with every thrust. We both moved in a fast and desperate rhythm... right until Ryker changed the rules again. He stilled, touching every part of me he could reach, kissing me. Knowing he needed to savor me like this was doing unspeakable things to me.

I ran my hands all over his back and arms, kissing his neck and shoulders—everywhere I could reach. I loved having those steel muscles against me, feeling the perspiration forming on his skin. When he started moving his hips again, I felt everything at a different level, as if we were even more entwined than before. I dug my hips firmly into the cushions, gyrating them, following his wild rhythm.

A loud, guttural sound pierced the air as I felt

him pulse inside me, chasing his climax.

Next thing I knew, he pressed his thumb on my clit, and I was done for. Where my last orgasm built up slowly, this one slammed into me so fast that it left me breathless. The aftershocks lasted longer this time. We were both fighting to regain our breath.

"I'm crushing you," he said after a few minutes, sliding off me. He drew the tip of his nose from my shoulder up the side of my neck.

"Yeah... but I kind of like it." I couldn't believe how earth shattering this had been. Ryker had made it so. He chuckled, sitting up straight. "You okay?"

I nodded, smiling. "Better than okay. Just not too sure I can get up right now. Or even sit."

Ryker took my hand, kissing it. It was the third time tonight my heart felt about to explode, and I was certain it wouldn't be the last time.

"Come on, let's clean up and head back out there," he said.

Holy shit! I'd completely forgotten about Avery and the ball and everything else. Adrenaline kicked in. I bolted upright so fast that my vision swam. I tightened my grip on Ryker's hand for support.

"Oh God, how long were we gone?"

"Heather, relax. We'll go out in a few minutes."

"It'll take me a bit longer to put myself together."

"Okay. Let's clean up, and then I'll go out

first while you finish touching up. There's a small bathroom in that corner. How does that sound?"

"Like a plan."

Ryker gathered his clothes off the floor and went first into the bathroom. I hurried to the mirror, checking my phone. The sitter hadn't called me. I exhaled sharply, then assessed my appearance. There was *no* hiding what had just happened. My hair was rumpled, and there was no way I could style it back in the elegant do from before. My cheeks were flushed, my lips a little swollen. There was also no erasing that smile on my face. I didn't even try.

Ryker came out of the bathroom the next second, fully dressed. He walked behind me, kissing my bare shoulder, looking at me in the mirror again. His eyes still smoldered.

"I'll wait for you outside." He spoke against my skin, feathering his fingers up my arm. I simply nodded.

After Ryker left, I hurried to finish cleaning up. My body was still humming from his touch. What would his love feel like? I smiled just thinking about it, even though I had a small knot in my throat. I'd set rules for myself, and I'd already broken them.

The ball was still in full swing. I searched the kids' corner for Avery, but she was nowhere to be seen. Then I noticed her curled up on one of the couches, sleeping. One of the sitters was next to her, along with Tess, who was speaking with Ryker. I headed their way.

"She just fell asleep a few minutes ago," the

sitter said.

"Thanks. Did she ask for me?"

"Not at all. Just came directly to the couch and lay down on it."

"Thanks a lot." She went back to the kids' corner, which was when I realized Tess's gaze lingered on my rumpled hair, and her lips curled into a smile. Could she tell what had just happened?

"I'm taking her home. She does this when she's excited. Plays until she's exhausted, then immediately falls asleep."

"I'll take you home," Ryker said.

"We can just uber." My face heated up just at the sound of his voice.

"We have a car service for our guests waiting outside," Tess said.

"I'm coming with you," he repeated in a tone that brooked no argument.

"But you still have to mingle with the guests," I said.

"Oh, please, do let my brother play the white knight. Otherwise, I'll have to deal with him. You'd be doing me a favor."

I laughed, looking between the siblings. Ryker was glaring at Tess, who just elbowed him in the ribs.

"What? It's true. I love you, but you know it's true."

"Did I or did I not help you get rid of that schmuck who followed you around at the last gala?"

"Ouch. Low blow, brother."

"Just pointing out that my skills can be

useful."

Turning to me, Tess said, "*Please, please, please* take him away."

"Okay, then," I conceded. "Tess, this has been a wonderful evening. Thank you so much for everything. Is Skye still here? And Cole? I'd like to thank them too."

"They're here somewhere, but I can't see them right now. I'll give them your thanks. And you're welcome."

"Ten o'clock at the store tomorrow?" Ryker asked Tess.

She nodded. "Thanks. We have about a million boxes to sort out."

"I can come and help too," I offered.

Tess waved her hand. "No need. Between my siblings, and our cousin and his wife, we're gonna be fine. Now, off you go before someone chats Ryker up."

After she left, I tried to lift Avery in my arms, but she woke up. Her eyes widened, but it was clear she was still sleepy.

"Are we leaving, Mommy?"

"Yes, we are. Ryker is taking us home. Remember him?"

Avery nodded.

"I've heard a lot about you, Avery," Ryker said.

Her eyes widened. "You did?"

"Yes. That you're a smart girl and like to collect coloring books."

I felt as if my heart was about to explode *again*. He'd listened to all that?

"Yes. Winnie is my favorite. But I'm a big girl now. I can't like Winnie anymore."

"Why not?"

"Because big girls don't watch cartoons."

Ryker winked. "All the cool people like cartoons. I also like anime and superhero movies."

Avery's jaw dropped open. "You do? But you're so old. You're like Mommy."

Ryker jerked his head back. I laughed, patting his shoulder. The contact zinged me. I withdrew my hand so quickly that it was awkward. I patted my hair to give myself something to do.

"Well, yeah. But even old people can enjoy animated comic movies. Tell you what…"

He looked between me and Avery. My stomach flipped. I leaned slightly forward, anticipation coursing through me. He was plotting something, I was certain of that.

"If you give me your permission, I'll take your mom to a superhero movie that just came out."

"Why?" Avery asked suspiciously.

"To show her that even old people can like them."

Avery clapped her hands. "YES! Then maybe she'll watch Winnie with me."

Ryker laughed. Avery beamed widely. I loved putting that smile on my daughter's face, but Ryker deserved all the credit for this. My heart wasn't just increasing in size, it felt as if it was about to leap out of my chest. I'd spent two years with a man who hadn't once put that smile on Avery's face, and yet Ryker did so effortlessly. Did he know how charming that was to me? How much it meant to me?

It just came naturally for him. Bonding with those around him, making them feel at ease. After all, I'd felt at ease around him the moment I'd met him, and I'd been fighting with my ex.

"What do you say, Heather? Go to a movie with me? Now that we have permission and all?"

Smiling, I nodded. Avery jumped up and down, and the three of us headed out. I was acutely aware of his hand on my arm as he led us both outside. His grip was possessive, as if I belonged to him. As if we both did.

"I know who you are," Avery said suddenly before we climbed into one of the cars waiting outside.

"Who?" Ryker prompted, raising both eyebrows.

"You're Prince Charming."

Ryker's eyes bulged. The two of them talked the entire ride home. I kept glancing between them, barely managing to get a word in. It was the first time Avery was so chatty in front of a person she'd just met.

When we arrived in front of my building, I was surprised when Ryker climbed out of the car too. "What are you doing?" I asked.

"What kind of prince charming would I be if I didn't walk you to your door?"

Avery squealed. Her happiness was contagious. I couldn't hide my smile as I opened the door of the car. Avery led the way. She had so much energy that it would take her a while to fall asleep.

Then again, it would take me a while too. Ryker went up with us.

As I unlocked the front door, I told Avery, "Say goodbye to Ryker and go straight to the bathroom and brush your teeth."

Avery sighed. "Do I have to?"

"Yes, it's late."

She held her tiny hand out to Ryker again. "It was nice meeting you, Mr. Ryker."

"Likewise, Ms. Avery."

Avery formed an O with her mouth, looking up at me, then back at Ryker. "I thought only old ladies are Ms. I can be a Ms.?"

"Of course. If you want to."

"I want to."

"Avery. Teeth," I repeated, fighting laughter.

"Goodnight, Mr. Ryker," Avery said, nodding eagerly before disappearing into the apartment.

I lingered in the doorway, even less ready to say goodnight than I'd been at the party.

"Tonight was... incredible," I murmured.

"Yeah, it was."

He pushed a strand of hair behind my ear. My entire body was on edge from that one touch.

"Do you have time for that movie tomorrow?"

"I have a deadline for an article on Sunday.

Next week?"

"We have a big project coming in on Monday… it will keep me at work until late in the evening. Next Friday?"

"Yes, that works."

He trained his eyes on me, and I was overwhelmed by the mix of heat and determination in them.

I had to be honest with him. "Avery asked me if it'll be just the two of us for a while, and I said yes. I don't think she wants us to have someone else in our life."

He cupped my face in both hands. "I'm going to do everything in my power to make sure that little girl feels safe around me. Make sure she's happy. And then we'll take it from there."

Oh, wow. What could I say to that? All I wanted to do was wrap my arms around him and pull him into a kiss.

"Between you and me, I think my chances aren't half bad. She gave me her permission to take you out to a movie pretty quickly."

"That's because you tricked her. You essentially made her believe I might watch cartoons with her if you take me to the movies."

Ryker grinned unapologetically. "Hey, I saw my chance, and I seized it."

"You most definitely did."

"And I'm not done doing that yet."

I laughed, and this time I *did* pull him into a kiss. One thing I knew about Ryker. If he didn't see a chance, he created one.

Chapter Fourteen
Ryker

The next morning, I was at my sisters' store at ten o'clock. To my surprise, only Tess and Skye were here. Tess was perched on a ladder, pushing merchandise boxes around on the last shelf. Skye was handing her boxes.

"Where are the rest of your helpers?" I asked, referring to Cole, Hunter, and Josie. Since the store officially opened on Monday, we had a lot of last-minute details to take care of.

"Cole's bringing breakfast, so he'll be a bit late. But Josie and Hunter should be here any second."

"Okay. Can't believe they're coming. Didn't they land last night?"

"I told them they can sleep in or just skip today, but they insisted," Skye said.

After they finished the boxes, Tess climbed down from the ladder. My sisters looked absolutely exhausted. They both had dark rings under their eyes, and Skye was paler than usual.

"What time did you two go to bed?" I asked them.

Tess waved her hand. "Don't make me think

about it. I think I slept two hours in total. But I haven't slept much the past week either."

"Yeah, I only got in one hour Thursday evening. Got stuck here sorting through inventory, and we had more deliveries coming in at six o'clock."

"You slept *here*?" I asked.

"Hey, don't judge. The couch is comfy," Skye said on a frown. I'd been naive enough to think that after they quit their day jobs, they'd be taking it easier.

"You two will burn out if you go at this rate."

Tess pointed a finger at me. "I'll make you a deal. You stop nagging us about that, and we won't ask about your plans for the date."

Skye jerked her head back. "Ummm... don't make deals in my name, sister."

I burst out laughing. This morning was off to a brilliant start.

"Besides, you're one to talk. Who was working a hundred hours a week to make director just a few years ago?" Skye asked.

"I was twenty-five, and it was only for a short time."

Tess gasped. "Oh my God, he just called us old."

"I didn't. Fuck, I did. I need coffee," I said on a groan.

Skye shook her head energetically. "No, no. It's easier to spill secrets when you're half awake."

The front door opened, and Hunter and Josie came in, as well as Cole carrying bags.

"You're saving my life," I told him. He placed the food on the counter.

"Dig in. I was hungry, so I bought half the store."

"Atta boy," Skye exclaimed, rubbing her stomach.

We all reached for the food so fast, one would think we hadn't eaten in three days. I wolfed down a ham and cheese sandwich before downing a coffee.

Out of the corner of my eye, I saw Skye pout. There went her strategy of keeping me away from caffeine so I was an easier prey for their questioning.

"Did I miss anything last evening?" Josie asked.

"Business as usual. The donation spreadsheets aren't done, but I think we've reached our usual target," Skye said.

"Oh, and Ryker here finally scored a date with Heather," Tess said.

Cole laughed, patting my shoulder.

"All our praising helped, right?" Skye asked.

"Yes, it did," I admitted.

"Wait!" Josie exclaimed. "What's that about Ryker going on a date? Who's Heather?"

I looked at my sisters. "Want to fill her in?"

"Of course. I volunteer," Tess said, and summed up everything in a few sentences.

"Well, well, *the flirt* has finally met his match," Josie said afterward.

Cole shook his head. "I'm gonna be the only bachelor in the family before long, I just know it."

He sounded so dejected that we all burst out laughing.

After we finished breakfast, Tess told us the game plan while we drank a glass of Dom Perignon, celebrating the opening.

Then I moved the couch with the guys before helping Skye carry some light but huge boxes into the back. After setting down the last one, Skye abruptly said, "Ryker, you're being careful with Heather, right?"

Okay... I hadn't expected that. My sister was biting her lip with worry.

"What do you mean?"

"Well, it's just that I know you don't take relationships seriously."

I could hardly say anything in my defense.

"It's all fun and good... but there's also a little girl involved. Don't... get her hopes up. Or if you do, don't disappoint her."

"I wouldn't do that."

I knew exactly how it felt to be disappointed by a parent, and so did Skye, hence her warning.

Skye closed her eyes. "You're right, you wouldn't. I'm sorry. I don't know why I said that."

"Skye, are you okay?"

"Yes, just exhausted. I think that tends to make me more emotional. Forgive me?"

"Sure."

"Okay, let's go see if there's anything else left to do."

When Skye and I returned to the main room,

the group was chatting about the nicknames Josie gave us when we first met years ago.

"I'm quite proud of mine," Tess said. They were all leaning on the counter, sipping from fresh coffee cups. Someone must have done a second run. I took one immediately.

"You deserve it. Hurricane through and through," Josie said.

"What do you mean? That I don't deserve being called the Charmer?" Cole asked, faking indignation.

Josie laughed. "Yes, you do."

"You know, I'm the only one without an official nickname. I feel left out," Skye said.

Josie narrowed her eyes, studying my sister. "I didn't mean to. Skye just stuck in my brain, you know? And I couldn't remember the boys' names and was so shocked that Tess had convinced a bunch of you to go bungee jumping, hence the hurricane thing. I kind of thought of you as a wallflower."

Skye's jaw dropped. "Ouch."

"Hey, I mean it in a good way."

"Uh-huh."

"You were shy and quiet. And now..."

"You're not," I finished for Josie. "How about 'dragon'?"

Everyone turned to look at me.

Skye was smiling brilliantly. "I like that. I have no clue how you got to that, but I like it."

"Anyone who's ever seen you upset will agree with me."

There was a general murmur of agreement around the counter.

I was still thinking about ways to help my sisters relax a little. They weren't taking my concerns seriously, but I'd seen plenty of colleagues on Wall Street burn out after a few years. When you set up your own business, you don't know how long the trudge will last until you "make it." I just really couldn't stand watching my sisters work themselves to the bone. "Skye, Tess, is the exhibition you wanted to see at the Guggenheim still on tonight?" I asked.

"Yes," Tess said.

"Why don't we all go?" I suggested.

Josie straightened up. "If you need someone to finish up here, I can do that."

There was a reason why Josie was a killer lawyer. She knew my sisters might say that and didn't want to give them a chance.

"We were planning on checking the inventory," Tess said. "We're the only ones who can do that."

"But the Guggenheim expo is only until tomorrow," Josie added. "Ryker's right. We can all go."

Cole grimaced. I glared at him until he got my drift. "Yeah, let's all go. And have dinner afterward."

Hunter looked at his wife in confusion. I knew his credo—and shared it: the second-worst activity after shopping was going to an art museum. But he nodded, lacing an arm around his wife's shoulders.

"You do love us, brother," Skye said.

"How is that news?"

She shook her head. "It's not, just... it's good to remember from time to time."

She saw right through my tactic, but I considered it a victory anyway.

Chapter Fifteen
Heather

On Thursday, I received a surprise phone call from Tess. I was in my kitchen, whipping up a quick dinner of ravioli and Romaine salad for Avery and me.

"Hi, Heather!"

"Hey, this is a nice surprise."

"So, listen, I've heard through the Winchester grapevine that you and Ryker are going to a movie tomorrow."

"That's right." I smiled, realizing slowly that there were no secrets in the Winchester family.

"Do you have someone to watch Avery? Otherwise you can bring her by at the store. Skye and I will stay here until pretty late. Now that we opened, our to-do list grew exponentially. Mom will also be here, and she said she'd love to spend some time with Avery."

They were offering to watch my daughter? That was so strange. They barely met us last week. But I had a hunch they were different from most people I met. They were warmer, and so was their mom. In fact, the whole family had been very friendly at the event.

"Thanks, but my neighbor and friend, Natasha, is watching her."

"Oh, I see."

Come to think of it, though, Natasha would probably love going to the store, and my girl always liked being in Manhattan. It would be more exciting for them than staying at home, waiting for me.

"You know what? I'll ask Natasha if she's up for a trip to Manhattan and let you know."

"Perfect. What time would you be here?"

"The movie starts at six o'clock, so maybe... five thirty?"

"Let's make it five."

"Okay. Oh, shit. I'm overcooking the ravioli. Call you later?"

Tess laughed. "No need. Enjoy your evening. Just let me know what Natasha says."

***

The next afternoon, Avery, Natasha, and I arrived at the store at five o'clock on the dot. My girl smiled from ear to ear when we walked inside.

"When I grow up, I want to have my own store, Mommy."

"If you work hard, you can have whatever you want, baby."

"This place is amazing," Natasha said. "Most lingerie stores intimidate me, what with the tiny situation here." She pointed to her chest. "But this is real nice."

Skye, Tess, and Amelia were at the counter,

fixing gift bags. They all beamed when they saw us.

"Girls, do you ever take a minute off?" I asked them after introducing Natasha.

"They don't," Amelia answered.

"Not right now. But we're planning to take a break as soon as things actually work around here. Should be sometime in the next ten years," Tess said.

"I'm honestly more relaxed now than when we still had our jobs," Skye said. "At least now I get to focus all my efforts on one thing. I even have time to go on a date later this week."

I gave her a thumbs-up. "Is this why you're in such a good mood?"

"Well, life is generally great. We've finally opened the store, and an investor is interested in us."

"Wow, congrats. Why do you need an investor?" I figured if they'd opened this without one, they could do it on their own.

"It's always good to have more money coming in—we could expand quicker," Tess said.

These women were an inspiration for me. They went after what they wanted at full speed, embracing all the risks.

"Avery, we have something for you," Amelia said. She pointed to a small table next to the counter. A Winnie-themed coloring book, a doll, and a puzzle were lying on it.

"And we have something for you too," Skye said conspiratorially while Amelia took Avery to the table. Natasha gave me a surprised look. I'd brought her up to speed on all things Winchester when I asked her if she wanted to come here, but clearly, I wasn't the only one amazed by how welcoming these women were.

Tess hurried to the door to greet a customer who'd just come in.

"What do you mean?" I asked Skye.

"You'll see. Come on."

She led me to a changing room where a gorgeous red wool camisole was hanging.

"Oooh, this is beautiful."

"Yup. Just arrived. I set aside your size."

"How do you know my size?"

"It's my job. Try it on. It'll go well with your dress and will keep you warm."

I was ecstatic. I didn't want to overthink anything tonight. I wanted to feel sexy. I was going on a date. I was wearing a sweater dress and high-heeled boots, and it was as if Skye had read my mind. I had wondered if I wouldn't shiver a little.

While I changed, Skye talked my ear off about Ryker.

I peeked through the curtains. "Skye, you don't have to talk him up. I've already agreed to the date."

Skye grinned. "Extra pimping doesn't hurt. And you look amazing. You can't even tell you're wearing a camisole."

"I agree. I'm buying it."

"No, you won't. It's our gift."

"No way."

"Yes way."

I couldn't accept it, but judging by Skye's determined look, I'd offend them if I didn't take it. And I loved it. I was going to rock this evening.

I strutted out of the changing room with a huge smile. Anticipation coursed through me. I tried to push down the mix of guilt and fear threatening to float up to the surface. It was just a night of fun. I didn't have to make a big deal out of it.

Avery and Amelia were busy at the table with the puzzle.

Tess was back at the counter, showing Natasha a bra.

"Hey, girl. We'll stay here for a bit and then go to the pizza place across the street, if that's okay with you," Natasha said.

"Sure. Text me when you go home."

"Will do."

Turning to Tess, I said, "Thanks for the camisole. How can I make it up to you?"

Skye wiggled her eyebrows. "Oh, we'll find a way. Now go, or you'll be late."

I kissed Avery goodbye, grinning from ear to ear as I stepped out of the store. I rarely came to Soho, and now I wondered why. It was wonderfully romantic. Everyone sitting outside was relaxed, not huddled over their warm drinks. The end of March was usually when the weather resembled spring more than winter.

Adrenaline was pumping in my veins. I was seeing Ryker in twenty minutes. I couldn't wait. I had a feeling tonight was going to be epic.

Chapter Sixteen
Heather

Friday nights were crazy in Manhattan, but despite being squeezed between other passengers in the subway, giddiness completely overpowered me.

I blinked at the explosion of lights and colors when I came out in Times Square, where I was meeting Ryker. We'd decided on one of the giant billboards as our meeting point. To my astonishment, I noticed Ryker coming out of the subway station as well. He stood out even surrounded by the mass of New Yorkers out to enjoy life. He simply had that magnetic presence that demanded to be appreciated. One look around revealed that I wasn't the only one affected by him. I counted at least five women appreciating the view.

My heart squeezed. Oh, shit. I couldn't be jealous... already. But I was. Ryker noticed me the next second.

"Hey!"

"You like to take the subway?" I asked, perplexed.

"Yeah. Cabs take longer in traffic. And why waste money when we have a perfectly good subway?"

I hadn't expected Ryker to be so down-to-earth. He certainly didn't have to worry about money.

"Shall we?" he asked.

I nodded, and we started walking in the general direction of the cinema. Ryker immediately put an arm around my shoulders, as if he was afraid he might lose me in the crowd. As if that was even possible. I was so aware of his presence, as if there was a palpable bond between us.

My heart rate sped up when he pulled me closer, touching the tip of his nose to my temple. A knot formed between my shoulder blades.

I can do this.

I'm ready.

I repeated the words a few times, but far from calming down, I was just working myself into a frenzy. My palms grew a little sweaty. I tried to hide them by putting my hands in my pockets. Ryker pressed his fingers into my arm, as if sensing I needed reassurance.

When we entered the cinema, he brought his mouth to my ear.

"You want me to bring you back to my sister's store?"

"N-no."

"That's not very convincing, love."

He let go of me, but our gazes were interlocked.

"Talk to me, Heather. What's going on in your mind?"

"I'm not sure I can explain. At least, not in a

way that makes sense."

He brought a hand to my face, caressing my cheek. I loved that he wasn't pressuring me, that he understood I needed to gather my thoughts at my own pace.

"I'm afraid that this is too soon after my breakup."

He frowned. "Heather, this is about discovering each other. So far, I love everything I know about you."

"You do?"

"Yeah. You're a fantastic woman, a great mother."

"There you go, being charming again."

He smiled. "I can't help it."

"I think you can, you just don't want to because you know it's irresistible."

"Glad to know it's working. I like you, Heather. But if you want to go back to the store, just say the word." He moved his thumb over my lower lip.

"What happened to seizing the chance?"

Ryker tilted closer until I felt his breath on my skin. "I didn't say I wouldn't try again."

I laughed. My pulse was jackhammering in my ears. His cologne and mere presence were so intense that I couldn't even think past how right this felt—his touch, his nearness. And those words. How did he always know what I needed to hear?

"Let's buy the tickets," I said softly. "And popcorn."

Ryker stepped back, smiling. "Popcorn for the lady, got it. Anything else?"

"Diet Coke."

"Got it. You go pick up the tickets from the prepaid counter. I'll line up for the food and drinks."

"Sounds like a plan." I nodded, full of excitement as I walked to the prepaid counter. Even though the line there was much shorter than Ryker's, it moved infinitely slower.

I was just about to take out my phone to check if Natasha had messaged me when a guy approached me.

"Hey, beautiful," he said lazily. "You alone? I'll keep you company."

"No need. I'm here with someone."

"Well, if he left you alone, that's his problem."

"He went to buy popcorn," I said coldly.

The guy didn't budge.

"What do you say we get out of here?"

"What do you say about getting lost?" I replied, in no mood to fend off anyone's advances. Another downside of going out on Friday evening. Some people started happy hour really early. The whiff of cheap whiskey told me that was the case with this guy. Out of the corner of my eye, I spied Ryker walking toward us with determined strides. Oh, this was going to be good.

I barely held back a smile when Ryker stopped right next to me.

"Get lost. She's mine."

Oh, my. That tone of voice was just delicious. It warmed my heart that he thought of me as his... but I didn't know what Ryker expected and if I was ready to fulfill those expectations.

The guy quirked up a brow. "Maybe I'll wait for her to tell me that."

"I already did. Ryker, let's move somewhere else."

"Get out of our way, or I'll remove you from this building myself." Ryker's tone was dangerously calm. The guy must have noticed that too, because he backed off. Either that, or he finally realized that Ryker was much, much more muscular than him. On top of that, Ryker gave off that dominant vibe that made you think he could win any fight he wanted—even if it was just a battle of wills.

"Let's get the tickets together," he said.

"What about the popcorn and drinks?"

"Bought them already but told the cashier to keep them there when I saw that douchebag."

"Okay."

He didn't want to leave my side? That was so... I didn't even know how to describe it, but I felt so important. Protected.

After picking up the tickets, we went to the food counter. I tried to hide my disappointment at the serving size he'd chosen: small. I was hungry, and this was going to be my dinner. His portion was small as well. I wondered if I could get away with stealing some of his.

As we headed to the theater, I took off my

jacket.

"Fuck," Ryker muttered.

I glanced up and nearly swallowed my tongue. Ryker's gaze was not just intense, but feral. He was looking me up and down slowly. I felt great wearing the new camisole underneath my wool dress, it just made me feel that little bit sexier. My choice of footwear was also intentional: sexy stiletto half boots instead of my usual flat, knee-length boots, and tights.

We were in a narrow corridor next to a small table in front of another empty theater. Ours was further down at the end of the hallway. Ryker set his popcorn bag and soda cup on the table, then did the same with mine.

I was about to ask what was going on, when his intent became clear. Interlacing one hand with mine, he pulled me into the room. It was completely dark inside. Ryker's mouth came down on mine the next second. His kisses were usually exquisite, but now he was taking everything to a whole new level. He explored me with an urgency that made me burn. And when he lowered himself on one of the chairs, pulling me in his lap, I curled my knees at his side instantly. His hand slipped under my dress. The contact electrified me. I pushed my hips into him, moaning softly. He pressed his fingers on my flesh, as if it was all he could do not to rip apart my tights. I felt his other hand in my hair, cupping the back of my head. He kissed me until I was so weak for him and so turned on that I could barely think.

"Heather, fuck," he murmured against my lips.

"I think our movie is going to start."

He made a sound I couldn't quite decipher before helping me climb down from his lap. As we left the room, I felt him look at me. In the dimly lit corridor, I glanced up. Oh, heavens... if I thought his gaze had been feral before, it was nothing compared to this. He looked as if he was having second thoughts about the movie and would much rather just throw me over his shoulder and take me out of the building.

I felt him watch me as I picked up my popcorn and drink. He followed suit, then guided me to our actual theater. I chuckled as we sat down. I hadn't gone on a movie date since college.

"You know, I've never made out at the theater?" I whispered to Ryker.

His mouth curled into a satisfied smile. I simmered. Simmered! And the man wasn't even trying to seduce me right now. Oh, heavens. How was I supposed to just sit with him for the next two hours?

By focusing on the movie, that was how.

It became clear within the first minutes that Ryker was a terrible person to go to a movie with. He kept trying to explain back stories and trivia, with the result that I spent more time shushing him than paying attention. On the bright side, he was so focused on explaining every detail that I'd managed to eat half his popcorn too. I'd wolfed down mine during the trailers.

"I'm never watching another movie with you," I announced when we returned to the main hall. "You're one of those awful people who talk through the whole thing. Worst movie companion."

"I promise I make a better dinner companion."

"What do you mean?"

"You didn't think I wouldn't take you to dinner, did you?"

"You didn't say anything about dinner."

"Didn't want to risk you saying no. I want to spend more time with you, Heather. And I'm starving. Aren't you?"

I narrowed my eyes. "You bought a small popcorn bag on purpose, didn't you?"

He grinned. "Guilty."

"Ohhh...." I'd just realized a tiny detail. "Skye, Tess, and your mom already know, don't they?"

"And Natasha. Had to tell her so she could make plans for Avery accordingly."

"How do you even know Natasha? And how to contact her?"

"I have my ways of finding out what I want."

"You thought about everything."

My pulse jackhammered in my throat, my chest, my ears. I couldn't focus on anything else except Ryker, as if we were separated from our surroundings by a veil. How could he do that? Reduce everything to a low background noise? Make my entire body hum with one look, one touch? Make me want things I'd been determined to avoid only a few weeks back?

"Okay. Where are you taking me?"

"I have a few surprises in store."

Like his sisters, Ryker didn't do anything half-heartedly. The restaurant he'd brought us to was on a ship on the Hudson river. Twinkling lights adorned the metal railing outside. The restaurant's walls were made out of floor-to-ceiling glass. We had an excellent view of the city.

"If I didn't know better, I'd say you're out to impress me," I teased.

"I am. Want to sit outside?"

"Sure."

It was a bit chilly here on the river, but they had gas heaters next to every table. Unfortunately, the heat was reflected from above, so my legs were cold within minutes. As if realizing that, Ryker asked for a blanket, placing it on my legs, tucking it in at the sides.

"So careful," I murmured.

"Just making sure my girl's taken care of. Don't want to give her a reason to say no to the next date."

My stomach flipped. "Already planning the next date?"

"Planning much more than that, but let's start small."

Well, what could I say to that?

There were only two set menus to choose from, each boasting five courses. Everything sounded delicious. We ended up choosing different menus, so we could taste what each had to offer. Despite being hungry, I was too captivated by Ryker to properly pay attention to the food.

"So, let's see if I got this straight," I said. "Tess is pretty balls to the wall when she's after something. And Skye is subtle—"

Ryker held up a finger. "Sort of. I mean, Skye is more laid-back than Tess, except in crisis situations. Then she goes from relaxed to... dragon."

I laughed, trying to picture Skye upset. "Yeah, I can totally see that. Let's talk about Cole. What is there to know about him? He made an impression at the gala."

"Did he now?" He cocked a brow.

I batted my eyelashes. "Oh, yeah. Your family is easy to like. I mean, your sisters just volunteered to spend time with Avery."

"They like Avery."

"Plus, they like torturing you."

"That too."

"I think they're very brave, just going for what they want."

"Yeah, they are. But I also think they're taking on a lot."

My heart squeezed at the way he genuinely worried for their well-being. Seeing all the Winchester siblings together made me think how great it would be for Avery to have a sister or a brother. I hadn't considered that before, but now I could imagine a toddler with dark blond hair and blue eyes.

Wow, I'd basically described Ryker. Holy shit, how had my mind jumped there?

"What are you thinking about?" Ryker asked.

I felt my cheeks heat up. Usually, I loved not filtering my thoughts around Ryker, but it was best not to voice this one. Way to send him running.

"Just... how nice it is to have a large family and all live in the same place."

"Where are your parents?"

"In Arizona. A small town near Phoenix. Avery goes to see them during school breaks. They spoil her all day long, undoing all my good work. Every time she returns, she's back to default factory settings."

Ryker laughed, helping himself to more wine. By the time we'd finished dessert, I wasn't sure I'd ever be able to eat again.

"This was delicious, but too much," I said.

"You still don't look completely relaxed."

I smiled, shrugging. "Sorry. I'm not sure I know how to completely let go. Haven't done that in a while."

"Leave it to me. I just have to up my game."

"Oh, and how do you plan to do that?"

"No heads-up. It's more fun if I show you. The evening isn't over yet."

"It's not?"

My heart rate quickened. I leaned forward in

anticipation. What else did this gorgeous man have in store for us? He was just full of surprises, wasn't he? And I loved every single one of them. "Have you asked for permission for that?" I teased.

He nodded, surprising the heck out of me. "Avery and I have our secrets."

"I can see that."

"Spoke to her that night we were at the gala."

Oh, shit. My eyes became misty. I glanced at my hands, trying to hide it. This man! He was getting under my skin. If he kept this up, he was going to stay there.

"I told you I'd take care of you. So I'll have to prove it. And I will, starting tonight."

"I thought you only asked permission for movie and dinner."

"I did, but I have my tricks to get what I want. And I'm sure Avery will be on my team. Besides, your shoulders are still up to your ears. It's my duty to make you relax."

"Your duty? That doesn't sound like fun."

Ryker winked, leaning into me.

"My duty and my pleasure. How does that sound, Ms. Prescott?"

"Like something I can look forward to."

"Right answer."

Chapter Seventeen
Heather

I texted Natasha to ask if they'd already left Manhattan, but she replied that they'd gone back to the store after dinner.

Avery pouted when Ryker and I arrived, clearly wanting to stay longer. She was sitting on the same chair where she'd been when I'd left, only instead of a coloring book, she had fabrics in front of her.

"Mommy, look what I made." She held up a red cloth covered in glitter.

Skye, Tess, and Natasha were leaning against the counter. There weren't any gift bags left. Wow, they'd sorted all those? After my dinner with Ryker, I saw the sisters in a different light. They did look tired.

"Avery got bored of the coloring book," Skye explained.

"So you sacrificed fabric instead?"

Skye waved her hand. "They were just leftover scraps from damaged items."

"Where's Amelia?"

"Left about ten minutes ago," Tess said, looking between Ryker and me, lips pressed firmly together. I could tell she had a million questions, and Avery was the only reason she wasn't firing away. Ah, what I wouldn't give to hear them quiz Ryker later.

"Avery, we have to go," I said.

"But I'm not done with the glitter."

"It's late, sweetheart."

"You can take the glitter bottle and the rest of the fabric with you. I'll put them in a box," Tess offered. Avery looked at her as if she'd hung the moon.

I helped Avery into her jacket while Tess packed the box. When she handed it to Avery, she clutched it in her arms as if it was her most prized possession.

"You know what, I think I'll stay out for a while longer," Natasha said, beaming. "Unless you need me to come with you?"

"We're good. Thanks a lot, Natasha."

"I'll order an Uber," Ryker said. I wasn't even going to ask again that he not come with us. And honestly, I wanted to spend more time with him.

"Can we go with the train?" Avery asked, looking between the two of us. Ryker deferred to me.

"Why not? The car isn't much faster."

The train was as full as expected on a Friday evening, but we still managed to secure three seats.

"Mom, did you like the movie?" Avery asked.

I didn't want to disappoint my daughter... but I also didn't want to lie to her.

Ryker must have noticed my dilemma,

because he answered for me. "We made progress. But I'll have to show her a few more before we win her over to our side."

"Ooooh. Can I spend time with Amelia or Tess and Skye when you take Mom to the movies?"

"If you want to." Ryker sounded a little too pleased. He looked at me over Avery's head, winking. "So, what other movies do you think I should take your mom to?"

Avery tapped one finger against her chin, the way I did it when I was deep in thought, before launching into a debate with Ryker. I just watched them, unable to get a word in—I honestly had no clue what they were talking about. Ryker was out of his depth too when it came to movies outside of the superhero genre, but he covered it well.

He wasn't one bit condescending or looking for a way out of the conversation.

"You think Mommy is listening to us?" Avery asked, snapping me out of my thoughts.

"Don't think so," Ryker replied playfully before lowering his mouth to Avery's ear, holding a hand in front of his mouth as he whispered something.

"Yes," Avery declared, giggling.

"Hey, I want to know what's going on," I protested.

Ryker shook his head. "Nah, we still have to keep our secrets."

"Ryker, I have a science fair on Thursday," Avery said. "Do you want to come?"

I froze. Damn, I didn't see this coming. Avery was shy, usually didn't like anyone else watching her except me. Ryker looked as stunned as I felt, but before I could come up with a smart way to answer, he said, "Sure. I'll talk about the details with your mom, but I'll be there."

There was no stopping that dangerous train of thought I'd embarked on at the restaurant, even though I was a little worried that Ryker had felt obligated to say yes. Was this too much? What was I thinking; of course it was. I had to offer him a way out before the night was over.

That worry intensified when we entered the apartment. The reality of single motherhood might put him off. I was a little jittery as I spoke next.

"Ummm... I have to help Avery go to bed."

"Go ahead."

I felt Ryker watch us as we walked to Avery's room. She talked about her evening through the entire routine. While I combed her hair with the Tangle Teezer, Avery looked at me in the mirror, clutching the teddy bear she slept with in her arms.

"Mommy, is Ryker going to come here again?"

I wanted to scream *Yes, yes, yes* at the top of my lungs. Instead, I hid my smile behind Avery's head.

"Do you want him to?"

"He's nice." Avery nodded excitedly. I couldn't help myself. I hugged my daughter, glancing at her in the mirror.

"I think so too. Come on, let's go to bed."

I was so full of this happy energy. Just knowing that Ryker was in the next room made me giddy. This man had entered into my life one month ago, and he was already such a huge part of it that I didn't know what to make of it.

After kissing Avery goodnight, I let myself out of her room, taking a quick trip to the bathroom, checking my appearance. Should I shower? No, that would take too long. Reapply makeup? That seemed silly. I just got rid of my tights. It was too hot for them inside the house.

Ryker is in the living room, waiting for me.

I had no idea how the rest of the evening would go. I'd signed up for a movie tonight and had ended up on the most swoon-worthy dinner date. What else did Ryker have in store for me?

Well... I had to join him to find out. Ryker was sitting on the couch when I returned to the living room, moving his finger in a come here motion. I practically flew to him. He patted the spot next to him.

"Finally going to reveal your tricks?" I teased.

"Neck massage."

I sat on the couch with my back to him. He lowered the zipper of my dress.

"That's necessary for a *neck* massage?" I asked.

"Definitely. Most points of tension are actually on the upper back."

Wow, his hands were pure magic. I wasn't

sure why this all got to me. Maybe because Ryker was doing all this without any expectation. He pressed his fingers on the pressure points on my shoulder blades, then the muscles along my spine. Every time he touched my bare skin, I shuddered. I couldn't help myself. It was an involuntary reaction. Oh God, if he kept doing that, I was going to ask him to stay the night, and I really couldn't go there. It would take this to a whole new level, and I wasn't even sure what *this* was.

But when Ryker dropped his hands, placing his mouth on my bare back, he wiped all thoughts from my mind except how much I wanted him here with me.

He touched his lips to my skin first, and then the tip of his tongue. My entire body already felt on fire. How was this possible? And how was I supposed to stop this when I wanted nothing more than to turn around and wrap myself around him?

He pushed the dress off one shoulder, moving his mouth over the exposed skin before slowly turning me around, pulling me into his lap. Ryker crushed his mouth to mine, and I responded to the kiss with no restraint. I'd never felt anything like this, and I didn't have to pause and think why: it was just Ryker. I couldn't be with him and not be completely consumed by him. I moved my mouth down his jaw and neck, sucking a little on his Adam's apple. He fisted my hair, keeping me close.

"Babe, wait," he murmured. I straightened up, noticing Ryker had clenched the blanket on the couch with his free hand. His knuckles brushed my thigh. He'd been seconds away from sliding his hand under my dress.

"If you continue that way, I'm going to try to seduce you, and we can't have that, because I wouldn't leave until the morning."

I'd completely lost track of... everything, and he was the one who remembered where we were? Sensed that I wasn't ready for him to spend the night here?

I might just have to do everything in my power to make him fall in love with me. I mean, what other option did I have to make sure I didn't lose him?

I chose my next words carefully. Hopefully he couldn't guess where my mind had just been.

"You're going to *try* and seduce me?" I teased. "What do you call what you've been doing until now?"

"Looking after you. If I wanted to seduce you, I'd do this."

He let go of the blanket, lazily stroked his thumb on my outer thigh until his hand disappeared under my dress. The second goose bumps formed on my thighs, our gazes locked. He slid his hands to my inner thighs, stopping just at the hem of my panties. He kissed one corner of my mouth before biting my lower lip. When he stroked over my panties, I shuddered, clenching my thighs. I wanted him so much, and the way he pressed the drenched fabric over my sensitive skin was pure torture.

"Baby, fuck. You're wet." His voice was almost a growl. My entire body was on fire... even more so when Ryker traced the strap of my bra with his other hand, as if he was seconds away from taking off my clothes. To my surprise, he dropped both hands.

"This wasn't part of the plan," he said.

"Enlighten me. What *are* you planning?"

"At least a couple more dates before we move on to the overnighter."

"Mmm, you think I'm so easy to win over, do you?"

"All evidence points that I'm on the right path. Plus, I'm willing to learn."

Oh, man. He was making it harder and harder for me to climb out of his lap and see him to the door, and that feral glint in his eyes made one thing clear: he was walking a fine line, and was very close to falling over the edge.

I had to be the one to keep my head cool. The only problem was that I already felt very... seduced.

Reluctantly, I climbed out of his lap. He immediately rose to his feet, walking away from the couch, as if staying too close made it too tempting to fall back into each other's arms. Well, the risk was very real.

As I walked him to the door, I suddenly remembered that Avery had asked him to come to her science fair.

"Ryker, I'm sorry Avery ambushed you with her fair. Don't worry about it. I'll tell her she can't invite people just like that."

"Heather, I want to come."

"Really?"

"Yeah."

"But it'll just be a group of kids standing next to posters. A bit boring."

"You'll be there?"

"Of course."

"Not boring, then."

I was smiling from ear to ear when we reached the door.

"What do you think, far enough from the couch?" he asked.

"Far enough for what?"

"Kissing you without the risk of wanting to yank off your clothes."

Ahh, by the edge in his voice, I had a hunch he still wanted that very much. Before I could answer, he gripped my hips and kissed me, deep and wet, and just didn't let go... not until I felt a hard surface behind me.

He chuckled. "Fuck, woman, I'll just pin you against the wall."

"You already are," I pointed out.

"I think not touching is a better strategy." He took a step back, holding his hands in the air. I was *that* tempting, huh? Good to know. Because I couldn't just shove him out the door like this, I gave him a quick peck on the lips before bidding him goodbye.

I did a little dance in my entrance hall after

Ryker left. I couldn't believe tonight. It had been... I didn't even know how to describe it. I just couldn't wrap my mind around everything... including all the budding feelings I already had for him. Ryker had swept into my life like a hurricane. I hadn't been prepared. I still didn't feel prepared. And yet I already knew that falling head over heels for this amazing man would be inevitable.

Chapter Eighteen
Ryker

"Mr. Ryker, did you like my poster?" Avery asked next Thursday, after we left the science fair.

"It was interesting," I replied. Out of the corner of my eye, I saw Heather was about to burst out laughing. *Interesting* was a very generous way to describe the few volcano drawings and pics on the poster. Honestly, some of the projects looked like they were an April Fool's joke, which was appropriate since it was the first of April.

That prompting was all Avery needed to go into detail about formation of volcanoes and whatnot. Then she switched gears, talking about her upcoming trip to her grandparents'. She was leaving next week for her Easter vacation.

On the way home, we passed an ice-cream parlor.

"Want to go for ice cream?" I asked. Avery practically lit up. Heather narrowed her eyes. She saw right through my tactic. I wiggled my eyebrows, putting an arm around her shoulders, pulling her nearer.

"You're cheating," she whispered.

"I know," I whispered back. But I didn't know the rules yet, and I planned to play the clueless card for as long as possible.

The ice-cream parlor was full, so we stood in line. It was almost our turn when Heather's phone rang.

"I'm going outside to take this," she said.

"Sure."

"What does your mom usually buy for you?" I asked Avery when we had to order.

"A cone with three scoops," she answered in one breath.

"Okay. Let's buy yours."

Avery was so ecstatic that I couldn't help grin. Was it really this easy to make kids happy? I'd always thought there was more to it.

Heather joined us just then. Her eyes bulged when she noticed Avery's cone.

"How much ice cream is that?" she asked.

"Three scoops," I said. "She said that's what you usually buy her."

"Kid-sized scoops."

I glanced at Avery. "You didn't tell me that."

Avery shrugged. "You didn't ask."

"Fair enough."

Heather laughed, pointing to a table. "Wait for us there, Avery. We'll buy ours and join you."

Avery practically ran away, as if afraid her ice cream might get confiscated. I took Heather's hand, pulling her closer to the counter. "What about you?"

"Mango. You?"

"Not really in the mood for ice cream."

"What do you want instead?"

I didn't answer. Instead, I ran my fingers lazily up and down her palm, making my intention clear. I wanted *her*. Heather cleared her throat, but her voice was slightly breathy when she ordered her mango ice cream. Her cheeks were a little flushed. Fuck, I loved seeing her react like this to a simple touch and implication. She was still blushing when we sat next to Avery.

She'd already finished hers, though by her appearance, she'd smeared half on it on her face, her hair, even on her jacket. She was already eyeing Heather's cup.

"So, Avery, what are your plans with your grandparents?"

"I will play *all* the time. I have a big room at their house. And they have a *huuuuge* yard."

"I think Avery would move there if she could," Heather joked.

"I love Arizona. It's warm, and I can always play outside."

"See? She crushes my heart every time." On a smile, she added, "We should get going. It's late. And you need to get to the Northern Lights, right?"

I nodded. "Yeah. My set starts in an hour."

"Mommy, the nice man at the counter said he'll give me cookies before I leave. Can I go get them?"

"Sure."

Heather kept an eye on Avery as she darted to

the counter.

"By the way, I'm coming in for a second round of interviews next week, just before I drop off Avery at the airport. Danielle—my editor—just told me she spoke to Owen."

"Perfect. Stop by my office when you have a break."

"Why? I'm not interviewing you."

I smiled, touching a hand to her cheek. "Interview isn't what I had in mind."

"Ryker...."

"Just come by my office," I repeated. Her eyes flashed. She licked her lower lip. I dragged my thumb over the same spot. Fuck. I just wanted to pull her behind the store and kiss her until she begged for more.

"I'll consider it." Her tone was teasing, but by the light tremor in her body, I knew I'd already won the battle. I liked that every time we were together, she gave in to me more easily, that she was more open. "Go, before you're too late."

I was shocked to discover I wasn't looking forward to performing as much as usual. In fact, I would've preferred to spend the evening right here. I'd never considered ditching a chance to perform for anyone except my family... until now.

***

The next week was brutal, full of ups and downs on the stock market. I kept my cool, as usual, which was one of the reasons I'd shot to the top as quickly as I did.

Whenever I had a spare moment, I messaged Heather, and even dropped by with dinner one evening on impulse. I barely kept from inviting myself over more often. I didn't want to push too much, too soon. I had no idea how my life could change so drastically in just six weeks, since I'd first noticed Heather at the Northern Lights, but I liked being with them—both of them.

Friday had always been my favorite day. This one even more so, because Heather was inside the building for another round of interviews. But right now, I had one of the city's heavy hitters sitting on the other side of my desk. He wanted reassurance. I was confident in my predictions, the advice I gave to clients.

"You know I'm right."

"You always are. You made me a lot of money."

"Then trust me on this one. The stock value will recover within a month. All indicators are in line with that prediction."

I got to my feet, signaling that this meeting was over. Usually, I didn't hurry clients, but I needed him out in the next few minutes. Heather had been here for a few hours. She was finishing the interviews in about ten minutes, and I didn't want to miss the window of opportunity to see her.

"Okay. Okay. Let's keep in touch next week."

"Of course. My door is always open."

Except now.

I showed him out, using the pretext to check where Heather was. Still in the meeting room. She had her back to me, but her interview partner, Melissa, waved when she saw me. That prompted Heather to look over her shoulder. Her eyes widened slightly. I didn't do anything to give us away, just walked back to my office and texted her. I was craving her nearness. I'd thought it was hard to behave around her the first time she was here for interviews... but now, after I'd touched her, after I'd had a taste of her, I couldn't be around her and not want to be *near* her.

I paced the office, smiling when I heard a knock. I went to open it right away. Heather stood there, looking sexy as hell in her little black suit.

I pulled her inside, locking the door.

"Did you just lock the door?" she asked.

"Yes."

"Why?"

"Don't want anyone walking in on us."

"And a locked door wouldn't give them any reason to question what's happening in here?"

She made a good point, only I didn't particularly care. I walked her backward to the wall, cupping her head as I pushed my hips against hers, and kissed her the next second.

She tasted like coffee and chocolate, and I fucking loved it. She moaned when I coaxed her tongue, pushed her hips into me when I skimmed my hands down the sides of her body. I tugged at her shirt before remembering where we were. Damn. I was hard. I pushed myself into her, wanting her to know.

She moaned again, rubbing against me. I planted both hands on the wall to keep from just yanking away her clothes. "Wow, that's a hell of a greeting," she murmured, but then wiggled out of my grasp. I noticed my right sleeve was loose. Heather had dislodged one of my cuff links. We both saw it on the floor. She blushed when I wiggled my eyebrows at her.

"Don't go. Stay just for a little while. We can make up a reason," I said.

"I wish I could... but I need to drop Avery off at JFK. Mom is arriving from Phoenix at four o'clock to pick her up. Then their plane leaves for Phoenix one hour later."

I wanted her to stay a while longer. What had I been thinking, imagining that a few minutes would be enough? Honestly, this was so new to me that anything I imagined was probably incorrect.

I stalked toward her, but she held up a finger. "No, no. I can already feel that my lips are swollen. Probably a bit red too. You can't kiss me again."

"Want to bet?"

She laughed, rubbing her neck with one hand. "When do you finish work?"

"Probably around seven."

"Want to have dinner together? At my place?"

"Fuck, yes."

"Okay. We've got a plan. Aaand I'm off before you try to kiss me again."

"Hey, you're the dangerous one." I pointed to the cuff link on the floor. She laughed, but she scurried out the door the next second, closing it behind her as if afraid I might go after her if she didn't. Well, there was a real risk I would. I couldn't believe that I felt euphoric just because she wanted to catch up later. It meant that she couldn't wait to be with me any more than I could wait to be with her.

***

Heather

The rest of the day was a marathon in the true sense of the word. Mom waited for Avery and me in front of the check-in counter, as usual.

"Hey!" I kissed her cheek, pulling her into a hug.

"My girls, I've missed you." She hugged us both before pulling back and giving me what I liked to call the Mom-check. I was still wearing the black suit I'd conducted my interviews in, but my hair was in complete disarray. My mother never left the house looking anything short of perfect: coiffed hair, flawless makeup.

"Hon, why don't you take some time off and join us?" Mom asked.

"I have a lot of deadlines coming up. I'll visit soon, though. I promise." I turned to Avery. "Be good, okay? And listen to Gran and Pops."

"Yes, Mommy."

"Okay, check-in all done. Say goodbye, girls,

we need to go through security," Mom said.

It always broke my heart just a little that Avery had no problems saying goodbye, while I just wanted to wrap my arms around her and not let her go, but this also meant that she was completely happy spending time with my parents. Whenever Mom picked her up, it was as if her life in New York didn't exist. It was all about her room in Arizona, her toys there, her chickens, and her pony. Their bonfires and exploration trips. It made me miss home like crazy, and I was happy my daughter got to experience a piece of my childhood.

The moment they were out of sight, I went into a frenzy. I still had so much to do today!

I had two hours left until Ryker would come to my place. I wanted to prepare the perfect dinner. Not just the food, but the ambiance too. I had that last part down: romantic, but not too feminine. Diffuse lighting but no candles. It would take me no time at all to set it up.

But the food... I had no idea what Ryker liked to eat. I tried to recall what he'd had the few times we'd met up... and came up blank. Holy shit, and I prided myself in having an excellent memory. But I'd been so wrapped up in him that I didn't even remember what *I* had eaten on those occasions.

I went to a shopping area near my place, but after entering and exiting the second store empty-handed, I decided that I needed a new plan. A better plan. I was going to call Skye.

Was I crossing boundaries by bringing his

family into this? Then again, he'd plotted first, when he'd conspired with them. Besides, he'd conspired with Avery too. Ryker wouldn't mind. Besides, it was better to cross boundaries than poison him. My food was mediocre at best when I cooked freestyle, but if I followed a detailed recipe, it was delicious.

I sat on a bench under a crab apple tree. The white blooms looked like something out of a fairy tale, and the sweet scent made me hungry. Mid-April was one of my favorite periods in the city. I couldn't wait to have some time to venture to Central Park and see the cherry trees in blossom.

Before I could talk myself out of it, I called Skye.

"Hey. Is this a good time to talk?" I asked.

"Sure. I'm just sorting out some inventory. Fire away."

"So, umm... Ryker and I have a date tonight, and I want to surprise him by cooking for him. What's his favorite dish?"

"Roast beef and au gratin potatoes."

"That sounds... like something I can completely screw up. Do you have a recipe? The more detailed the better."

"I'll look one up and send you the link. Just give me a sec."

"Thanks! You're a lifesaver."

"No one's asked me this before," Skye said. "I think my brother's hit the jackpot with you."

I laughed nervously. "Wait to see the result of dinner before you praise me too much."

"Oh, I trust you, Heather Prescott."

I was still in a frenzy after hanging up. While waiting for Skye to send me the recipe, I decided to take a time-out. I found a vintage coffee shop and sat at one of their tiny round tables. The white paint was chipping off, but in a lovely rustic way. I ordered a cappuccino and a scone.

Damn, big mistake. I was already jittery, and the coffee didn't help. Neither did the sugar. By the time Skye messaged me, I was so nervous I could barely sit.

And that recipe, oh God. It had a million steps. It also required a meat thermometer, which I didn't have. Okay, I could do this. I could definitely do this.

I went to the butcher across the street. A panicky feeling overcame me when the butcher glanced at the recipe and proclaimed it was all kinds of wrong and that I'd ruin a great piece of meat by following it. Well, that *was not* helpful.

I just smiled politely, paid for the products, and darted out of the store before he could scare me some more.

By the time I arrived home, I didn't have *that* much time left.

I could shower and get all pretty and fancy for Ryker while everything was in the oven. Yeah, I could do that.

Five minutes into following the recipe, I realized it was even harder than I'd anticipated. Still, I persisted. I'd even bought one of those fancy thermometers. When everything was in the oven, I hurried to the bathroom. I was late. Ryker was supposed to arrive in forty minutes, yet the beef needed ninety in the oven. Oh well, I just had to entertain him until it was done... and I was quite good at that.

After a quick shower, I put on a short, silky dress that just spelled seduction and sprayed on a new perfume. I didn't style my hair aside from blow-drying it, but it fell into loose curls all around me.

I was ready for the evening to start.

When the bell rang, I had to reconsider that statement. My heartbeat went from normal into overdrive in a fraction of a second. I pressed a palm on my chest, hoping to calm down, but feeling the wild pulse under my hand only made me more aware of it.

I hurried to the door, opening it with a big smile. He'd taken off his coat already, giving me a prime view of his suit. My gaze automatically went to his right cuff link—the one I'd dislodged today. He'd fastened it back.

"Already thinking about tearing it off again?" he teased, putting me at ease a little.

"Of course, but not before I feed you."

I'd asked him here on a spur of the moment impulse, before I had time to second-guess anything. And right now? My stomach was full of butterflies, and I hadn't even let Ryker in yet.

Chapter Nineteen
Ryker

"Heather, you look amazing."

"Thanks. Come in."

"What's that smell?" I asked as she led me to the living room.

She glanced at me over her shoulder. "Roast beef."

She'd cooked for me? That was... I had no idea why that got to me.

"It's my favorite."

"I know. I asked Skye."

"You called my sister to ask what my favorite meal is?"

"That's right. I'm excellent at following recipe instructions. And I'm proud to announce that I now even own a meat thermometer and know how to use it. At least, for your sake... I hope I do."

I swallowed hard. She'd called my sister? Just to surprise me? No one had done anything like that for me. Her gaze turned from playful to uncertain.

"I overstepped boundaries, didn't I?"

"What? Hell, no." I grabbed her by the waist, turning her around so she was facing me.

"You just surprised me, that's all."

I captured her mouth. I'd been dying to do that ever since she'd been at my office today—kiss her like I really meant it... which lately translated to not stopping, not wanting to let her go. Especially right now, after this welcome.

"Thanks, Heather. You didn't have to go to so much trouble."

"It wasn't too much trouble."

"Liar."

"Fine, I am lying. I spent the entire afternoon running around like a crazy person. So even if you don't like it, you have to say you like it."

She was avoiding my gaze, moving up and down on her toes.

"Am I making you nervous?" I brought my hand to her face, touching her lips with my thumb.

"Yes."

"Why?"

"I... I don't know," she said.

"There's no reason to be nervous. It's just me, baby."

Coming home to you.

The thought just popped into my brain, completely unexpected. But hell if it didn't sound right. Feel right. I'd never had anything like this before.

"And I'll like your roast beef even if it's burned to a crisp."

She buried her head in my neck, chuckling. "Hey. Don't jinx it."

"Come on. Let's check on it together."

"Okay."

She led me to the kitchen, proudly pointing to the oven.

"How does it look?"

I knew before I even opened it that the beef was completely dry. But she was so nervous already that hell would freeze over before I admitted it.

"Like it's ready."

I carried the food to the table while she brought plates.

"How did Avery take leaving for Arizona?" I asked as we were about to sit.

Heather looked at me warmly. "Thanks for asking. She was psyched. She's always over the moon when Mom takes her. I'm more emotional than her. I'll be melancholic the whole week."

She sighed deeply, her smile fading. I moved closer, touching her neck with the back of my fingers. "I'll distract you from that."

"You are amazing at distracting me, that's true."

"And I haven't even used my best weapons yet."

"Oh, I see. Keeping the best for when we're alone?"

"That's right."

That brilliant smile was back on. Mission accomplished. I skimmed my hand down her body, cupping her ass, pushing her hips against me. Damn, I was already turned on. Her eyes widened.

"Wow. You plan on starting right now?" She

batted her eyelashes, running her hands down my chest.

"No. Just giving you a taste."

She frowned, stepping back. "Tease."

I grinned, happy I'd managed to take her mind off Avery's trip.

"Let's eat. I'm starving," she said.

We sat at the table, helping ourselves to beef and potatoes. Heather watched me intently.

"Why are you looking at me like that?" I asked.

"Trying to check if you really like the food."

I had a great poker face. Staying calm and composed despite the stock market's volatility was a job requirement. But in my personal life, I'd rarely had to use it.

"Heather, stop fretting. What are your plans for the week?" I changed the subject smoothly.

"I have a few deadlines coming... but I'll come by the Northern Lights and watch you play." In a lower voice, she added, "Then I'll take you backstage and jump you."

"Why are you whispering?"

Giggling, she shrugged. "Habit, I guess. When are you playing?"

"Tuesday."

"I'll be in the front row. I can't wait. You're walking seduction with that guitar."

I touched her legs under the table. "Don't need a guitar to seduce you."

She blushed, biting her lower lip. "That's true,

you don't."

We chatted about our day until we cleared our plates, because neither of us had really eaten much of the meal. It wasn't bad, just well cooked—I'd have to interrogate my sister to see what she was up to.

Heather jumped out of her seat screeching, "Oh my God, I completely forgot the wine."

She started to go to the kitchen, but I caught her hand, pulling her back, and sat down with her right into my lap.

"Heather. Stop. Fretting."

"Yes, sir." Grinning, she placed her hands on my shoulders. "I just want you to feel good here. Maybe you'll stop by again."

"I will. You're not getting rid of me, Heather."

"Yeah?

I kissed up her neck, nibbling at her earlobe before rising from the chair and placing Heather on the empty portion of the table. She leaned back on her palms so I had all the access I wanted. I moved my mouth down her chest, teasing that soft skin, claiming it inch by inch.

I needed her, and I needed her right now. I couldn't focus on anything other than kissing her, touching her, but one thought nagged at the back of my mind: I wanted to be more than a fun time for Heather. I wanted to be so much more. Claim every part of her, make her mine.

Odd thoughts for a flirt like me but that's how it had been since the beginning with Heather.

Just one look and I was hooked.

Her dress had three buttons running from her neckline to just above her stomach. Opening them only gave me a teasing look at her soft skin and bra, but I needed more. I pulled her dress over her head before taking a step back so I could see her better. She was wearing a flesh-colored bra and matching panties. They drove me crazy. How could she be this beautiful? I wanted to touch her too much to linger at a distance. I lavished her breasts with attention, kissing the upper part that rose out of the bra cup. She wrapped her legs around me, her heels digging in the back of my thighs.

Jesus, I needed to move her somewhere more comfortable before I completely lost control, or I'd fuck her right here on this table. I pulled back, laughing when she looked up at me with a pout.

"Let's go to the bedroom."

"Why? I like the table."

"I need a bed for what I have in mind."

"Ooh. Okay, then."

She pushed me away playfully, jumping down from the table. I kept my hands to myself while she led me to the bedroom. The second we were inside, she turned on a lamp.

"So... this is my humble bedroom." She paused and looked nervously around. "A bit small—"

I didn't care about any of that. I pinned her against the door with my hips, licking her lower lip. I unclasped her bra before lowering myself on my haunches. I dragged my fingers from the sides of her knees up her thighs, watching her skin turn to goose bumps. Her breath quickened as I moved higher. She gave me a nervous laugh when I hooked my thumbs in the elastic band of her panties.

She had absolutely nothing to be nervous about, but I knew telling her that wouldn't help. I was going to show her. I lowered her panties down her legs, watching her, looking her straight in the eyes as she stepped out of them. Then I hooked her right knee on my shoulder, kissing her inner thigh until I reached her apex. I kissed that soft skin until she scratched at the door.

"Ryker," she whispered before burying her fingers in my hair. Feisty. I loved it. I moved my mouth on her, feeling her breath become increasingly more labored.

Fuck, I was so hard it was painful. I needed to be inside her, but I wanted her to come first. When the leg she stood on wobbled, I cupped her ass cheeks, supporting her. I pressed my fingers on her skin, tilting her ass forward, changing the angle a bit. She was just where I needed her to bring her over the edge.

I pulled her clit between my lips until she came hard, curling her fingers in my hair. She almost lost her balance.

"Ryker," she whispered in a shaky voice as I kissed up her body. I wanted to claim every inch of her as mine. When I captured her mouth, she hummed against me before biting my tongue teasingly. I blindly pulled at the buttons of my shirt.

"You're going to ruin your shirt."

"Don't give a fuck. I need you now."

She smiled against my lips. "I'm on board with that."

Between the two of us, I got naked real fast. Heather drew her fingers down my chest while I walked backward. With a sassy smile, she pushed me down onto the bed, climbing on top of me. I loved watching her take what she wanted. She kissed my right shoulder before moving down my chest, licking and nipping. I fisted her hair, tilting her head until we had eye contact.

"Heather...." My voice was almost a growl.

"I am finally getting a chance to explore," she said with a grin. "And I'm going to take advantage."

I cocked a brow. I was so hard that I was seconds away from claiming her. I kissed her long and deep. I sucked on her tongue, pulling her flat against me so my cock was trapped between us. She moaned, gripping my shoulders, pushing her hips forward, rocking herself against me. The skin-on-skin contact drove me insane.

I gripped her hips, moving her on the bed so she stood on her knees. Then I turned her around, pressing down on her back until she was on all fours.

I leaned over to kiss her back, starting from the base of her spine, moving up slowly. I wanted to draw every drop of pleasure from her. When I leaned forward even more to kiss the back of her neck, I trapped my cock between my pelvis and her right ass cheek. I groaned, gripping her hips with both hands. I couldn't prolong this anymore. I needed to be inside her too much. I nudged her clit with my tip, then teased her entrance, dragging the tip along her opening, sliding in just an inch, then pulling back out and continuing to tease her.

When she stuck her ass out, searching for me, I pulled back even more, then dipped, biting her ass cheek lightly. She yelped, face-planting on the pillow before bursting into laughter. I took advantage of the fact that that beautiful ass was still stuck up in the air and bit the other ass cheek. Heather looked at me over her shoulder, amusement and lust dancing in those green eyes. Straightening up, I slid my cock between her thighs, rubbing her clit with the tip.

"Ryker," she gasped, fisting the pillow under her head with both hands. "Ryker. Please."

"I'll fuck you so good. I promise. So, so good."

Her thighs shook lightly as I continued to tease her clit, and then she buried her head in the pillow. I could still hear her though. And now I couldn't hold back any longer. I *needed* to be inside her. I drove inside the next second. She was so tight that pleasure shot through me instantly.

"Fuuuuuck." I was already so close. So damn close. I slid in and out of her wildly, chasing my orgasm. She pulsed around me, clenching tight. I reached out for one of her hands, taking it in mine as we moved in sync. I wanted to be intertwined with her every way there was.

It seemed impossible that I already felt so strongly about her, but I wasn't about to question the best thing that ever happened to me. I just planned to go along with it, fight to make it last.

I slipped a hand to her clit, feeling her tighten around me even more. When she moaned into the pillow, I moved even faster. I was just on the edge. Her inner muscles pulsed around me once more, and then I was a goner. I gave in to my climax, driving in and out of her until I was completely spent.

I collapsed next to her, pulling her into a messy hug. We were both sweaty, and barely regaining our breaths, but I wanted as much of Heather as possible.

"Hey, you're sweaty," she teased, pinching my arm. I pulled her under me, kissing her thoroughly.

"That's what I get for pinching you? Good to know."

"When did you get so sassy?"

"I've been cutting my teeth on you. I'm getting better and better, am I not?"

I kissed her again. Seriously, I just couldn't be this close to her and not claim her mouth.

"You're getting too good," I admitted.

"Whatcha gonna do about it?"

In response, I pinched her nipple lightly. Her eyes widened.

"Oh, so playing dirty is on the table?"

"Playing dirty is *always* on the table, Heather."

She grinned. "Good to know. That will make getting my way so much easier."

Her grin was infectious. Just looking at it made me immensely happy.

"So, what's the plan for the rest of the night?" she asked.

"How do you know I have a plan?"

"You always have one. Usually involves seducing me *or*... seducing me."

"Not telling you exactly what I'm planning, but I can tell you it'll include both."

"Upping the ante, aren't you?"

"Have to do my best. How else will I earn the right to another sleepover?"

"And when do you want to do that?"

"Tomorrow. This whole week."

She stilled, watching me intently. All my muscles were strung tight. I cupped her face with one hand, not breaking eye contact.

"I want us to be together for more than a few hours here and there, Heather. I love being around you."

"Yeah?" She smiled.

"Yes."

"My semi burned roast beef won you over."

"Love, it was burnt to a crisp."

She poked my chest. "Not true. You said you liked it."

I grinned. "I did like it. But... it was still burnt."

"Lesson learned. You're more honest after an orgasm."

"More like I'm too spent to have any

brainpower left."

"Why did you say you liked it?"

"Because A, I did. B. You put a lot of effort into it, and I like that."

"I might have forgotten to add water a few times. I got caught up thinking about you."

"So it's my fault the beef was dry?" That might have been partly to blame for the dryness, but I think sis extended the cooking time.

"Indirectly, yeah. No good deed goes unpunished, huh?" She squirmed under me. Feeling her naked body was torture. "I can try my hand at cooking it again this week."

"So that's a yes to us spending the week together?"

She nodded, but even though she was still smiling, I noticed a slight unease in her eyes.

"Tell me what you're afraid of," I urged.

"I don't know exactly." She swallowed, looking away. I could feel her heart beat faster. "Seeing Avery hurt, I think. Being hurt too."

"I'd never hurt you or Avery." I captured her gaze so she could see the sincerity in my eyes, because what I was saying was the truth. They both had become very special to me.

"I know... it's just... the fear is there, you know? My recent track record lends to my apprehensiveness too, I suppose. But I won't let that hold me back. I promise."

"And I promise you that this will be amazing, Heather. What we have together is nothing like anything I've experienced. I'd never treat you the way your ex did. Never."

She smiled, and I cradled her head in my hands. She closed her eyes. I kissed each of them, holding her until I felt her relax underneath me. When she kissed my jaw, her lips were curled in a smile against my skin.

"Let's go shower," she whispered. "Before we go from sweaty to stinky."

I pushed myself up on an elbow, liking the levity of her comment but still leveling a mock glare at her. "I was being romantic."

"I know. And I love it. But... being clean is also romantic." She grinned, shrugging one shoulder before darting out of the bed. "Come on. If you don't catch me before I get to the bathroom, I'll shower alone."

I chased after her, catching up right before she went inside. Curling an arm around her waist, I brought my mouth to her ear. "I'm faster."

"I was hoping for that."

I fondled her ass with my free hand.

Heather giggled. "Hey, why did you do that?"

"It's my reward."

***

"Want to spend some time on my balcony?" Heather asked after we showered and dressed.

"You have one?"

She jerked her thumb in the direction of the

window. "Oh, yeah. My own personal heaven. Avery's not allowed out there."

She led me outside, where she'd put a table and a huge armchair. She had potted plants hanging from the ceiling and strings of lights around the railing.

We spread one of the blankets we'd brought on the armchair. I sat down first, then pointed to my lap.

"Come here. I'll keep you warm."

"That's what the blankets are for."

"Skin on skin contact works better, and you can wrap the other one around us."

She whistled, clapping her hands once. "And you called me creative."

"Heather. Sit. Now."

"Yes, sir." She waggled her eyebrows before lowering herself on me. I put an arm around her waist, keeping her back flat against me. She threw the second cover over us, tucking it in at the sides.

We had a great view of the sky here. With all the lights in the city, you couldn't see the stars, but I simply enjoyed sharing this quiet moment with her.

I'd been so on edge when I'd arrived, still running high on the adrenaline of the day. Usually, nothing helped me come down except performing at the Northern Lights.

But being here, just holding Heather, filled me with a sense of happiness I'd never known in my entire life.

"You're quiet," she whispered. "That's very

unlike you."

"I'm just enjoying you." I pushed her hair to the side, kissing the back of her neck.

"Let's play a game."

"I'm all ears."

"A question for a question."

"I like the sound of that."

She squirmed in my lap. Groaning, I clasped her hips. "Heather, stop."

"Ah, my bad. Wasn't intentional. I have an idea. Since dinner wasn't all that great, do you want some cheese and crackers?"

"Sure."

"Okay. Stay here. I'll be right back."

While she went inside, I inspected the surroundings. The balcony was on the second floor, and the inner courtyard was dark except for light from someone's TV to the far left.

Heather returned with a plate full of crackers and cheese. "So, let's change the rules. Answer a question, and I'll give you a bite of cheese and cracker."

"Sounds kinky." I winked and immediately pulled her back into my lap.

"I'll start?" she asked, and I wasn't sure I liked the grin she had on her face.

"Sure. Shoot."

"Do you like musicals?"

"Huge no."

She sagged against me. "Damn. But here, have a cracker."

"Favorite spot in the city?" I asked after swallowing a mouthful.

"Central Park. Yours?"

"The Rockefeller Center."

"You're a building lover, and your favorite building isn't even one that belongs to your cousin?"

"Now you know my secret. Don't tell anyone. Especially not my sisters."

"Don't worry, I won't give you away... unless...."

"Unless what?" I pinched the side of her torso, close to her armpits. She yelped, pressing her arms to her sides, cutting off my access. She thought that would deter me?

I always found a way of getting what I wanted. Her feet were lying at the side of my thigh as she sat across my lap, soles upward under the blanket. I tickled her there, and she shrieked with laughter, immediately taking her legs away, crossing them in front of her. She was still laughing, juggling our snack on her lap. The sound reverberated in the yard between the buildings.

"Hey! Some of us are trying to sleep," an angry voice shouted. Heather spun around, burying her face in my shoulder, *still* laughing. I ran a hand up and down her back, attempting to calm her down, fighting the urge to burst out laughing myself. There was no stopping us if I gave in. It took Heather a solid few minutes to calm down. Tears were streaming down her face when she came up for air. She wiped them away before pointing a finger at me.

"I was going to say unless you play dirty, but I see you've got that down to a science."

"That's right."

"Don't make me laugh again. I can't stop."

"Learned my lesson."

"So you won't do it again?"

The corners of my mouth twitched. "Didn't say that. I'll just keep it indoors."

"Why would you do that?"

"I like hearing you laugh. Besides, if we keep it indoors, I can turn tickling into something... else."

"Damn. If there's a not-so-innocent part in any plan, you'll jump on it."

I grinned. "Glad we cleared that up."

"Well, I feel like staying out here for a while longer. And nothing you do will change my mind."

"I beg to differ."

She pressed her arms to her body, clearly thinking I was going to tickle her. I wasn't an amateur. I didn't use the same strategy twice. I kissed her, tangling our tongues, pressing her hips into me until she moaned against my mouth.

"Ryker," she whispered in a shaky voice, tugging at the collar of my shirt. "Let's go inside."

"Why? You think you might do something indecent if we stay out here?"

She pulled back, narrowing her eyes and pinching my arm. "Yes!"

"Why did you pinch me if you agree?"

"Because I'm only *grudgingly* agreeing. Thought I'd let you know." Not that I believed her; she was as

hot for me as I was for her.
"Duly noted."

Chapter Twenty
Heather

On Tuesday, I'd decided to go into the newspaper's headquarters only because I was meeting Ryker later at the Northern Lights.

I spent the day cooped up in one of our multifunctional offices—a fancy name for a room with multiple bean bags. Reporters didn't have designated offices, since we were either in the field or working from home.

I also asked my editor when the article on Pearman would be published—I was almost done editing it.

"Honestly, it's up to the bosses. You know how these things are."

Well, that was no help. Articles weren't published in the order I wrote them, but the clock on my lease was ticking.

I pulled up my account on my phone and paid in advance one more month of rent... and that was the last of my savings. If I didn't get the bonus paid out within a month, I'd have to move us to a cheaper apartment.

I didn't want to seriously consider that possibility, though—not yet.

At six o'clock, I sprinted out of the building. It was a gorgeous mid-April evening, so I planned to walk the few blocks to the Northern Lights. With kids being on Easter vacation, one would think that the city would be emptier—it had been like that in my hometown growing up, but it wasn't the case with New York.

When I arrived, the bar wasn't as busy as usual. Happy hour hadn't started yet, but I was just on time, because Ryker was up on the stage. I took a moment to admire him before I made my presence known. God, he was just perfect. Everything from the way he moved to those sculpted muscles. He hadn't changed out of his suit, but honestly, that just made him more alluring. Our gazes crossed while he took his seat on the stage. He lifted a brow. I flashed back a sassy smile. Why not own up to checking him out?

Cole was there, with a man who seemed vaguely familiar.

"Hi, Cole!"

"Hi, Heather. This is Hunter." Ah, that's why he looked familiar. I'd seen him in magazines. Ryker jumped down from the stage, greeting me with a kiss.

Cole wiggled his eyebrows at us both.

"Hunter, why don't you keep an eye on Cole? Don't know if he can behave," Ryker said.

Hunter grinned. "And you want to impress, I get it."

Ryker groaned before focusing on me.

"Heather, stay as far as you can from these two buffoons."

"Why? Your sisters sang your praises. Maybe one of them will actually tell me the truth."

Cole held his hand up. "I'm your man."

Hunter held his fingers to his throat. "Abort mission man, or we won't be allowed here again."

Cole winked. "I'll take my chances."

"Here's a brave man," I said.

"I know, right? Where should we sit?"

"Unfortunately, Cole and I actually have to go. We're having a late night at the office and just came for a break," Hunter said.

"And to annoy Ryker, who *didn't* mention you'd be here," Cole said with yet another eyebrow wiggle. I laughed, bidding them goodbye as they left. Ryker jumped back on stage, and I took a seat right in front of it.

One of their waitresses brought over a cocktail on the house. I had no idea what it was—something orange that tasted a lot like sherry. It was delicious.

The place started to fill soon after the guys sang the first notes. I wasn't really paying attention to the music though. I was too lost in *him*. God, the way he looked at me... as if there was no one else in the room. As if he sang just for me. My heart was beating wildly.

Sighing, I tore my gaze from the stage, because I needed to calm my racing pulse, and it was obvious I couldn't do that while holding eye contact with this sexy man. To my dismay, when I went to the bar to get a second drink, I realized two women sitting there were shamelessly eye-fucking him.

"God, he's hot," one of them murmured. "I'm bagging him tonight."

"Is he single?"

"Ryker? Please, he's perpetually single. Why would he tie himself down? I mean, look at him. He can probably get a different woman every night."

I forced myself to go back to my seat after getting my drink and focused on the music. A ball of unease lodged in my chest. Ryker's personal life was so easy and free. He was under constant pressure at his job, so he liked to let off steam in his down time. My life was different—planned to the minute. I loved it, and spending time with Avery was my favorite thing to do… but I couldn't imagine Ryker wanting the same thing.

These few days were different, because it was just the two of us, but what would happen at the end of the week, when my baby was back home? Ugh, why did I have to get negative? *Geez, Heather, enjoy the moment.*

I stared into my orange cocktail, playing with the tiny umbrella that came with it, making myself a promise.

I'd just enjoy this week, without any what-ifs. After all, I kept telling myself I didn't want to jump in with both feet again, so why even consider what would happen at the end of the week?

Looking up, I had my answer right there, on

the stage, the second our gazes connected. I always felt so immensely happy when I was around Ryker, as if I was more aware of myself. He magnified every sensation. I hadn't even known it was possible to feel this way.

When the set finished, he jumped from the stage right in front of my table. I rose to my feet, grinning.

"Well, if it's not the most handsome performer tonight. And the most talented one too."

"I did my best. Wanted to impress my beautiful date."

"Oh, me?" I feigned surprise. He laughed, tugging at my hand, then kissing me right there in front of everyone. I gave in to him completely, and holy hell, in seconds my underwear felt on fire. Ryker didn't know how to kiss any other way than smoking hot. "Do you want another drink?" he asked when we pulled apart. The two women I'd overheard earlier looked at us in shock. I tried not to look too smug but failed utterly and completely.

"No, I'm good. What do you want?"

"To kiss you some more." His voice was a little gruff. I loved it.

"Want to get out of here?"

"Yes, ma'am."

Out of the corner of my eye, I noticed a familiar face. Hank Dawson—he was one of the best reporters in town and had left the competition to build his own news website. What was he doing here? He approached us when he noticed I was watching him.

"Heather! Haven't seen each other in a long time."

"Hank, hi. Ryker, this is Hank. A brilliant reporter."

"Ryker, you're just the Wall Street man I was hoping to run into. I was wondering if we could chat a bit about the whole Pearman debacle?" Hank took out his phone, no doubt preparing to record. I stilled. Wait, what? He wanted to interview Ryker?

"That won't be necessary. Heather's already got everything covered."

"So I've heard."

"How?" I asked.

"Word gets around." Hank placed his phone back in his pocket. What was going on? He'd come here just for that?

"Ryker, if you change your mind, here is my card."

He stretched out his hand.

"I won't," Ryker said in a clipped tone. "Heather, are you ready to go?"

"Yes." Draping an arm around my waist, he turned me in the general direction of the door, and we started to make our way through the crowd.

"Hank just showing up here isn't good," I said.

"It's a hot topic, Heather."

"Hank came here specifically to interview you. He knew you were performing, and that means he's already put solid work hours into this."

I shivered when we stepped outside. The temperature had dropped by a few degrees since I arrived two hours ago.

"Don't stress about it, Heather. Not right now, anyway." He cupped the sides of my neck with his palms, splaying his fingers wide.

"I don't think I can stop."

He flashed me one of those panty-melting smiles. "Then I need to take your mind off it, don't I?"

"I guess you do." I leaned into him, needing the heat of his body.

"Are you cold, babe?"

"A bit. It was warmer when I came."

"Here, take this."

He shrugged off his jacket, draping it around me. I was already wearing one, but his was so huge that I could just wrap it around me on top of everything I had on. But now he was only wearing a thin shirt.

"Ryker, you'll get sick."

"Nah, I never get sick. Besides, we'll get in a car in a few minutes."

I cocked a brow, attempting to shrug out of his jacket. Ryker kept his arm firmly around my shoulders. His gaze was unrelenting.

"You're so stubborn," I murmured. "Fine, I'm keeping the jacket."

"Right answer."

I was melting at his determination to keep me warm, but I didn't share his confidence about being immune to sickness.

We bought hot dogs from a stand near the bar and wolfed them down while we waited for our Uber. The second I slid inside the car, it hit me that I was going to Ryker's place, and I became jittery. I had no idea why I was nervous. After all, he'd been to mine.

Ryker lived in a gorgeous two-story apartment on the fifty-fourth floor of a Manhattan skyscraper. The master bedroom was on the second floor, the living room and a guest bedroom on the first level. It was exactly what I'd imagined his bachelor pad to look like.

Modern art paintings were hanging on the pristine white walls. The furniture was in shades of black and dark brown. And the view... oh, the view.

"Ryker this is beautiful," I murmured. The city looked so different from up here, magical somehow. It was dark already, but I could imagine that this place was flooded with light during the day.

I felt him come up behind me, touching my arm, resting his chin in the crook of my neck.

"I'm glad you like it. I don't plan to let you out very soon."

"Oh, and what do you have in mind to make that happen?"

"I have a few ideas." He moved his mouth up my neck, teasing the sensitive skin with his lips. When I felt the tip of his tongue, I shuddered. If there was a better feeling than being wrapped in this man, I didn't want to know it.

"Do you want a drink?" he asked.

"Yes. First things first. You should drink tea."

He looked perplexed. "Why?"

"Preemptive measure against a cold."

"Babe, I'm fine."

"I want to make sure you're fine tomorrow too."

His gaze softened. "Okay."

Adrenaline pumped in my veins. When I was with him, I was able to let go in a way I never had, and just have fun.

And my belly? A crazy number of butterflies roamed around. I'd *almost* pushed the incident with Hank out of my mind.

"You ever work from home?" I asked him.

"Rarely."

"If I lived here, I think I'd never leave. But I can work from anywhere."

"You always wanted to be a reporter?"

"I've always wanted to write. Well, books, but you know, I got this job and sort of put everything else on the backburner."

"You should try it," he said with a smile that was contagious. What was it about him that made it so easy not just to voice my dream, but also imagine what it would take to go after it?

***

Ryker

"How long have you lived here?" she asked

while we were waiting for the water to boil in the kitchen. I hadn't even known I had tea, but Heather found everything in one of the drawers.

"Two years. Lived further away before, but I wanted to cut the commute as short as possible."

"Is this one of Hunter's buildings?"

"No. They don't do too many residential projects. I just saw an advertisement for this. After checking it out, I came back with my siblings and Hunter to get their opinion."

"You do everything as a group, huh?"

"A lot of things, yeah. I just trust them, so I know they'll tell it to me straight."

"What do they say about me?"

"That you're just what I need."

"And what do you think?"

"They're right, as usual."

She smiled brilliantly. "I like a man who's not afraid to admit others are right too."

I chuckled, taking the cup of tea she handed me. We went to the couch, and I pressed a button to open the doors of the dresser where the TV was hidden.

"Wow. You have one of those fancy TV sets. It's like a home cinema."

"It's pretty great, yeah. Want to watch something? Here's the remote."

"Ha! Don't give me control of that, or you might regret it."

"Have at it." I watched her flick through channels, but I could tell she was still worried about the run-in at the bar.

I pulled her into my lap. She yelped, letting go of the remote.

"I can feel you stressing," I said.

"I don't know how to stop."

"I do."

I ran my fingers from her ankle to her inner thigh, feeling her muscles tighten with tension—but a different kind than before, which was my goal. When I reached the hem of her skirt, she grinned, turning around and straddling me.

I'd gotten used to being on my own in the apartment, but I wanted this woman here, with me, and I'd never had this impulse before: to want to do everything together, even something as simple as watching TV or talking. It was the first time I was experiencing this, and I wanted to explore every facet of it with Heather.

We barely slept that night, but I figured we could just sleep in the next morning, since I didn't have to go to work too early. Except I woke up to a thunderstorm. They weren't common in April, so the sound startled me out of a deep sleep.

"Morning." Heather stood in the doorway of the bedroom, hair damp, wearing my robe. Fuck, she looked good wearing that, walking barefoot around my apartment. I wanted her to feel at home here.

"Morning. Want to grab breakfast across the street? I have some time before I need to be in the office," I said.

"I don't know. Not really get-out-of-the-house kind of weather."

I wiggled my eyebrows. "Are you talking dirty to me?"

"Nah, just pointing out that staying indoors is a great idea."

"I agree. I just have one request."

"What?"

I made a "come here" motion with my finger, and when she was close enough, I undid the tie of her robe. I pulled her closer, until her breasts were right in front of me. I captured one with my mouth, twirling my tongue around the nipple. Heather moaned, tugging at my hair, pressing herself into me. I loved how easily she responded to me. I ran my fingers up her inner thigh slowly, savoring every inch of soft skin I touched. I'd never tire of exploring her, of finding new ways to turn her on, to bring her pleasure. Her skin turned to goose bumps as I touched her further up. I smiled against her breast. Heather groaned, taking a step back, carefully tying the belt again.

I grabbed her by the waist, pulling her closer, until she toppled on the bed.

She shrieked with laughter.

"What are you doing?" she asked in between fits of laughter.

"Having my way with you."

"Oh, I see. By all means, don't let me deter you."

"So you're surrendering, just like that?"

She batted her eyelashes, pulling me closer.

"No. I'm going to use it as a negotiation point later on."

"I see."

"I'm redefining the parameters of staying inside. Let's stay in bed."

She flashed a wide smile, throwing herself on her back before turning on one side and shoving a pillow under her head.

"I can do that. I'm glad you don't have a cold."

"Told you I never get sick."

"Well, since we're staying indoors, I can make us some breakfast."

"That can wait."

She gave me a shrewd smile, narrowing her eyes. "If I didn't know better, I'd say you're enjoying this."

I reached for her, cupping her cheek. I wasn't sure how to put everything into words. How much I liked what we had.

"I like having you here." In an instant, I pulled her underneath me. Her eyes widened, but her mouth tilted up at the corners.

"Heather, I like spending time with you more than anything else. No matter what we do, I always think about you. You're always on my mind."

"Does that scare you?"

"No. Because I know I'm exactly where I need to be."

Her eyes widened, as if she hadn't expected this. I hadn't really expected it either, but it was exactly how I felt, and I wanted her to know it.

I moved my mouth on her jaw until my lips hovered just over hers. Lowering a hand between us, I went straight for the belt, undoing it, letting the robe fall to the sides, running my mouth downward in a straight path. I'd been clamoring for this skin-on-skin since I woke up. I took my time, touching every curve with my fingers before running my mouth over them too. Her skin turned to goose bumps. When I kissed a straight line between her breasts, she opened her legs wider. I was already rock-hard, but this one gesture just drove me insane.

She looked down at me while I was teasing her navel, running my tongue around it before dragging the tip of my nose down her pubis. She dug her fingers in the mattress, pulling at the sheet. I could feel her hold her breath in anticipation of me going even lower. I moved up instead. She groaned in protest.

"You're cheating," she whispered when I was face-to-face with her again.

"Thought you didn't want to play along."

She narrowed her eyes.

"I didn't say *that*. Just thought we should get breakfast first."

"And what's the verdict?" I asked in between kissing her shoulder.

"That you're at peak performance even on an empty stomach."

"I love how easily I can win you over."

"Hey, I'm a tough negotiator, but I accept a

good argument when I get one."

"And promising to make you come is a good argument?"

"The best one."

"I'll keep that in mind."

She grinned. "Please do."

I tickled her, and she just dissolved into laughter. This felt so incredibly powerful. The way she gave in to me more every time. She was exploring this with me, each of us going at our own pace. But the one thing she didn't know yet was that I had big plans for us this week.

Chapter Twenty-One
Heather

Ryker somehow talked me into staying with him the whole week. I didn't even remember how that came about, but safe to say, the man was *very* persuasive. I'd worked out of his apartment, except for a morning I went into headquarters to talk to Danielle about Hank. She was just as in the dark as I was and advised me to forget about it and focus on my article.

"Damn, how did this week go by so fast?" I asked Ryker on Sunday evening.

"Time flies when you're in great company," he said. We were in his master bathroom, each at a sink. He'd just finished shaving and was now applying aftershave. I was pulling my hair into a ponytail.

I grinned in the mirror, elbowing him lightly. "You're a bit too full of yourself, you know that right, *Flirt?*"

"You mean I don't deserve the moniker?"

"Hmm... I don't know. I think I need some time to make up my mind."

I lowered my eyes to the sink, washing my hands carefully. We hadn't spoken about what would happen once the week came to an end. I had to pick up Avery from JFK in two hours, and then what?

"Well, why don't I convince you some more over dinner. Steaks?"

"Oh, I can't. I'm picking up Avery soon."

I phrased it as neutrally as possible, not wanting him to think I had any expectations. I was still washing my hands under the warm stream of water, though there wasn't any soap left. When Ryker turned off the tap, I snapped my gaze up, wincing when I met his eyes in the mirror. It was hard and focused, determined.

"*We're* picking Avery up." He came right next to me, bringing one hand to my face, tilting my head up, watching me, his eyes unwavering.

"I didn't... I didn't want to assume," I whispered.

"Heather, this wasn't just a week of fun for me. I want to be part of your life. *Avery's* life."

I couldn't look away even if I wanted to, but I didn't. I wanted to listen to this man forever.

"You mean it?" I whispered. Damn, why did I have to sound so insecure? I was a grown woman, and I'd come through even when life had thrown huge curveballs my way.

He whirled me around, cupping my cheek, looking straight at me, as if the eye contact through the mirror wasn't enough and he wanted the real deal.

"Fuck, yes, I mean it. What we're doing here means a lot to me, Heather. I know it's not what either of us was expecting, but that doesn't mean it's not real. It fucking is—the most real thing that's ever happened to me—the best. You're mine, Heather."

I was speechless. I had no idea what to say back. My whole body was vibrating with awareness, with the need to be even closer to him. I tugged at his shirt, bringing him an inch closer. I caught a glimpse of his smile before he kissed me so hard that I had to grip the sink for support with one hand. I wrapped the other one in his shirt, not particularly caring that I was wrinkling it. I just wanted him to feel how much his words meant to me, how desperately I wanted this to work even though I was still terrified I might end up brokenhearted.

Ryker's kiss was feral. He bit my tongue lightly before exploring me further. He was kissing me as if he wanted to claim me right here, right now, and I wanted nothing more than to surrender.

How could he reduce everything around us to background noise every time? Wipe every thought away, erase any fears? He had so much power over me that it scared me.

I was trembling lightly in his arms by the time we both came up for air. I was still fisting his shirt. Ryker had me trapped against the sink.

My heart was beating at a lightning-quick rate. He wanted to come with me, to spend more time with me *and* my girl. The light tremor intensified as this sank in.

Ryker watched me with a satisfied smile, skimming his thumb from my shoulder down to my arm, where goose bumps broke out on my skin.

"And you still think I don't deserve the praise?" he teased.

I rolled my eyes, playfully pushing him away. "Let's go. If we're late, Avery won't be your number-one fan anymore."

"Impossible."

"Don't push your luck."

He held up his hands in defense. "Wouldn't dream of it."

***

On the way to the airport, I was full of so many emotions that I felt as if my chest was about to explode. I couldn't put everything into words, but Ryker seemed to feel that I needed his touch, because he pulled me in a half hug, keeping me against his chest the whole cab ride to JFK.

I just loved being squeezed against his hard, toned chest. I moved my hand all over it, right until Ryker caught my wrist, stopping me.

I grinned against his arm. When I looked up, I was startled by the heat in his gaze. Holy hell, this man had three intensity levels: hot, hotter, and inferno. Right now, he was on the latter, and I had to find a way to bring him down. In other words, I had to behave. Easier said than done. I just wanted to feel part of him. As if I was here to stay and he couldn't shake me away even if he wanted to.

We arrived at the airport too soon for my liking. Ryker got out first, keeping the door open for me. He took my hand, helping me out, but then kept our fingers interlaced as we headed inside.

JFK was extremely crowded on Sunday evening. New Yorkers were returning from their weekend trips. Tourists were leaving. It was absolute madness. Ryker didn't ease his grip on me. I was so nervous!

My fears stemmed from a couple of things. This was the first time my mom was going to meet him. And Avery would know, just with him accompanying me, that something had changed. I hoped I was doing the right thing. I didn't want my daughter to feel as though something or someone had come between us.

This felt so perfect though, as if I was supposed to be exactly here… trusting him with my heart and my happiness… as well as Avery's. I couldn't be that wrong, could I?

Ryker must have felt my tension, because he looked at me over his shoulder, bringing our hands up, kissing the back of mine.

"Babe, I'm right here with you, okay?"

I smiled at him, even though I was still a little afraid of this huge step we were taking.

"I'm not afraid."

He cocked a brow.

"Okay, I am. A little."

"I can't tell you not to be. Just know that we're in this together."

My cautious smile morphed into an explosive grin all on its own. Despite our best efforts, we arrived a little late. Mom and Avery were waiting by arrivals.

Avery squealed so loud when she saw Ryker that several people turned to look at us. My girl made a beeline for us—correction—for Ryker.

She hugged him hard, squealing some more before hugging me too. The little traitor. She was already hugging *him* first? My mother was looking between the three of us with a curious expression, but she wasn't as taken aback as I'd expected. Avery must have told her about Ryker. He held out his hand to her.

"Ryker Winchester, Mrs. Prescott. I'm glad to meet you."

"Avery told me about you." She looked pointedly at me.

"I meant to tell you," I began, but she waved away my words.

"We don't have time to chat now. Plane's leaving soon, but call me."

"Mom, are you sure you don't want to stay? At least one night to rest?"

I didn't understand why she was always so stubborn. It was a long journey. She always insisted on picking up Avery, so Dad drove her to the airport in Phoenix, then she flew to New York and made the return journey the same day.

"No, no. I'm going to sleep on the plane anyway. And I can't be away too long from the animals. It was nice meeting you, Ryker."

They shook hands again before Mom hugged

Avery. She then turned her attention to me, pulling me into her arms, speaking in a soft voice.

"He's a fine man. A detail obviously Avery didn't mention."

"Umm, thanks."

Mom continued, "Just be careful."

"I am."

I could practically feel Mom trying to assess the situation, but lucky me, she didn't have too much time.

After walking Mom to the departures terminal, Ryker grabbed Avery's bag, and we all headed toward the exit.

"How was your week?" Ryker asked her while we fought our way through the crowd.

"Amazing. My pony isn't tiny anymore, Mom. He grew up."

"I know. Gran sent us pictures, remember?" I said.

"Yeah, but he's even bigger than in the pictures."

"You have a pony?" Ryker asked. "What's his name?"

"Tony."

"Tony the pony?" Ryker asked on a laugh. I smiled to myself. Avery nodded proudly.

"Do you have other animals too?"

"Yes. A chicken and a rabbit. And Gran said she'll buy me a goose this summer."

"My mom is basically luring her to Arizona with animals to make sure she spends every vacation there," I explained.

Ryker nodded. "Sounds like something Mom would do if she had grandkids living in another state."

We flagged a cab, and after we loaded Avery's luggage in the back, we all slid onto the back seat. Avery was in the middle. Ryker kept asking her about her vacation, and my girl sure didn't keep anything back.

"And then we went to the mall, and Gran bought me everything I wanted."

She loved talking to Ryker even more than she loved talking to me.

"Avery, I want to take you and your mom to dinner tonight. What would you like to eat?"

Avery squealed again. The cabbie glared at us in the rearview mirror.

"Can I have ice cream?"

"Real food," I answered, voice firm.

Avery pouted. "But Gran gave me ice cream whenever I wanted."

Right... factory settings were definitely back on. Truthfully, I'd eat ice cream all day long too, but eh... I had to be responsible for her sake.

"How about steak?" Ryker asked.

Avery sat up straighter, nodding. Interesting... if I had suggested this, she wouldn't have been so keen.

I looked at Ryker suspiciously, asking, "Did you conspire with her again?"

"No, I guess I'm awesome enough that she

wants to spend more time with me."
I laughed but didn't give him any shit, because he had a point. He reached out over Avery's shoulders, touching my arm. That euphoric feeling was back in full force, just threatening to spill out of me.

Ryker took us to a restaurant on the Upper West side that looked like one of those fancy wine cellars, with red brick arches and diffuse lighting.

We stopped in front of the sign that said Wait to be Seated, but there was no one behind it.

"I'm going to ask a waiter for a table. It'll be quicker this way," Ryker said.

"Thanks."

After he left, I asked Avery, "So you like steaks now?"

She shrugged, playing with her fingers. What was going on?

"Avery?" I prompted.

"I like burgers more… but if I impress Ryker, do you think he will like us more?"

I swear, I could feel my heart cracking. I lowered myself on my haunches until I was level with Avery and took her little hands in mine, holding them tight.

"Love bug, Ryker likes us just the way we are. You don't have to impress anyone."

She frowned, looking at the floor for a few seconds, as if she was mulling over my words.

"Are you sure?" she whispered.

"Yes, I'm sure."

"So you think he'll like us even if I have a burger?"

"Yes, lovebug."

When I looked up, I realized Ryker stood just behind Avery. He winked before saying, "They have a table for us."

The three of us walked toward the back. When we sat down, Ryker looked straight at Avery and said, "Avery, I don't know about you, but I'm more of a burger guy."

My girl practically lit up. So did I, barely able to hide my grin behind a menu. I pressed a palm to my belly. I always felt every emotion in my stomach: angst, fear, euphoria, excitement. I'd just realized something very important: Ryker was going to make me fall head over heels in love and break all the rules I'd set for myself.

Chapter Twenty-Two
Ryker

The following Tuesday morning, Tess called to ask if I could stop by the store to help them set up some new shelves. When I arrived, Cole, Hunter, and Josie were also there, all gathered in the back room, sitting on the floor. They'd also brought breakfast—sandwiches and waffles. Great, because I was starving.

"Food first, then we get to work," Tess announced.

I sat on the floor too, grabbing the nearest takeout box—mozzarella and tomato sandwich. One of my favorites.

"So... whole family is here," I said between mouthfuls. "Coincidence?"

Tess grinned. "Obviously not. But since Skye and I have bailed on the last working lunches, I thought it was high time we all gathered here."

Cole and I exchanged a glance. If our sisters didn't want to wait for another working lunch, it meant they needed extra attention. It had always been a telltale sign, even as kids.

"We just missed spending time with you as a group," Skye said.

We hadn't had another Ballroom Gala since the one in March, so we'd spent even less time than usual together. Since the last one raised a hell of a lot of money, we'd almost made our yearly target. We just needed one more event this season, and it would take place in June.

"We're here," Cole said through yawns. "Sorry. Date yesterday went until late, but I'm all yours now."

"Following in Ryker's footsteps, Cole? Who knows, maybe you'll be the one surprising us at the next gala, bringing a woman," Tess said.

"It was just a date," Cole said. It was my turn to laugh.

"Well, if the Flirt can get serious about a woman, I'd say the Charmer also stands a good chance," Josie said. Only a few months ago, I would have laughed this off, but now I could see myself in that position. More than that, I *wanted* to.

"Ryker, this would be the moment for you to step in and save my ass," Cole said loudly. "Hunter, you can help too."

Hunter held up his hands, shrugging. "Can't contradict my wife this early in the morning. It's bad luck."

"And I'm enjoying this too much. So, is there any work to be done, or are we just catching up? I'm okay either way, just want to know." I'd been so hungry that I'd already finished my food.

Skye sighed. "No, we actually do have shelves to put up. Tess and I were going to do it ourselves, but I feel like my arms are going to fall off from carrying boxes around and folding merchandise."

Josie looked between my sisters for a beat before announcing, "Spa day tomorrow. My treat. I'm not taking no for an answer."

Skye blinked at her. "You're not taking no for an answer? I see our cousin's bossy ways are rubbing off on you."

Hunter looked very pleased with himself.

Josie grinned brilliantly. "I'm a fast learner."

"You know what? I'm actually all for it. Can we go tomorrow evening?" Skye asked.

Tess pouted. "Skye, we have inventory to do."

Skye waved her hand. "We'll do that... whenever."

"Tomorrow works," Josie exclaimed.

Well, fuck. If Skye willingly tore herself away from the shop, it meant she was exhausted.

"Okay, let's get to work now," Tess said.

"By the way, Ryker, how did Heather's dinner turn out?" Skye asked.

"Did you tell her to cook the roast for ninety minutes?"

Skye widened her eyes. "Oh my God. I did? I meant sixty. Crap. She didn't realize that was too long?"

"No. I thought you did it on purpose, as a joke or something."

"Ryker. I'm not that cruel."

"Noted. Anyway, Avery was at her grandmother's house for spring break, and Heather and I practically spent the whole time together."

Skye widened her eyes. Tess's jaw hung open. Even Cole, Hunter, and Josie looked perplexed.

"Holy shit, this is amazing," Skye exclaimed. I would have taken it as a compliment, but her voice was so incredulous that it sounded almost like an insult.

"You know, one great thing about Hunter and Ryker leaving the bachelor pack is that I finally don't have to compete with you guys anymore on our evenings out," Cole said before adding, "Not that I wasn't always winning by a decent margin."

Everyone burst out laughing. As if on cue, a group of women stopped in front of the shop, looking at the merchandise... and then right at my brother. One of them even winked at him. As if only then noticing the rest of us, they hurried away. I was laughing so hard, I was afraid I'd crack a rib.

"Aaaand I rest my case," Cole said, and I couldn't contradict him for once.

We started on the shelves right after that. I could feel my sisters' gazes boring into the back of my head. I was sure that one of them would volunteer advice before the morning was over. My money was on Tess.

It turned out, both of them thought I needed advice. They flanked me while I was setting up some extra shelves in the back.

"Sooo... what's your next move?" Tess asked.

"I don't know. I'll play it by ear," I said.

"Sounds good. If you need advice, you can

always call us." Skye was smiling brightly. There was something different about her this morning.

"I'll keep that in mind." I pointed a finger at Skye after I finished securing the shelves I'd been working on. "You look more cheerful. Any reason for that?"

She exchanged a glance with Tess, and even with Josie, who looked our way when she heard my question. Wait a second, what was going on?

"Well, things with our investor are going great," Skye said.

"And?" Cole urged. Clearly, he'd picked up on this strange energy in the room. Even Hunter was paying attention.

"If you must know, I'm dating someone. And it's going *really* well," Skye declared.

"Define really well," I said.

"He's not dating someone else at the same time. That's a winner in my books."

Cole groaned. "Sis, your standards are just too low."

She shrugged. "I'm not demanding. I'm hoping he'll join me at the next Ballroom Gala. Then you'll all get to meet him."

That meant they were serious. Things were changing for everyone. I'd come in here thinking I just had to put up some shelves…

But then again, things in the Winchester clan rarely went according to plan.

We finished just in time for Skye and Tess to open the store. I was the first to leave, because I had an early meeting at the office. On the way, I took out my phone, calling Heather. We hadn't made plans after our dinner on Sunday, but after the conversation with my family, I wanted to see her tonight.

She didn't answer, but I shot her a message.

Ryker: Dinner tonight, if you don't have plans?

Heather: YES! Now I finally have something to look forward to. It's going to be a crazy day.

I was right there with her. Wall Street was a fast-paced environment to work in even on calm days, but when international key performance indicators were confusing, fast-paced turned to breakneck speed. It was paramount to calm everyone down, talk them out of hasty transactions.

After my twenty-third phone call for the day, I went for a coffee break. Several of my colleagues were gathered there, discussing today's developments in hushed voices. Most had their shoulders up to their ears from stress. I was just bone tired.

"How can you be so relaxed?" one of them called to me while I filled a cup with coffee.

I shrugged. "When you're relaxed, you pass that calm on to the clients."

"I'm shitting my pants right now," he said.

"Stop. They'll feel it. That's the only piece of advice I can give you."

He rolled his eyes. "Drinks after hours? To blow off steam?"

"I already have plans," I said before strolling back to my office.

Meeting Heather and Avery for dinner sounded a million times better than going out drinking and mourning over the day.

Only a few months ago, I would've looked forward to performing tonight, or just enjoying a glass of whiskey in the quiet of my apartment. But now the things I was looking forward to were different.

Back in my office, I saw a missed call from Heather and called her back right away.

"Hey! So, I can't make it tonight. A source I've been after forever just agreed to meet with me for an interview. I can't say no. I sorry."

"No problem. We'll have dinner another day."

"Thanks. I would rather be with you, but I just can't pass this up."

"I understand. But who is watching Avery?"

"Oh, I was thinking about talking to my neighbor. Natasha has always been supportive at the last minute, and Avery likes her."

"Or... I can spend the evening with Avery."

Was it too fast? Too early? I didn't really know what I was doing. I was playing this by ear, following my instincts.

"Wow. Really? She'd love that. I'd love that too."

Her voice was bursting with excitement. I liked that I was the reason for that.

"Perfect. What's the schedule?" I asked.

"Well, the two of us are home already. I need to leave in about three hours. Isn't that too early for you though?"

Damn, it kind of was. On days like this, I had to be on top of things even after the stock market closed.

"I'll be there on time and just bring my laptop with me," I said. I wasn't missing out on time with my girls for anything.

***

I was at Heather's place at six o'clock on the dot. She opened the door for me with a huge smile. She looked phenomenal, wearing a black suit. The skirt reached just above her knees. Her legs looked endless in high heels.

"Fuck, you're beautiful."

"Good evening to you too." Her smile grew more pronounced. She took my laptop bag, placing it on the small chair next to the closet. I kissed her as soon as I stepped inside the door. I hadn't seen her in two days, but this hunger I felt for her was insatiable, as if it had been two weeks. I wrapped a hand in her thick hair, tilting her head, kissing, claiming, marking her as mine. Her lips were slightly swollen when I pulled back. I ran my thumb over her mouth, pressing on the upper bow.

"Ryker, don't," she whispered weakly.

"What? Just kissing you for good luck. So you can focus better."

"Well, if you keep it up, all I'm going to

accomplish is to daydream about you during the interview."

I took a large step to one side, keeping my hands up in surrender.

"I don't want to jeopardize your professionalism. Where's Avery?"

"In her room. So, I've left puzzles out, and if she wants to watch cartoons, she'll tell you what her favorites are on Netflix."

"Babe, we're going to be fine," I assured her. "What time will you be back?"

"Nine or ten."

We heard Avery stomp through the apartment, running toward us.

"Ryker, you're here!"

"I am."

"Be a good girl, okay, Avery? Listen to Ryker," Heather said.

"Yes, Mommy."

"Okay. I have to go. Call me if you need help with anything."

She fiddled with the strap of her bag, clearly wondering if this was a good idea.

"I've got this," I said. "Go. Don't be late."

She smiled before taking off.

Once it was just the two of us, Avery took my hand, bringing me to the kitchen.

"Can we order pizza?" She pointed to a take-out menu pinned on the fridge. "We always order from there."

"Sure."

"Yes." Avery clapped her hands, instantly lighting up. Should I be suspicious? I almost texted Heather to ask if there was some rule on pizza, but I'd just told her I had everything under control.

After ordering one pizza for us both, I told Avery, "It'll take forty minutes for the delivery. What do you want to do until then?"

"I want to paint." That brilliant smile was still on.

"Okay."

I had no experience whatsoever with kids, but I was a fast learner. Within five minutes I realized there was a fundamental rule: I had to be very specific.

Case in point: I should have asked exactly what she wanted to paint. I assumed she'd bring out a coloring book, but instead Avery wanted to paint her own palms.

"Wait, let me see if that's safe," I said.

The package said it was water soluble, which was reassuring. I opened my laptop, checking the latest emails from clients while she played. By the time our pizza was delivered, Avery was walking around with blue palms, despite washing her hands once.

The delivery guy nearly broke a rib from laughter when Avery held up her hands, proudly declaring, "We can't wash it off. I have blue hands now. But if you put the pizza on my arms, I'll be really careful not to get paint on the box."

She stretched her tiny arms, pointing with her

chin to them. I placed the box on her arms, watching her walk slowly to the kitchen, balancing it carefully, as if it was a prized possession.

"Even if it says water soluble, try shampoo," the delivery guy said once Avery was out of earshot. "My three-year-old painted his whole body once."

The trick worked. Avery pouted while the color washed off, but her good mood was back once we were sitting at the table, devouring the food.

"This is an awesome evening," Avery declared, taking a huge bite from her slice of pizza. Damn, how could it be so easy to make this little girl happy?

"What do you want to do afterward?" I asked her.

Avery chewed slowly, frowning, as if she was deep in thought.

"I have a kitchen in my bedroom. Do you want me to show you how to play with it?"

"Sure. We can start right now if you want, and just take our food with us?"

"We're allowed to take pizza to my room? Ooooh, that's so cool."

Right. That enthusiasm clued me in that Heather must have some rule against eating in the bedroom, but fuck it. I'd already screwed it up, why take it back?

"We're making a huge exception. Just for this evening."

Avery practically jumped out of her chair. "Ryker, you are the *best*." She threw her little arms around me in a hug. I laughed, ruffling her hair. We took the cartons and napkins to her room, putting everything on the floor.

"Only cool people are allowed in my room," she exclaimed.

"So I'm cool?"

"Yes."

The thought that this small creature was already so attached to me was getting to me in a way I couldn't even describe. There wasn't much space to move around between her toys and the furniture. She'd have a whole lot more space at my condo. Even the smallest room was bigger than this one.

Jesus, my own thoughts were scaring me... but not enough to keep from imagining the logistics of this, how everything could work out.

For the next half hour, she patiently explained how the "kitchen" worked, and I tried real hard not to tune her out. I failed more times than I succeeded.

"Avery, your pizza will get cold." In her excitement, she'd forgotten to eat.

"Okay. Okay." She sat down cross-legged, eating with small bites, glancing around her room. Her gaze stopped at her desk, and then she kept looking between me and the desk, as if trying to figure out something.

"Ryker, can I draw you a friendship card?" she asked after a while.

"Sure."

"So you want to be my friend?"

I winked. "I thought I already was."

She looked at me wearily. "So I don't have to call you Dad?"

I'd started gathering our pizza boxes, but froze in the act, swallowing hard.

"Do you want to?"

She shook her head. "No. I want you to be my friend. Because friends always stay."

Avery sounded satisfied, as if she'd found the perfect loophole. Pressure gathered in my chest in a matter of seconds. Jesus, I couldn't believe my ears. It wasn't just her words, but the way she'd said them, with so much nonchalance, as if she was informing me it was cold outside tonight. It slayed me. I tried to see things from her perspective, and it was remarkably easy. Kids' worlds weren't complicated. She'd been disappointed before, so that was the only thing she'd come to expect. Disappointing children should be illegal. If I had a kid, I'd never leave it. Ever.

I had no idea what to tell her. Should I even say anything? Explain that things weren't black and white? No, I had to talk to Heather first.

After we took the empty pizza box back to the kitchen, Avery brought a sheet of paper and crayons into the living room. I was sitting on the couch, she was lying on the floor on her belly, bent over the paper. She scribbled "Friedsip card" on it and drew two figurines just below it. Didn't take a genius to figure out it was supposed to represent the two of us, even though we looked nothing like the drawings. She shoved the card in my hands after she was done.

"Thanks, Avery."

I detected a hint of wariness in her eyes. Damn, I wanted to erase that. I knew how it felt to have that security blanket stripped from around you. It sucked. I wanted her to have the safety of knowing that both her parents would be there no matter what. But what did I even know about that?

Chapter Twenty-Three
Heather

"Troops, I'm home," I called the second I entered the apartment. No one answered. In fact, the whole place was suspiciously quiet. I returned earlier than I'd thought so it wasn't Avery's bedtime yet. Considering she usually fought tooth and nail for any additional minute, I wasn't sure what was going on.

Tiptoeing to Avery's bedroom, I discovered her sleeping soundly. Oh, wow. That was a first.

Hearing the water running in my bathroom, I headed that way. Ryker was showering. Oh, yum. He was just... perfection. Taut skin and toned muscles everywhere I looked. I rarely had the opportunity to just drink him in like now, so I planned to take advantage of it for as long as possible.

"Had your fill?" Ryker asked in a teasing tone.

"Not by a long shot." I grinned, shrugging. I'd been so lost in the act of admiring him that I hadn't realized he was watching me.

Ryker's mouth curled up in a smile. He moved one finger in a come here motion. I walked toward him slowly, eyeing the spray of water. I stopped at the edge of the shower, heart beating wildly. Was this drop-dead sexy man really here, in my shower? Or was he a vision? I ran a hand from one shoulder to the other, tracing a pattern over his chest, feeling his wet skin under my fingers. He kissed me the next second. Oh, yeah. He was real.

The touch electrified my lips, and the way he explored me made me weak in the knees. I clasped his shoulders, needing more support. Next thing I knew, Ryker's hands were gripping my hips. What was he planning?

He pulled me with him under the shower, getting my clothes completely wet. I half laughed, half yelped.

"What are you doing?" I asked.

"What's it look like?" He grinned widely. I was full-on laughing now.

I wasn't spontaneous, but Ryker was making me discover all sorts of things about myself. Like the fact that I relished these small, unexpected moments.

He kissed me again before I could answer. Pressing my back against the tiles, he deepened the kiss, exploring me with so much urgency that I felt on fire. Not just the simmering kind, but a full-on inferno.

I felt wanted, claimed with every stroke of his tongue, every inch of skin he bared.

I had no idea when he'd undone the zipper of my skirt. I'd been too consumed by feeling his hard, naked body pressed against mine. When I was buck naked, he turned off the water, and we both stepped out of the shower. He wrapped a towel around me and another around himself before pulling me in a bear hug.

"My clothes are drenched," I said, glancing at the pile. I would have pinched him, but he had me firmly captive in his hug. "Why did you pull me in the shower?"

"I didn't plan on it."

"So you just couldn't help yourself?"

"Exactly. Just saw you standing there and wanted you with me."

I sighed, just sinking against him. Well, I was completely disarmed now. I disentangled myself from his arms, turning around, running my fingers over his chest.

"What are you doing?" he asked.

"Getting my fill of you. And shhhh... your voice is too sexy. It's distracting me."

"Yes, ma'am."

He was silent right until I reached the hem of the towel he'd wrapped around his lower body.

"Heather...." His voice was dangerously low.

"All done, had my fill."

"Really?"

"For now," I amended.

"We'll see about that." Ryker's smile was wolfish now. And his voice was still in that lower octave that made my entire body tingle. "How was your evening?" he asked.

"Excellent. The interview was just what I needed. I'm going to edit it tomorrow morning while it's still fresh."

"You can do it tonight if you want."

"Ha! I've got you here to kiss and touch as much as I want, and you think I'll waste my time editing?"

"Happy to know I'm more important than editing." He wiggled his eyebrows, but then he swallowed hard, looking at me intently. "I want to talk to you about something."

"Okay."

"So... Avery made me a friendship card today."

"Oh, that's cute. She does those sometimes."

"Yeah... but she made that after telling me she'd prefer if I was her friend, and not her dad. Because dads leave."

My vision faded at the corners. I blinked a few times. My throat wasn't just dry now; I had a lump the size of a fist at the base of it too.

"She... she said that?" My voice was shaky.

"Yes. And I was thinking, why don't you two spend some time at my apartment too? Maybe then she'll trust that I want to stick around. That I'm here to stay."

Air rushed out of me. I hadn't expected this, not in a million years.

"You want us at your apartment?" I whispered. Yes, I was double-checking, but I just couldn't help myself.

"Yes. I want you two to be part of my life. You're more important to me than I even thought possible, Heather. Both of you."

"Ryker... wow, this is so surreal," I

whispered.

He frowned. "And you don't want it?"

"I do. I do. I've just been so concerned with looking out for us... you know, just trying to protect us from being hurt, that I'm not even sure I know how to be truly happy without worrying about losing that happiness. Oh God, I'm not even making sense." I buried my face in my hands. I wasn't coherent. What was wrong with me?

I felt Ryker lean in, clasping his fingers around my wrists, lowering my hands.

"You are making sense, babe. And don't worry, you'll be so happy that you'll just forget to be afraid. I'll simply leave you no choice."

He was beaming widely now. I laughed as some of that anxiety just melted away. I was so immensely happy. He wasn't put off by my fears. He wanted to fight them alongside me.

"I know how Avery is feeling," he said, pushing strands of my wet hair behind my ears. "My dad left when I was young. I don't even remember him too much, honestly. But I do remember how shitty everything was for my family. How abandoned we all felt, like we were just afterthoughts. Leaving kids should be illegal."

"Yeah, it should," I whispered, wiggling my arms around his torso, wanting to be a little closer to him. I wanted to protect him. From what, I wasn't sure. It wasn't like he needed my protection anyway, but maybe I could take his mind off those unhappy memories. Yes, I could definitely do that.

"I don't know if I can give you two something I didn't have, or at least don't remember. But I sure as hell want to."

I couldn't believe he actually doubted himself.

"I think you can do anything you want." I looked up at him, kissing his jaw, feeling like my heart was about to explode.

"Oh, yeah?"

I nodded firmly, kissing down his neck.

"Didn't know you held me in such high esteem."

"I definitely do."

"And you didn't tell me before... why?" His teasing tone was back. Mission accomplished. I'd distracted him.

"Doesn't quite pack the same punch if I say it repeatedly. I've been saving it for a special occasion."

"I see."

I smiled against his chest when he gripped my hips, pulling me flush against him. I continued kissing down his torso as if nothing had changed... even when he undid my towel, letting it fall to the floor. I'd discovered a new side to Ryker tonight, and honestly a new side to me as well.

"You're very important to me, Ryker," I whispered against his skin, taking off his towel as well. He tilted my head up, drawing his thumb under my lower lip.

I was going to combust under his gaze. I just knew it. He pulled me back up until our lips were level.

"What are you doing to me, Heather?" he murmured. "Since I met you, I keep wanting things I never even thought about before. I imagine them down to every last detail."

I couldn't believe he wanted me and Avery to spend more time at his apartment, to be part of his life. I'd never felt so... precious. As if he was willing to do everything for me.

"I want you so much. All the time," he went on. We moved to the bedroom, walking clumsily, too busy touching each other to pay much attention to our surroundings. Ryker tilted my head back, just holding me like that for a beat before sealing his lips over mine. I groaned at the primal way he claimed my mouth—passionate and demanding. He was pure fire. He skimmed his hands down my body, teasing the sides of my breasts with his thumbs before descending even lower.

Sliding his hands under my ass cheeks, he lifted me up. I groaned, digging my fingernails in his arms when my clit collided with his hard-on. He hoisted me up slowly, drawing the entire length of him across my opening, teasing my clit more and more until my legs were shaking before lowering me down so I was sitting on the edge of the bed.

***

Ryker

One taste was all it took for me to become insatiable. I just couldn't get enough of her lips; I wanted to explore them every way imaginable. Gentle, and hard, then gentle again. I was in completely over my head. It hadn't ever felt this intense. I pushed her hair to one side, gathering it in my fist, tilting her head so I could explore her neck all I wanted. I drew my mouth slowly over her skin, enjoying every time she caught her breath, the way the muscles in her entire body seemed to strum together as I went lower. When I reached her shoulder, I changed course, moving lower toward her breasts. I let go of her hair, looking up at her when my mouth hovered just over her nipple.

Heather's eyes were wide and full of lust. I could ask anything of her, and she'd give it to me. And that was exactly what I wanted: her complete surrender.

I licked her nipple once, smiling when she jerked back on instinct, just out of my reach. I needed her in another position: more at my mercy. Like this, sitting at the edge of the bed, she could get away too easily. She looked up at me with a hint of shyness.

"You're beautiful, Heather."

I stayed where I was, a good two feet away from the bed, drinking in every part of her. When our gazes locked, she licked her lower lip.

"You like watching me get naked?" I asked.

"Might be among my top ten favorite views."

I laughed, stalking toward her.

"Top ten, huh? Not even top three?"

She rolled her eyes playfully, running her hand

down my chest, making a circle around my navel before lowering her hand even more.

"We have to be quiet," she murmured.

I gripped the headboard when she wrapped her hand around my cock, circling around the crown with her thumb before tracing that same path with her tongue.

"Fuck!" I hadn't expected it to be so intense. Everything was heightened with Heather. When she looked up at me, I just wanted to bury myself inside her, but instead I let her take charge... for now.

She took me in her mouth, slow and deep. Fuck. *Fuck*. I was going to splinter the wood or sprain my hand if I gripped the headboard any tighter. I was breathing in through my nose, out through my mouth, pacing myself. Pulling back, she licked up from the base, going slowly, driving me crazy. When she pressed the flat of her tongue against it, I dropped my head back, groaning. She clamped her lips tight around my cock, and on instinct, I moved my hips back and forth, watching her. Her eyes glinted playfully as she gripped the base of my cock with one hand, my ass with the other. Her nails pressed into my skin. She moved her mouth up and down, slowly and then faster, increasing the rhythm. Energy shot through me. Fuck. I ran one hand through her hair before fisting it.

Leaning to one side, I reached between her legs. When I traced my fingers down her pussy, realizing how wet she was from having her mouth on me, I nearly lost my mind. I circled her clit slowly, until she grasped the sheet with her free hand. Her moans reverberated against my cock, sending a jolt of pleasure through me.

"Babe!" I groaned, pulling out slowly. I pushed her back on the bed, spreading her legs, leaning over her. I moved my mouth up one inner thigh while dragging my fingers up the other one. Her skin turned sensitive everywhere I touched or licked.

When I pressed my tongue flat against her clit, I heard her swallow hard, felt the muscles in her belly contract in anticipation.

"*Rykeeeer.*"

I held her thighs firmly, watching her come apart with every lash of my tongue, until her thighs were shaking.

"Please, please," she whispered.

I moved my mouth up on her body in a slow, lazy rhythm. She writhed under me in protest.

"Ryker, touch me. Please."

Smiling against her skin, I touched two fingers to her clit, applying pressure again. Damn, it was a fucking privilege to feel her come apart, to wring every drop of pleasure from her.

I wanted to be etched so deep in her body and her mind that there was no place for any man except me. I *needed* to be important to her. I kissed up her neck, groaning when my cock rubbed against her stomach. Pulling back, I positioned the tip at her entrance. She pulsed around me the second I slid inside. Her eyes widened, as if she wasn't expecting this any more than I did.

"Let go, beautiful. I want to feel you come," I urged, sliding in deeper, faster. She was so turned on from our foreplay that I knew it wouldn't take much to push her over the edge. My pelvis pushed against her clit on every thrust. She grew tighter, and then tighter still, and then she came hard, tugging at the sheets. A shot of pleasure rippled through me, so intense that I buckled over her, nearly crushing her. Fuck, no.

I pulled out, pacing myself, waiting for her to regain her breath, kissing her breasts and neck before I hooked my elbows under her knees, lifting her legs up.

She gasped in surprise, but that didn't keep her from surrendering to me just the way I wanted her.

I smiled when she reached a hand between us, gripping my cock, bringing it closer to her pussy. I drove inside her the next second. She gasped, thrusting her hips upward. I was deeper inside her than before and knew this was so intense for her that she wouldn't last long. Fuck, it was intense for me too. She clenched around me on every thrust.

I placed one of her legs back on the bed. She had more leverage like this, and I had a free hand. I could touch her. I teased a nipple before lowering my hand. I loved that damp skin, her cries of pleasure—they were all because of me. They were *for* me. I rested my palm on her pubis to increase the pressure while nudging her clit with my thumb.

"I love feeling you so tight around me, so close," I said. "I love you."

"Ryker, I'm going to..." Her words were completely lost in her cry of pleasure. I couldn't last one second longer. This was so intense that I could barely think, barely breathe through the pleasure, and when she grabbed the headboard with both hands, squeezing her inner muscles even tighter, I let go completely.

"Fuuuuuck." My vision faded at the corners. I shut my eyes, wanting to block out everything except how damn intense this felt. Pleasure zipped through me with a savage intensity. I kept thrusting, even though every muscle burned and tightened. After I was completely done for, I buckled forward, resting my forehead on the pillow, still inside her, unwilling to sever our connection.

"Wow," she whispered.

"Yeah. Wow."

I rolled over next to her, laughing when she made a little sound of protest.

"We weren't exactly quiet," she said on a chuckle. "But the walls are thick. We're good."

I turned on one side, just looking at her before reaching out and drawing my fingers up and down her stomach.

"Heather, I meant what I said earlier. I love you."

I caught her smile before she rolled over, hiding her face in my chest. "I'm not saying it just because you're saying it, but I love you too."

"And you're scared about it."

She pulled back, looking up at me. "A little."

"Don't be."

"You're not allowing me?"

"Damn right, I'm not."

"Wow. That's impressive."

"So it's working."

She grinned. "I'd say you're on the right path."

Chapter Twenty-Four
Ryker

Heather and Avery came to my apartment the following week. I realized within a few hours that my place was boring as hell for a kid, so I made plans to take them shopping on Saturday.

As I prepared to leave my office on Friday evening, Owen knocked at the door. "Got a minute?"

"Sure."

"A reporter might contact you. Hank Dawson."

I stopped in the act of shutting of my computer. "He already tried to approach me. What's his deal?"

"I contacted him. Thought it wouldn't be bad to have various publications on top of this. He wants to write a story on this."

"I'm not talking to him."

"He can write the article even without your contribution."

"You know Heather's taken a risk by writing a piece that paints us in a positive light, right? The least you can do is make sure it's exclusive."

"We all take risks."

"This is bullshit, Owen, and you know it."

"I see what's going on. This isn't strictly professional for you, is it?"

"Heather and I are dating, but that's none of your business."

He shoved his hands in his pockets, shaking his head. "Maybe not, but the people who make it on top in this business are the ones for whom work comes first."

"Then get to the age of fifty and take trophy wives twenty years younger. I don't need advice on that topic."

I didn't give him a chance to say anything else, just shut off my laptop and walked straight past him. I was still furious by the time I was out of the building.

I dropped by my sisters' store. I'd possibly done it out of instinct, because I hadn't heard from them in a few days. I expected to see my sisters inside, either huddled over their laptops at the counter or arranging merchandise on shelves, as usual.

I had *not* expected to see the store closed. It was only seven o'clock in the evening. Their usual opening hours were until nine. Again, instinct told me something was wrong.

I took out my phone, calling Tess. It went straight to voicemail. Shit, what was happening? I called Skye next. She didn't pick up, but at least it didn't go to voicemail, so I tried again. The fourth time, she picked up.

"Ryker," she greeted. "Sorry, I'd put it on silent."

"Hi! I'm in front of your store."

"Oh, we're not there."

"I figured that out. How come?"

Skye didn't answer. I ran a hand through my hair, trying to summon some of that calm I was so known for.

"We've decided to cut the opening hours shorter. We're both so tired, and we need to rethink some things."

"What happened?"

Again, silence. It was freaking me out. Skye had two modes: dragon mode or pacifier mode. Silence meant she was in so much trouble that she had no idea how to get out.

"Where are you?" I asked.

"At Tess's place."

"I can come over."

"I have a better idea. I'll meet you in the city. Being inside isn't helping."

"Okay. Is Tess coming too?"

"Nah. She's asleep. Don't want to wake her up."

"She's sleeping at 7:00 p.m.? Skye, what's happening?" I pressed my forehead against the cool window.

"It's been a rough week."

"Rough how? Can I help?"

More silence.

"Skye, what's wrong? This isn't like you."

"The investor we were talking with decided not to work with us anymore."

I clasped my phone tightly, balled the other hand in a fist.

"Shit. Anything else?" It was more of a rhetorical question, but I braced myself when Skye exhaled sharply.

"The guy I was dating said I was a buzzkill and no fun, and he didn't need that in his life."

"He just told you that after you've had one of the roughest weeks ever?"

"Yes. So I've been a bit out of sorts. Tess has dealt with a bunch of paperwork all by herself, and now she's exhausted." Her voice wobbled on every third word. I prided myself on being a relaxed, take-life-as-it-comes guy. I'd been that way for as long as I could remember, and my strategy had helped me deal even under stress. That strategy didn't work when shit hit the fan in the family. I went from being calm to wanting to punch the window in front of me.

"Where do you want to meet?" I asked.

"The viewing deck on the Empire State?"

My sister loved viewing decks. She always had.

"Sure. I'll be there in half an hour."

"Ryker, you don't have to do this," she said, almost as an afterthought. "I'm a big girl."

"Still my sister. Come on, don't argue with me. Just meet me there."

She chuckled. "Yes, sir."

After hanging up, I ordered an Uber. On the

way to the building, I tried to calm down. The problem with being in a rage was that I couldn't think clearly. It was the reason why I'd lasted so long on Wall Street, why I was so good at what I was doing. I compartmentalized anger and fear easily to focus on finding solutions. But I couldn't compartmentalize jack shit when it came to family... or Heather. I was still processing my conversation with Owen, trying to foresee the ramifications of his decision and any preemptive measures I could take, anything to protect Heather. I was far too upset to come up with anything.

After buying my ticket, I went to the deck. Skye had texted me that she was already there, and I spotted her immediately. Years ago, it used to be very crowded, but now there were so many viewing decks in New York that you actually had *some* space to move around here, admire the view. It was still a major tourist attraction, but it wasn't too full currently.

"Remember the first time we came here?" Skye asked.

I chuckled. "Yeah. Gave Mom a scare and we were grounded for a month."

"It was worth it though."

"Every minute of it."

We'd just moved to New York, and we were dying to explore the city. Skye had pleaded with all of us to come here.

So one evening, when Mom was supposed to be working late, we'd all snuck out here. Once we found a corner to ourselves, we celebrated by drinking soda from the cans we'd brought.

We made a pact. It was a silly, childish adventure, but the memory was branded in my mind. We'd promised to always stick together, have each other's backs. I remembered feeling all powerful and protective... right until the police showed up. Someone had reported four minors to the authorities. They escorted us back home. Mom was in tears when we arrived. She'd left work earlier than anticipated and had panicked when she'd found the house empty.

We made another pact the very next day: not to give Mom more headaches. She'd had enough on her plate already.

Glancing at Skye, I was trying to decide the best course of action. My goal was simple: get her to let me help. Amazing how I could decide over million-dollar portfolios in a matter of minutes by only factoring in several key performance indicators, but despite knowing Skye my entire life, I still couldn't tell what strategy would work best. Women were complicated.

"You do remember the pact, right?" I asked.

"The one where we promised not to give Mom any more headaches?"

"No, the one before."

She elbowed me, grinning. "Of course I do. Our family lives by rules, pacts, and policies."

I'd found my angle.

"You and Tess always hold the no-secrets

policy over my head. I'm going to pull the brother card here. We made a pact. Always look out for each other. I want to cash in on it."

She smiled, touching my cheek. "You do that constantly. Remember all those shelves you put up?"

"I'm serious, Skye. Investors are my job—"

She dropped her chin to her chest. "Jeez, you're stubborn. We told you that we don't want you to risk your reputation with us."

"I don't give a damn about my reputation. You're my sisters."

"What exactly would you like to do?"

"I can get you a bunch of investors."

"No, no. That's a surefire way to get people to whisper that you're doing deals for your family. Just protecting you from yourself, little bro. You're impulsive and headstrong, and sometimes you don't weigh all the risks when you want something. Especially when that something is family related."

I glared at her. "I hate it when you're right. In my defense, I only shot myself in the foot once. And I was sixteen."

"And that time you were twenty-three. And that other time last year."

I threw my head back, laughing. "Okay, okay. Point made." On a serious note, I added, "I just don't want to see you two struggle."

She leaned closer, smiling. "We won't struggle forever. All beginnings are hard, right?"

I said nothing. Skye poked my arm.

"Back me up. I've made a mile-long list of

motivational quotes. I need you to approve every single one of them."

"Yes, ma'am."

"Tess and I will regroup, okay? Don't worry that much. It's just been a very rough week."

"I didn't know you and that guy were so serious," I blurted.

"We weren't." She looked in the distance, frowning. "I mean, you know I'm laid back about these things, but I didn't think he was going to just run off when things got a little rough." Her voice was small. I hated it, and what I hated even more was that I couldn't do anything about it.

A beeping sound came from her bag. Skye rummaged through it, taking out her phone.

"Tess woke up and texted me." She looked up at me, eyes wide, as if she'd suddenly had an idea. I braced myself but made an inner promise to just go along with whatever she wanted, because tonight was all about Skye.

"How much do you love us?" she asked, batting her eyelashes.

"Very much."

"Enough to go with us to an outdoor movie screening? Tess said they're showing *Gone with the Wind* in Central Park."

I really didn't have a choice. At least it wasn't a museum.

"I'll do one better. Why don't we call Cole too? We'll make a party out of it."

Skye grinned from ear to ear. "My favorite

people in the world *and* a movie screening? I can't say no to that."

I was banking on it. We made a beeline to the elevator, but I waited to call Cole until we were back out on the street again. The wind on the deck was too strong to have a phone conversation.

While Skye ordered an Uber, I called my brother.

"What are you up to?" I asked the second he picked up.

"Nothing."

"Can you meet me, Skye, and Tess in Central Park?"

"Sure. What happened?"

One of the things I loved about my family? We could tell when something was off before the other even spelled it out. Walking a few steps away from Skye, I filled Cole in quickly.

"That motherfucker."

"Which one? The investor or Skye's guy?"

"Both. Who are they?"

"I don't know."

"They screwed with our sisters. We need their names."

"Cole. Central Park. Twenty minutes. Don't bring up the topic at all. Just managed to stop Skye from beating herself up."

Cole was my opposite in many ways... except when it came to impulsiveness. Growing up, we'd competed in who was the most hot-headed, as if we were trying to win a medal for it. Luckily, our sisters had tempered us down. They were successful... most of the time.

Unlike the Empire State Deck, Central Park was crawling with people. Despite the vastness of the place, the perimeter of the movie screening was claustrophobic. But a deal was a deal, and Skye already looked more cheerful.

After I bought us hot dogs from a vendor passing by, Cole texted that he and Tess had found an empty patch of grass.

"Oh, look, Tess is waving at us," Skye said. We bought two more hotdogs and then did our best to reach our siblings without stepping on anyone.

"Jesus, I can't understand why it's so crowded. The movie's been out for fifty years," Cole said.

Our sisters glared at him as the four of us somehow crammed in on the blanket Tess had brought.

"Yes, but it's still more amazing than 99 percent of the stuff they make nowadays. So, let's set some rules," Tess said. "We won't talk shop tonight."

"Or about romantic stuff," Skye added.

"Deal," Cole and I said at the same time.

"You're in for brothers of the year, both of you," Tess declared.

"You only have two brothers," Cole teased.

"Yeah, if we're going to compete, it's going to be among each other," I volleyed back. "Personally, I feel like I'm in the lead by a solid lap."

Skye rolled her eyes, taking Cole's arm. "He's

less bigheaded. I'm siding with him."

Tess crossed her arms over her chest, looking between the three of us.

"Tess, I'm going to be real mad if you don't side with me," I warned. The corners of her mouth tilted up.

"Of course I'm going to side with you. It's all about balance in this family."

I cocked a brow at Cole. "See? We're even."

"Only because you begged," Cole teased.

"I only laid out my arguments. That's not begging. It's common sense."

"By the way, why did you even go by the store tonight?" Skye whispered as the beginning credits started to roll on the huge portable screen at the other end of the perimeter.

"Avery and Heather are coming by my place tomorrow. We're going shopping so Avery can have some stuff at my apartment. Thought you could give me some tips."

My sisters gasped. Cole choked on the last bite of hot dog.

"Why didn't you say anything until now?" Tess asked.

Then we got shushed. "Keep your voices down. Some of us actually want to see the movie."

I shook my head, shrugging. Only in New York could people take the screening of a fifty-year-old movie so seriously. I blocked out most of it, thinking about Owen again. I wanted to find solutions for everyone I cared about, but it wouldn't be tonight. Right now, all I could do was entertain my sisters.

Chapter Twenty-Five
Ryker

I arrived at home after midnight but couldn't fall asleep. I'd always been able to push work-related worries to the back of my mind, or if they were too pressing, a session at Northern Lights was everything I needed to unwind.

But there was no unwinding when my family or Heather was involved. My brain just worked tirelessly to come up with a solution, and when I couldn't find one, like now, frustration with myself just ate me up from inside. I didn't want Heather to run into any issues. I wanted to protect her. I wanted to protect my sisters too: from this madness, generally from ups and downs... from everything I could. We had a pact, a promise. Sure, we'd been kids back then, but I liked to make good on it as often as I could.

I only slept a few hours, so I was exhausted the next morning. I tried to push everything out of my mind when Heather and Avery arrived, but I couldn't do it.

"Earth to Ryker?" Heather asked, smiling.

"Sorry, I wasn't paying attention."

"We brought breakfast." She held up two

paper bags. "If today is going to go the way I think, we'll need sustenance."

"Good idea."

"I already ate. Can I go to my room?" Avery asked, almost breathlessly. I'd shown her the guest room last time they were here, and when I said it was hers, she'd been so beside herself that she kept working *my room* in every sentence.

"Sure."

Heather and I went to the kitchen. I took out plates, but she didn't open the bags.

"What's up with you?" Heather asked.

"Just tired. I didn't sleep much last night."

"We can go shopping another time. Or... we don't have to go at all." Her eyes were loving and concerned, and I needed that.

I almost took her up on her offer, but I knew I'd be letting Avery down if we canceled everything.

"It's fine," I said.

Heather frowned. "Ryker, is something wrong?"

"No. Just tired," I repeated. I didn't want to bring my crap into our relationship; she didn't need to deal with it.

"Okay." She began opening the paper bag, then stopped. "You're sure it's not something else? Look, if you don't want to go shopping, it's no big deal. I understand if you got a little overwhelmed last time."

"What are you talking about?"

She twiddled her thumbs, averting her gaze.

"I don't know. Did you change your mind? If you don't want us here—"

I closed the distance between us before she could even finish the sentence, cradling her head with both hands.

"Of course I want you here. Don't even think that."

"You're sure? Because you're... distant since I arrived."

"Yesterday was...." I hadn't wanted to ruin her day first thing in the morning, but maybe it was better if she knew right away. "Owen said he was the one who contacted that Dawson guy, asked him to write about the company too."

Heather gasped. "Shit! Why? I thought it was clear that we were expecting this to be an exclusive story."

"I know, babe. I'm sorry."

"Damn. I'm going to have to email Danielle and let her know. Did Owen tell you when Dawson's article is coming out?"

"No. I don't think he knows either." I placed my hands on her shoulders. "Babe, I'm right here with you, okay? We'll figure everything out."

"You really mean that?" She sounded surprised.

"Of course I mean it."

She gave me a guarded smile. "Is there anything else on your mind? You're still tense."

How could she tell that? It dawned on me that I wasn't used to talking about family stuff with anyone *outside* the family. It was just one of those things I'd always compartmentalized. But I could practically see Heather folding into herself just standing here, feeling left out, perhaps still fearing I didn't want them here. I could do this. Just let her be part of everything.

"Skye and Tess lost the investor they had."

"Oh my God. So what are they going to do?"

"Find another one, but it'll take a while. I'm worried about them. They're stretched so thin, and that guy Skye had been seeing dumped her, and I'm frustrated as fuck that I can't be of more use."

"Ryker," Heather said softly.

"I'm worried."

"We can brainstorm ways to help them out."

"We?" I asked. She nodded, placing her hands on my chest. She wasn't just brushing off my concerns. She wanted to be involved in this. I couldn't believe that she got me so completely. I kissed her—hard, deep, until she moved those hands up around my neck, pulling me closer to her. I felt the tension melt away from my body.

She smiled when I pulled back, tracing one finger on my forehead, down my temple, to the corner of my mouth. She tilted her head, as if considering some options.

"What are you thinking about?" I asked.

"That maybe we should take a trip to the Northern Lights tonight. You said that playing makes you relax."

It did, though nothing got me out of this

headspace when I was so wired up. Except this, right here.

"But then I can't spend time with you."

"You'd rather spend the evening with me than at the Northern Lights?" The look on her face was priceless.

"I'd rather spend time with you than do 99.9 percent of anything."

"What's the 0.01 entail?"

I brought my mouth to her ear. "If you want to know, you'll have to get it out of me."

Pulling back, she narrowed her eyes. "And you don't think I can do that?"

"No, no. I have full confidence in you."

"You're full of shit."

I laughed, curling an arm around her waist, keeping her close. I rested my forehead in the crook of her neck, drinking her in.

"Stay here. It's been a fucking hard week, and I just need you for a bit."

It felt good to say it out loud.

***

Heather

I ran my hands over his shoulders again and was pleased to discover they weren't as tense as a few minutes ago. I really was helping him relax, and that made me so happy. I wanted to be a positive influence in his life, just as he was in mine.

Before I realized what was happening, Ryker

slid his palms under my ass. I assumed that meant he wanted to scoop me up in his arms, so I helped by jumping him. A fraction of a second too late, I realized he'd had much simpler intentions: he'd just wanted to feel me up. He lost his balance, and for a beat, I was sure we'd crash, but then he recovered, placing me on the counter. I clutched my knees tightly at his sides. I was laughing so hard that I was afraid I'd crack a rib. Ryker wasn't faring much better.

"Woman, are you trying to kill us?" he asked in between guffaws.

"How was I supposed to know that you're just trying to feel me up?"

"Maybe because I'm always trying to do that?"

"Hmm... you do have a point." I blew air out of the right corner of my mouth, because my hair was sticking everywhere. He pushed some strands away, tucking them over my shoulder. I loved that I was his confidante, the person he came to no matter if he had something good or bad to share.

"Mommy, can we go now?" Avery's voice sounded from the corridor.

"We'll be with you in a minute," Ryker said. "Wait for us by the door."

Avery squealed. "Okay."

"Why did you tell her to wait there?" I asked, jumping down from the counter.

"So I could do this." He brought a hand to my waist, pushing me against the door. I only caught a glimpse of the lust in his gaze before he brought his mouth down on mine. The second our lips touched, my nerve endings leapt to life, fire dancing along my skin everywhere he touched me. His hands pressed on my waist before skidding down to the hem of my dress. He slid one hand under the fabric before pulling back completely, as if afraid that if he didn't put distance between us, he'd lose his head.

He didn't say one word, but the way he kept his palms pressed against the wall was enough to give me a taste of all that passion he was barely keeping at bay.

"Sneaky kissing. I like it," I whispered, grinning.

He grinned back. "There'll be plenty more when we come back."

"Why not now?" I teased.

"Because if I get another taste, we might not leave at all."

His tone was playful, but that intense glint in his eyes told me just how plausible that scenario was. He grabbed the paper bag with breakfast in one hand, and we headed out to the corridor. My heart was beating insanely fast, as if we'd just been caught doing something wrong.

"Ready to go shopping?" Ryker asked Avery.

"YES," Avery practically yelled. Yeah... she was definitely my daughter. No danger of hospital mix-ups there. If there was any opportunity to shop, Avery didn't want to miss one minute of it.

"After you, my ladies." Ryker opened the door. Avery skidded out first, mimicking a runway walk all the way to the elevator.

"What's the first stop on the list?" I asked as we rode down. "Or wait, is there a list? Do we have an itinerary?"

I caught Ryker and Avery exchanging a glance. They'd been conspiring again?

"Bergdorf Goodman," Ryker said.

Holy shit, that had escalated quickly. I'd expected Costco or Target.

"What exactly are we shopping for?" I inquired. This wasn't my usual playground. It was out of my way, and honestly, above my paycheck.

"They have toys," Avery declared. "The special collection Barbie dolls."

"And we can't find those anywhere else?" I asked.

"No, it's an exclusive line. Some girls at my school have it."

I barely hid my smile. My mother bribed Avery with actual animals. Ryker had only gotten to dolls. I didn't know if I should consider myself lucky or brace myself for an escalation.

I took my phone out, sending a quick email to Danielle. I resolved not to think about any of this today and just enjoy our time together. I wasn't going to let Ryker worry about anything today either. Usually, something like this would have sent me spiraling out in a panic, but I felt oddly at ease, feeling it in my bones that we really could work out everything together.

Chapter Twenty-Six
Heather

Saturday in Manhattan was crazy busy, especially on a gorgeous day like this one. It was the beginning of May, which meant half the flowers in the parks were in full bloom. Everything was green anyway.

I felt like royalty from the moment I stepped inside Bergdorf Goodman. Everything from the way the merchandise was arranged in displays and on shelves to the faint jasmine smell in the air dripped with elegance and luxury.

We went directly to the children's section. Avery and Ryker were in the lead, whispering. It felt like we were a little family, traipsing around and discussing the pros and cons of every toy.

Ryker kept taking out his phone from time to time, typing notes on it.

"What are you doing?" I asked.

"Writing down potential investors for Skye and Tess."

I'd resolved to not let him worry, but this was something else: he was finding solutions. I barely refrained from suggesting he take a seat in the coffee shop across the street and finish his list. He'd insisted that he did want this shopping trip... but he already had so much going on. An old worry resurfaced, wondering if this change in lifestyle was too much, but I pushed it away, choosing to focus on what was in front of me.

When Avery stopped to inspect a huge, turquoise Smurf figurine, I pulled Ryker to one side.

"How many items did you negotiate?" I asked him.

"What do you mean?"

"How many items is she allowed to choose?"

Ryker cocked a brow.

"Please say you've told her how many items she's allowed."

"That's no fun. We'll just play it by ear."

"Have you ever been shopping with a seven-year-old before?"

"No."

I pressed my lips together, but still couldn't hold back laughter.

"I've got this," Ryker said confidently.

"Okay. You do your thing. I won't interfere."

I was curious to see his tricks. After all, he'd cut his teeth on Wall Street wolves. Fifteen minutes later, I realized Ryker's trick was saying yes to everything. Clearly, his Wall Street rules didn't apply to Avery. We already needed a cart to carry around our acquisitions.

I'd said I wouldn't interfere... but he needed saving from himself. I was torn between saying something and just watching Ryker and Avery. They were having so much fun that I just couldn't bring myself to interfere. Midway through the spree, I went to buy water. Upon my return, there were three more items in the buggy: a mini skateboard, a mug, and a candle. I wasn't sure who was trying harder to pretend that the items weren't there: Avery or Ryker. I decided not to call them out on it. Five minutes later, it turned out they thought they'd fooled me, because they attempted the same maneuver. I had gone to ask where we could find sheets, and upon my return, there was a tea set in the pile that most definitely hadn't been there before. Yeah... definitely time to interfere.

"What's that?" I asked, gesturing to the tea set.

Avery pointed an accusatory finger at Ryker. "It was his idea."

Ryker laughed, crouching until he was level with Avery.

"Avery, a partnership works only if we don't rat each other out."

Avery shrugged. "Yes, but then Mommy would be mad at both of us. Now she will only be mad at you."

He laughed, standing up, turning to me. "She has a point."

"I'm not mad at either of you. But we've got enough things. You already have enough toys to keep you busy for a while."

Avery pouted, looking from me to Ryker, who nodded.

"Excellent. So we're done?" I asked.

"Avery wants to check out the playground," Ryker said. "We can drop her there while we wait for the store to bring the sheets from the storage room."

We dropped Avery off at the playground, where a supervisor assured us she wasn't letting the kids out of her sight.

"Just say it," Ryker said as we went up again on the escalator.

"What?"

"I know you're dying to make fun of me."

"Well...."

"I just don't know how you say no," he said.

I wiggled my eyebrows. "Practice."

"Doubtful. She just has this look in her eyes, like her entire world revolves around buying this next thing."

I was on a higher step than him, so I easily laced my arms around his neck, playing with his hair.

"Yeah... she's good at blackmailing without even using words."

Once we reached the floor, Ryker put one arm around my shoulders, keeping me close. When he nibbled at my earlobe, I elbowed him lightly.

"What are you doing?" I whispered.

"I've been dying to touch you for hours. Didn't want to do it with Avery watching."

"How about everyone watching right now?"

"Don't give a fuck about them."

Warmth coursed through me, rising to my cheeks.

"Fuck, I love seeing you blush. Especially because I know how far this blush spreads." He dragged the back of his fingers from my cheek down to my neck, and then lower still, only stopping at the neckline of my dress. That warmth instantly turned to heat. I licked my lips, pulling slightly away, needing fresh air. The combo of cologne and testosterone was not easy to resist.

The bedsheets were supposed to be delivered to the cash register on the main floor, but the woman working behind it informed us it'd take a while until they'd be here.

"You're welcome to look around until then," she finished.

"Thanks," Ryker said. We moved along the counter toward the back, where there were no buyers.

Now that we had time for a breather, I took time to admire him for the first time today. He wore a light blue shirt and jeans and looked simply delectable. He was just getting hotter by the day.

"What are you thinking about?" he asked.

Blushing, I turned around, glancing down at the glass counter.

"That you're basically like George Clooney. Getting sexier all the time. When you're fifty, you're going to be winning sexiest man of the year awards, and I'm just going to keep out of the pictures so I don't cramp your style."

"Already imagining us at fifty?"

I gasped. My stomach tightened the very next

second. "I was just... I mean, I know how that sounds."

"Sounds like you believe in what we have. I know I do. And today I just had this glimpse of what it feels like to have a family, and I want it, Heather. With you. And I bet you'll be hot when we're fifty." He lightly bit the side of my neck, laughing like we were just playing around, when he was claiming more of me with every word.

I want it, Heather, he'd said. But we'd known each other for two months only. Was he ready? Was I ready? I had no answer, but I knew one thing: I loved being wrapped up in him like this. He was holding me tightly to him. If I stood still, I could feel his heartbeats echoing against my body.

"Choose something," he whispered in my ear.

"What?"

"Anything. I want to buy you a gift."

"That's not necessary. And you've already bought so many things that we'll need a truck to transport them."

"I want something just for you." He pushed my hair to one side. I felt his breath on the exposed skin behind my ear.

"Choose something, Heather. Or I'll choose for you."

By the way his voice had taken on a rougher edge and his fingers pressed on my belly, he'd choose something dangerous. I wasn't sure in what way, but I wanted to find out. I just wanted to be surprised, and that was saying something, because I usually liked to be on top of everything.

"You choose," I said.

He laughed softly, moving his fingers in the shape of a small eight on my belly. I sucked in a breath, hoping to steel myself against the contact. Somehow, it had the exact opposite effect. Goose bumps broke out on my skin. How on earth could that touch affect me like this?

"Fine. A few rules."

"There are rules to getting a gift?"

"Yes. You're not allowed to refuse it, or to return it."

I whirled around, looking him straight in the eyes.

"Will I regret this?"

His mouth curled in a devastating smile. "Probably."

"Give me a hint. So I can brace myself."

"That wouldn't be a surprise now, would it?"

I pouted, holding up my thumb and forefinger. "Just a tiny little hint?"

"You belong to me, Heather. Every part of you. I want everyone to know that. Our families, friends, strangers."

Oh, wow. I didn't even know what to say.

"Am I scaring you?" he asked.

"A little," I admitted.

"You trust me?" he asked.

"Y-yes."

"That was a stutter. Not very encouraging."

That devastating smile was back.

"Should I give you tips?"

He laughed, looking at me incredulously. "No. It's a surprise. Turn around. Go down to Avery. I'll come get you later."

He placed his hands on my shoulders, actually turning me around, then walking me in the general direction of the escalator. I was so giddy with anticipation. Couldn't I just watch him buy it? Come to think about it, that would probably take away half the fun. But what if he bought me something outrageous? Or just something that didn't fit me at all?

"I can't believe you're bossing me into accepting a gift," I teased.

"This isn't bossing, Heather. This is me being on my very best behavior. Wait until we're home and I have you naked in my bed."

"Ryker! You can't say those things when we're out in the open."

"Yes, I can. You're mine, Heather."

I licked my lips. My body was already humming with anticipation... and not about my gift.

Ryker only let me go when I stepped on the escalator. I looked at him over my shoulder, intending to tease him, but the sheer intensity he was emanating was magnified by a factor of ten when I made eye contact.

I waited at the edge of the playground, glancing toward the escalator every few minutes. Avery was too busy playing to pay any attention to me. Ryker finally joined us half an hour later.

"Ready," he announced.

"So, where's my gift?"

"Hidden in one of the shopping bags waiting for us at the entrance. I'll give it to you at home, when we're alone."

I groaned. "I knew it. You bought me something totally inappropriate."

"You want something inappropriate? I'll make another trip upstairs. I'll be real quick."

"That's not what I mean."

"Isn't it?" His eyes raked over me playfully. I averted my gaze, because who knew what I'd say if I kept eye contact for too long.

Avery barreled toward us right away.

"Let's go, young lady," Ryker said.

We walked out of the store with what felt like a million bags. The Uber we ordered gave us the side eye when he picked us up, but I couldn't care less. Ryker was happy, my little girl was happy, and so was I.

Avery was wedged between the two of us on the ride home. The excitement of the past few hours had been too much for her. She fell asleep in a few short minutes. My heart flipped when I noticed she was holding my jacket with one hand, Ryker's with the other. A small knot formed in my throat. When I felt Ryker's fingers nudge my shoulder, I realized he'd been watching me. He gave me a smile that made the knot instantly loosen.

Avery woke up the second we arrived. She always did that, almost like she had an internal clock.

As soon as Avery entered the apartment, she announced, "I want all the toys in my room. Ryker, can you help me?"

She darted toward her room before Ryker even answered.

"I think I'm her favorite person," he said as we stepped in the enormous living room. We placed the bags next to the couch to give our hands a short break.

I grinned. "I wonder why."

A strand of his dark blond hair fell over his forehead. I pushed it back, craving to touch more of him. But I had a plan, and I needed to be alone to put it in motion. I was hoping he wouldn't take all the bags to Avery's room right away.

"Off you go," I encouraged. "Wouldn't want you to lose the favorite status."

Ryker tilted his head to one side, studying me. "You're going to rummage through the bags for your gift, aren't you?"

Oh my God. That was so spot-on that it was scary.

"Yes," I admitted, because there was no point denying it.

"You keep wanting to change the rules."

"You didn't say anything about not looking in the bags at home," I pointed out.

"You'll get it when we're alone," he repeated, voice strong and determined. My entire body hummed. I wanted to rile him up a bit but didn't get the chance, because Avery called out from her bedroom.

"Ryker?"

He grabbed the bags, walking backward, keeping eye contact until he left the room.

Even though Avery specifically asked Ryker for help, I ended up joining them too. Between the three of us, we got everything unpacked and put together in no time at all. I'd never seen Avery so excited. She spread out her toys everywhere and insisted on having the new sheets on the bed right away. I liked to wash bedlinen before using it the first time, but when Avery looked at me with wide eyes, saying, "Pleaaaaaaaaase, Mommy," I gave in. Guess I wasn't that good at saying no either.

Ryker ordered dinner to be delivered, but Avery fell asleep before the food arrived, and I decided not to wake her up.

I stood in the doorway even after I turned off her lights, remembering that evening when she'd asked me if it could be just the two of us. And yet here she was, starfished on the bed as if determined to occupy as much space as possible. She loved it here, there was no denying it. She was a kid. Giving her heart away was natural for her. It was my job to look out for her... and yet I was head over heels in love with this man. I couldn't even guard my own heart, let alone Avery's.

"Babe, I can feel you overthinking this," Ryker whispered, startling me. I hadn't realized he was behind me. Taking my hand, he led me to the living room. My heart was beating at a million miles an hour. Yes, I was still a little afraid that we were just jumping into this, and I was still not sure if we quite fit in his life.

"Don't know how to stop doing it," I admitted.

He caressed my cheek, looking at me intently. "How about I distract you from it?"

"What do you have in mind?"

Grinning, he searched his pocket, taking out a gorgeous watch. The face was round, with a dark blue background that showed the mechanism.

"Ooooh, my present. Thank you."

I bounced up and down on my toes as he clasped it around my wrist. I loved it.

"Time for some adult fun. I'm proposing something decadent," I announced, nudging his shoulder. One of the perks of a huge apartment? We didn't have to worry about Avery hearing us. The living room was separated from the guest bedroom by a corridor and two doors. The master bedroom was upstairs.

"I'm all ears."

And hands, and lips. He pounced on me the second we stepped inside the living room.

"I meant we could order some dessert."

"I already did. Ordered pizza and dessert."

"Wow! Right now, you're *my* favorite person."

"I see. So ordering dessert is the way to win that title?"

"One hundred percent. You have a talent for picking out delicious treats."

Ryker's gaze turned from playful to intense. He closed the distance between us, pressing the back of my thighs into the armrest of the couch. He kissed from the corner of my mouth up to my cheek before moving on to my ear, biting the shell lightly.

"What are you doing?" I whispered.

"Reminding you of my other talents."

"Oh, by all means. Go ahead."

He laughed in my ear, continuing his ministrations. God, I loved having his mouth on me, and his hands. I considered telling him that I'd been waiting for hours for this moment... but I had a hunch that meant I'd have an even harder time getting him to keep his hands to himself next time we were out in public.

The sound of someone knocking at the door interrupted our moment. I pursed my lips when Ryker pulled away.

"What's with that pout?"

"Just let them go away and come back to what you were doing."

Ryker laughed, running his thumb over my lips.

"Don't say that twice, or we're going to starve."

I grinned. "Oh, that's right. Our pizza and dessert! Can't believe I forgot about that."

"I kissed you that well, huh?"

"You know you did."

The sheer intensity in his eyes told me he was seriously considering not opening the door.

"What's this? Ranking me above dessert?" he asked.

I laughed, stroking my chin in an exaggerated gesture. "I'm conflicted. If I say yes, does that mean I'll get more kisses? Or more dessert?"

"Whatever you want."

I wiggled my eyebrows. "Dessert it is then."

Ryker lunged for me again, but before he could reach me, the doorbell rang.

"No, no, no. That'll wake up Avery, and I'm *still* hoping for adult fun."

His gaze smoldered on the word "adult." Oh, yeah... we weren't going to sleep much tonight. Avery was going to my parents' again in two weeks. Memorial Day was coming up, and she'd spend an extended weekend in Arizona.

I could already envision Ryker and me not sleeping much the entire time. Ryker went to open the door, thanking the delivery guy. We ate at the kitchen island, straight out of cartons.

"This is delicious. Hands down the best pizza and doughnuts I've had," I announced, licking my fingers once I was done. To my surprise, Ryker laughed.

"What?" I asked.

"You're cute. I'd rate it as good, but not the best."

I shrugged one shoulder playfully. "Maybe I'm just in a good mood."

"Or maybe it's the company." He wiggled his eyebrows.

"Still in competition with the food, I see."

Chapter Twenty-Seven
Heather

For the next two weeks, I kept checking Dawson's website every day. My article was scheduled to come out in six days, in the third week of May, which seemed an eternity away. I couldn't pay in advance another month to reassure my landlord, so I needed that bonus right away. But big newspapers moved slowly. Since he was in charge of his own platform, Dawson was more flexible.

On Thursday Mom was flying in to pick up Avery and fly back to Phoenix with her. Memorial Day was on Monday, of course, but my girl's school had given them Friday off as well.

The damned article popped up just as I was heading to pick up my girl. She was watching a play downtown with her class.

I started reading the article while I was still in the subway station, stopping next to a busker singing a Michael Jackson classic.

Oh, crap. It was a nightmare. The title was "Frauds and Fears."

The rest of the article was even worse. What the hell? This was *not* the angle I'd thought he'd take. I doubted this was what Owen had had in mind when he contacted him. I stared at the screen of my phone, trying to plan my next steps. Call Ryker? Danielle? Had they already seen it?

I had my answer the next second when Danielle called. I hurried away from the busker to a somewhat secluded section of the station before answering.

"Did you read Dawson's article?" she asked the second I picked up.

"Just finished it."

"It's a disaster. The bosses just called me. We're not publishing your article."

"What? Why? Wouldn't now be the time to point out the article's inaccuracies?"

"It would make us look like we're desperate to pitch in. Especially after how scathing Dawson's article was. I'm sorry. I know it's disappointing for you."

That was an understatement.

"I already told Owen it's not going to be published. He wasn't too happy, but considering he was the one who brought Dawson into this, I don't give a damn."

But I did. I needed to speak to Ryker right away, but before that, I needed to address another point. Even though I knew already what the answer was, I asked anyway. "My bonus?"

"I can't make that happen. I'm sorry. My hands are tied. But it doesn't mean it's not doable; you've got until the end of the year."

Except I needed the paper slip confirming the

bonus right now. My landlord wasn't going to give me another extension, I was sure of it.

"Right. Okay," I mumbled. "I've got to go. I'll send you the draft of my current article in a few days."

"Sure, take your time. No pressure."

I walked out of the station after hanging up, breathing in deeply once I was outside. I slipped into the coffee shop next to the theater where Avery was, buying myself a decaf mocha latte. I sat at a window seat and called Ryker.

We'd made plans for a late lunch so Avery could say goodbye before flying to Phoenix, but I wanted to talk to him about the article right now.

"Heather," he greeted.

"Hey! Just wanted to tell you about the art—"

"I know. We've all seen it… and we were also informed that yours won't be published. I'm sorry."

"Just spoke to my editor about it. How is the mood at the office?"

"Our PR team is flipping out. We're going to have a meeting about it today."

"Okay. We're still on for lunch?" I asked.

"Sure. In two hours, right?"

I just wanted to be with him so we could regroup together.

"Yes."

"Sure, babe. Just come here. Love you."

"I love you too."

I smiled, feeling a lot lighter after hanging up. I sat in the coffee shop long enough to finish my decaf mocha before heading to the theater. Avery and her group were already in the lobby. She barreled into me, wrapping her arms around my middle, grinning up at me.

"Hey, lovebug. How was the show?"

"Super boring. Are we still going to see Ryker?"

"Yes, we are. Come on, let's go."

I chuckled, hugging her with one arm. After thanking her teacher for making attendance the next day optional, we headed to Central Park. We still had an hour and a half until we were meeting Ryker. It was going to be a short (and very late) lunch, because we still had to make it home in time to get Avery's bag and head to JFK. We ended up taking a long stroll through the park, and when we arrived at the fund, the receptionist handed me a visitor badge automatically. I wasn't there on official business, but eh, she didn't need to know that minor detail.

Once we were on Ryker's floor, we stealthily made our way to his office. No one paid attention to us. It seemed even crazier than usual; everyone was running around in a frenzy. Even Ruby lacked her usual spark. Her hair was in disarray, as if she'd run her hands repeatedly through it. I waved at her, but she didn't notice me.

I was surprised to find Ryker's office empty.

"Let's wait in here," I told Avery. "He'll come soon."

She immediately sat in his leather chair, spinning around, grinning from ear to ear. I intended to call him, then noticed that his cellphone was lying between two stacks of paper on his desk. Okay, nothing to do but wait, then. I sat on the other chair.

"Avery, please don't touch anything," I warned.

"Yes, Mommy. I'm a big girl. I'm careful." She touched one of the stacks, just barely, but it tumbled down from the desk the next second. I jumped from my chair, trying to catch them all, but only managed to get a paper cut on my left palm. The papers just spread everywhere. *Jesus*! I went to my knees, gathering them. Shit, I didn't know how to put them back in order. The pages weren't numbered. I just placed them back on the desk as best as I could.

"Heather?" Owen's voice sounded from the doorway. Crap.

"Hi, Owen. This is my daughter, Avery."

He stepped inside, glaring at the disorderly stack of papers. "Those are confidential documents."

"They just fell on the floor, and I put them back."

"They fell because of me," Avery said apologetically. "But I don't know how. I was being careful."

She was still sitting in Ryker's chair, which Owen definitively didn't appreciate.

"What are you doing here, Heather?"

"We're just waiting for Ryker so we can go to lunch."

"He can't take a lunch break today. He's in a huge meeting."

"Oh. Okay. We'll just wait for him."

"It's going to take hours. You can't wait here. This is not a place for children."

I straightened up, jutting my chin forward. "I know. It's.... Can I talk to Ryker for a minute or leave him a message?"

"No. Look, Ryker needs to focus right now. He doesn't have time to chase children around the office or clean up after them. He's got more important things to do." His voice was so harsh that Avery gasped. Her eyes widened. She clutched the armrests with her tiny hands. I rolled my palms into fists.

"I know you're pissed about the article, but honestly, it's your fault for bringing Dawson into this in the first place." Now, why I went and said that I'll never know, but attacking my girl just pushed me a little too far.

"I can do whatever the hell I want."

"Yes, but I'm not going to let you take it out on my daughter and me."

"Don't wait up here." With a dismissive nod, he turned around, leaving the office. I hurried to Avery, who was rubbing her eyes. *Oh, no.* She was crying.

I crouched to her level, cradling her head with both hands. "Baby girl, why are you crying?"

Avery let out a heart-wrenching sob. "Ryker doesn't want to see us."

"It's not that, baby. He's busy."

"He forgot about us." Her lower lip was

trembling.

"Sometimes, you only find out you have a meeting a few minutes before. Like Mommy sometimes has to go for interviews, you know?"

"But now we're here, and he's not coming to see us," Avery insisted. "What if he doesn't want us anymore?"

My heart just cracked. "Avery, of course he does."

"But that mister said that Ryker has more important things to do than us."

"He only meant the meeting."

"How do you know?" Avery asked, tearing up again. "How do you know?"

I had to change topics, take my girl's mind off it.

"I just know, honey. Please trust me. Listen, why don't we go home? We need to take your bag and leave for the airport anyway. Then you'll be with Gran and Pops and all your animals."

Her sobs subsided a little, but she held out her hands. Oh, no! Lately, she only wanted in my arms when she was inconsolable. I carried her all the way out of the building. On the cab ride to the apartment, I tried to talk more about her animals and her best friend there, Jillian, but she only gave me monosyllabic answers.

Once we were at home, we ate some leftover pasta, and then I did the last checks on her luggage. She was usually so bubbly and happy before leaving for Phoenix. But now, she was just sitting on her bed, dangling her feet. I sat next to her, caressing her cheek.

"Honey, what's wrong? You don't want to go?"

"I have to go. Tony misses me. And Gran and Pops too."

"That's right, they do."

"Can you come with me?"

"To Phoenix?"

"Yes. *Pleaaaase.*"

Oh, God. I couldn't just buy a last-minute ticket to Phoenix. But I also couldn't just let my girl leave like this. She needed reassurance, and all the love I could give her. I just had to pack in a hurry and buy a ticket. It was only the weekend after all, and I could edit my articles out of my parents' place too. Jesus, I already didn't know my ass from my elbow. I checked the price of a last-minute ticket, because this was honestly the deciding factor. I blew out a breath of relief when I found one that fit in my budget.

Two hours later, when we met Mom at the gate, I was a mess, and so was Avery. I'd thought I managed to soothe her but quickly realized I hadn't because my girl had wanted to stay in my arms most of the time. We barely made it on time to the airport. I'd texted Mom on the way to let her know I was traveling with them as well. Thankfully, she hadn't asked why. She gave me the usual *Mom-check*, and her eyebrows went high up her forehead. She opened her mouth, but I shook my head lightly, pointing toward

Avery. Mom pursed her lips but focused on Avery.

"Sweetie, Tony misses you. He can't wait to see you."

Avery sighed. "I miss Tony too."

"I need to make a phone call before we board the plane. I'll be right back."

I walked a few steps away, because I didn't want Avery to know I was calling Ryker. I hadn't had time until now. I couldn't wait to hear his voice. Only... he didn't pick up. He was still in that meeting? I panicked when the ding for the voicemail came. Crap. What was I supposed to say?

"Ryker, hi! It's me. I mean, you know that, of course.... Listen, I don't know if Owen told you that he talked to me when we were in your office. Anyway, he was out of line, said things that upset Avery. She thinks—" Another deep breath. "—that you don't want us anymore. And I just don't know how to calm her down." My voice wobbled. "Anyway, she asked me to come to Mom's too, in Phoenix, and I couldn't say no. I'm at the airport now. I'm staying this weekend—"

A ping informed me I'd used up all the seconds in the voicemail. I dialed his number again, then disconnected the call, because I had no clue what to say.

We still had a few minutes before boarding. Maybe he'd see the call and... call back? I'd really been hoping to hear his voice. When the flight attendant announced that passengers with kids were invited to board, I sighed, slipping the phone back in my purse.

Mom was magic—she really was. Within a few minutes, she managed what I hadn't in hours: she shifted Avery's focus completely. By the time we were sitting inside the plane, Avery was telling us both everything she wanted to feed Tony... right before she fell asleep.

Mom waited exactly five seconds before pouncing on me.

"Want to tell me what's going on? I'm happy of course, but why are you coming with us?"

"Avery asked me to." Mom listened closely while I half whispered everything, afraid to wake up Avery.

"She's a little emotional," I finished.

"And how are you?"

Good question. I was...

"Tired. Guilty. Wondering if I'm selfish."

"For what?"

"Not keeping it just the two of us, like I promised her all those months ago."

"Don't you think like that."

"I know, I know. I'm just a mess."

Mom put a hand over mine sympathetically. I was so glad that she was here. "I'm going to take care of both my girls. You just wait."

Chapter Twenty-Eight
Ryker

I was blurry eyed by the time the meeting with the PR team ended, hours later. It had been a complete clusterfuck, and it wasn't over yet. Our PR people were desperate enough about Dawson's article that they'd brought the heads of all departments into this, and the directors. Tomorrow everyone was meeting again.

I went into my office, slumping into my chair. It was seven o'clock already. This day had just been insane. Then I remembered that I'd made plans with Heather and Avery for lunch too, so I could say goodbye to Avery before she left for Phoenix. Goddammit. How had I forgotten?

I was about to call Heather when my phone rang. Skye was calling and I picked up immediately.

"Dear brother, have you forgotten about us?" she asked.

"Sorry, I got caught up in a meeting. Heather and I were supposed to meet you at the Irish pub."

"Yes. Half an hour ago. Anyway, Heather messaged to tell me she can't make it."

"Why?"

"I don't know. Thought you'd tell me."

"I'll talk to her and then call you back." I sat straighter. What was going on?

"Okay."

When I hung up, I jumped out of my chair, about to call Heather, when I was interrupted again. Owen came into my office.

"Ryker, we should finalize the—"

"I'll do that tomorrow. I need to call Heather. I completely forgot I made lunch plans with her."

"I saw her in your office, with her daughter, just before I joined the meeting."

"Why didn't you tell me?"

"You were already in the meeting room."

"I could've just stepped out for a few minutes."

"Look, I needed you to have your head in the game."

"When have I *not* had my head in the game?" I barked.

"Lately, your focus has been split. A general piece of advice: those who make it far in this industry know where their priorities lie. You don't have time for chasing kids in your office, and I told them as much."

"You fucking didn't."

"I did."

"I don't need your advice on how to lead my personal life. I deliver results, that's all that concerns you. Refrain from any other comments." I spoke through gritted teeth, barely keeping my temper in check. "This is your fuckup, Owen."

Owen narrowed his eyes but didn't say anything else. Good for him, because I was pissed anyway. I walked out of my office, heading straight to the elevators, intending to call Heather on the way, then noticed I had a voicemail from her. Had something happened to her and Avery? Why didn't she make it to the pub?

I slid in the empty elevator, listening to the voicemail on the way down. Panic crawled up my body from her first word, and then it just kept magnifying. Holy shit, she sounded on the verge of tears. My woman was almost crying! When she mentioned Avery, I nearly lost it.

I listened to the voicemail again as I left the building, as if that would help me digest it better. It didn't. Once outside, I leaned against a wall, closing my eyes, just trying to calm down, but it was impossible. It was as if I had a stone lodged in my throat, pressing on my chest.

I wanted to go back up and take my anger out on Owen, but that wouldn't help jack shit. What would help? I had no idea.

I unhitched myself from the wall though, because just hanging around here sure wasn't going to solve anything.

I'd almost forgotten about my siblings *again* when Skye messaged me.

Skye: Are you coming?
Ryker: On my way.

My family was just what I needed. I walked at a brisk pace, bypassing a group of tourists that had come to a night tour of the city, blocking out the guide's voice rattling information about Wall Street's history.

In fact, I was trying to block out everything: the sound of cars, the occasional billboards... I wanted to focus on my own thoughts, but it seemed impossible at the moment.

The Irish pub where I was meeting everyone was just a few blocks way. The crowds thinned the closer I got. Cole had a knack for picking spots that were central but not overrun.

When I reached the pub, I noticed my siblings through the window, at a table. I made my way past a group of smokers holding beers in front of the building. As soon as I stepped inside, Cole waved at me. He looked so relieved to see me that I was willing to bet anything our sister had just cornered him about something.

"Sorry I'm late, everyone," I said, sitting next to Skye, opposite Tess and Cole.

Tess winked. "You're here, though. Thought you forgot all about the ruse."

"What ruse?" I asked, trying to sound innocent.

"You know... pretending you need our help just so you have an excuse to make sure you feed us and get us out of the store."

Damn, they'd caught on so fast? That explained why Cole had looked so cornered when I arrived.

"It's nothing you haven't done before," I

volleyed back. "Remember my first few years at the bank? When you took turns dropping by my apartment? Sometimes with food, sometimes just to check if I was alive?"

Since they were a little older, they'd already had the tough years behind them by the time I embarked on the hamster wheel.

Skye nodded. "It's true. We did that. To be honest, I quite like having all of you coddle us. By the way, Ryker, did you find out what's up with Heather?"

I swallowed hard. "She flew to Phoenix with Avery and her mom."

Tess frowned. "Did something happen? She's not exactly the type to decide in less than a day to jump on a plane."

I didn't know how to explain everything, so I asked them to listen to the voicemail.

Tess flinched, looking at me with pity.

"Oh, poor Avery," said Skye.

Their reactions just intensified my own anguish. How was I supposed to reassure Avery and Heather? How was I supposed to be the person they needed me to be?

"So, I know that you've come here this evening to coddle us, but I think the roles just reversed," Tess said. "And coddling requires me to sit next to you, so scoot over a bit."

I laughed as Skye and I shifted on the bench, making space for Tess. I felt so confused and exhausted at the moment that I didn't think I could be of any use to them anyway.

"Holy shit," Skye said, eying me wearily. "You're not even pretending to have it all under control. That's so unlike you."

Tess turned to Cole. "You know how Skye and I used to joke that Ryker wouldn't realize he's in love even if it smacked him in the head? We take it all back. Means there's hope for you too."

Cole cocked a brow. "You can tell you were wrong because he looks miserable? You're not exactly selling me on love right now."

Skye groaned. Tess shook her head.

"No, silly. We can tell that by the fact that he's all over the place because Avery and Heather are hurting," Skye explained.

"Being all over the place is still not a good selling point," Cole pointed out. "But let's focus on the important part: Avery and Heather."

Tess rubbed her forehead, laughing. "You're right. We'll circle back to your odd views on love another time. Now we have to focus our efforts on Ryker."

"Yes, please do," I encouraged them.

Skye patted my shoulder. "I know why you're beating yourself up. Stop doing it."

"How? We've been in Avery's shoes. We know how it feels... not to be wanted," I said.

"This isn't the same thing. Dad *left* us," Tess said, glancing at Skye and Cole as if inviting them to chime in with their opinions.

"I know, but I'm still—"

"Questioning yourself?" Skye asked sympathetically.

I nodded, relieved that she got it.

"Hell, no," Tess exclaimed. "No. No. Absolutely not. We won't let you do that."

"Jesus!" Cole exclaimed. "I was going to order a beer, but I need something stronger if we're getting into that. Anyone else?"

Tess clapped her hands. "I'm with you. Something that will inspire me to come up with motivational quotes… but also keep my mind clear."

"Just water for me," Skye said. "But I do want some food. I give really bad advice on an empty stomach."

"You do," Cole agreed. "How about—"

I interrupted him. "Cole! Don't hijack our sister's attention. I still need it on me. All of it."

Chapter Twenty-Nine
Heather

Being under my parents' roof was always a treat, but never more than now. This was like a time capsule from my childhood. They hadn't changed any of the furniture. I was sitting on one of the neon-orange chairs at the enormous kitchen island. They contrasted starkly with the polar white kitchen. Dad had left early this morning to go to his chess club, as he'd done every day since retiring. Business as usual. Avery was still asleep.

As Mom and I started baking all my favorites—blueberry pancakes, chocolate muffins, and apple tarts—she mentioned that Avery had gotten up briefly this morning to feed Tony, and that she'd seemed very happy.

And just like that, I remembered Avery's heartbreak yesterday and my eyes started burning. I blinked quickly, hoping to keep the tears at bay. I swallowed hard a few times, breathing through my nose. The burning sensation descended, lodging in my chest. Not even the smell of my mom's cooking was lessening it.

As if sensing I needed a distraction, she

pointed to the oven.

"Want to do a quality control on those?"

"Oh, yes."

Grabbing a toothpick, I opened the oven door, poking the first few muffins. They were just perfect. My mouth watered with anticipation.

"I know you want to steal one. Go ahead. I'll pretend I didn't see," Mom said.

I jutted out my lower lip. "But half the fun was always sneaking them."

"Ah, my dear girl. You honestly thought I never counted the muffins?"

I laughed and took out a muffin, biting into it before it had a chance to cool down.

Holy shit, what had I been thinking?

"Heavens, girl, no need to burn your tongue." Mom handed me a glass of iced tea. I gulped it down as quickly as possible, but the damage was already done. I wouldn't taste much for the next few days. It was only then that I realized Mom was watching me intently. She hadn't asked many questions after our conversation on the plane. I'd thought she wanted to give me a chance to get a good night sleep, but she's been suspiciously quiet this morning. In retrospect, that should have clued me in that something was awry. Mom's credo was that it was her prerogative to question her daughter as she saw fit—so she could dish advice, whether I wanted it or not.

"Have a seat," Mom instructed, in the exact tone of voice that usually preceded one of our "serious" talks. I climbed back on one of the orange chairs.

"You shouldn't stay locked up in the house all morning. You need to go out, enjoy the sun a bit," she said as she arranged the muffins on a plate.

"I'm not sure what I need. To relax a little, I think. I can't stop thinking about all the things I need to do back in New York... like pack up the apartment."

"What's Ryker got to say on the topic?"

"I don't know. We haven't had a chance to talk about it." I'd emailed my landlord this morning, asking for an extension, and received a no within minutes.

"Listen, Heather, I'm so proud of you, you know. I don't say it very often, and I'm sorry for that. That was how I was raised, but I should tell you more often than I do. You're a dreamer, and a fighter, and I couldn't be more proud of you. You didn't have it easy, but you fought tooth and nail to make New York your home, to give that little girl everything she needs."

"Thanks, Mom."

"I heard what you said last night. You can't protect Avery from getting upset now and then. You have nothing to be guilty about. You deserve to be happy, Heather. You and Avery. And Ryker *is* making both of you happy—I've never seen you two like this. And he wants to be there for you through everything."

I chuckled. "That sounds like something he would say."

Mom averted her gaze.

"Wait a second... that sounds *exactly* like something Ryker would say. Mom..., have you talked to him?"

She didn't answer. My ass slid so close to the edge of the chair that I nearly fell off.

"Mom?" I urged.

"Well, I'm not supposed to tell you anything about it."

"Mom!" I repeated, tone stronger this time. "Tell me everything. When did you talk to him? What did he say?"

"He called me last night."

"What? How did he even have your number?"

"Asked for it on Facebook."

"What did he want?" My heart rate was out of control. I placed a hand on my chest, as if that could help calm down my pulse.

"I can't say."

"Mom!"

"Stop Mom-ing me. I won't tell you anything, except that he was very charming."

I chuckled, dropped my chin to my chest. "Of course, he was." Then I decided to try another angle. "Why did he call you and not me?"

"Because he needed to know—" Mom stopped midsentence, narrowing her eyes. "Heather! This is foul play."

I held up my hands in defense. "I had to try."

I climbed down from the chair, suddenly feeling jittery and so pumped up with energy that I could run a marathon. I felt as if the walls of the house were closing in on me.

"I'm going for a swim in the pool," I announced. Swimming was even better than running when it came to calming myself down. The community had built a residential pool two decades ago. It had been the highlight back then.

"Oh, now you're going to leave me? Just when I'm about to start cooking lunch?"

"Would you rather I stay and help you?"

Mom waved her hand dismissively and teased me. "Go, go. You're not needed here. Are you going to stay at the pool the entire time?"

"Probably. Why?"

"So I know where to find you if I do need you. Your dad and I will take Avery and Jill to the fair as soon as she wakes up, so we might not be home when you come back."

Jill was Avery's best friend in Phoenix.

"Okay." I took another muffin from the plate Mom had carefully arranged.

"Hey!" Mom admonished.

"What? I deserve this for having to live knowing that you've been having conversations behind my back."

Mom laughed. "Fair enough."

"Are you sure you can't tell me anything?" I asked, gripping the muffin so tightly that the base disintegrated between my fingers.

"No."

"Not even a hint?"

Mom shook her head. I stole yet another muffin. "You know what? I don't think I'll need lunch after all."

"That is not a healthy meal, young lady."

"Oh, I know. But it's food for the soul, you know? Especially when you discover that your own blood is up to no good."

Mom didn't have any comeback. After finding a bikini in my room, I darted out of the house.

The heat in Arizona was so different compared to New York. I'd gotten so used to the humidity permeating the air in the summer months, it was shocking how dry it was out here. It was almost as if I could feel the dust particles from the scorched earth whirling in the air.

I walked lazily toward the pool, soaking in the sun. Why had Ryker called Mom? She'd called him *charming*, so it had to be good, right?

My heart felt lighter with every step. I hadn't even realized it had felt heavy as a stone until now.

***

Ryker

I flew into Phoenix early the next morning, then took a cab to Heather's parents' hometown. The driver had no problems finding the address Mrs. Prescott had given me. I got out of the car in front of a white house with a bright green roof and a generous front porch. The door opened just as I reached the landing.

Mrs. Prescott came out, smiling at me.

"I see you found the house easily," she said.

"Yes, ma'am. Nice to see you again." We shook hands just as a man I assumed was Mr. Prescott joined us.

"I'm Ryker, sir. Nice to meet you." I shook his hand firmly.

"Son, you just missed Heather. She went to the pool."

"I'll just meet her there, then."

"Nonsense. Come in and have a drink first. You must be tired," Mrs. Prescott said.

She was right. I was tired, but not because of the journey. I'd been up with my siblings until late. Then I headed home, packed a small bag, slept a few hours, and after I got up and showered, I went straight to the airport. I called in sick at work.

Following the Prescotts inside, I dropped my luggage next to the entrance and then went into the kitchen.

I took the glass of lemonade Mrs. Prescott handed me, gulping it down. I didn't want to sit, though. I wanted to see Heather, but first I wanted to talk to them both about their daughter and Avery before doing anything else.

"Is Avery with Heather at the pool?" I asked.

"No, actually Avery just woke up. She's in the back yard," Mr. Prescott said. "We're going to pick up a friend of hers and then go to the fair."

"I'd like to talk to her before, if there's time."

"Sure," Mr. Prescott said. "We weren't

planning on leaving for another fifteen minutes or so. Come on, I'll take you to her."

He led me to the back of the house, out the door where we stepped onto another large porch that spilled into a huge yard, with a doghouse on the side. Three golden retriever puppies were poking their heads out, looking at Avery.

Avery was sitting on the steps of the porch, sorting out straws.

"Hey, Avery. Look who's here," Mr. Prescott said.

"Ryker!" Her eyes were wide and probing. She also gave me a smile, but it was small and tentative, as if she wasn't sure she *should* smile. Damn it!

"Avery, Ryker wants to talk to you."

"Okay. You don't have to stay, Pops, I'm a big girl," Avery replied, gathering her straws closer to her.

Mr. Prescott opened his mouth, closed it again. He gave me an encouraging look before going back in the house.

"Can I sit next to you?" I asked Avery.

She nodded, shifting a little to make space for me. The second I sat down, she asked, "What are you doing here?"

"I came to talk to you and your mom."

She looked down at her hands, playing with her thumbs. One of the puppies came running out of the doghouse, straight into Avery's lap.

"But why? You didn't want to see us at the office."

"I couldn't, Avery. I was in a meeting. I'm sorry I forgot you and your mom were coming for lunch."

"But that man said that you don't have time for children." She hugged the tiny furball tightly to her.

Her voice was wobbly, and it fucking slayed me.

"He was wrong."

She glanced up at me warily. "But it has to be true. He's an adult. Adults always know best."

"Well, some adults think they know everything and like to speak even if they don't know all the facts. Owen didn't know how much I love you and your mom."

Avery's mouth formed an O. "You love us?"

"Yes."

"Are you sure?"

"Yes."

She still didn't look convinced. "But then why didn't that man know?"

"I hadn't told him. But everyone else knows. My whole family, even your grandparents."

That seemed to win her over, because her little face lit up with a smile that rivaled the one she gave me when we went shopping at Bergdorf.

"So you still like us?" she asked, as if it was just a normal fact to check.

"Yes, I do. I always will. I promise."

Before they came into my life, I would've stayed at the office to make sure I was on top of the situation at hand, but last night, I hadn't even hesitated to book my ticket. I'd never give Avery or Heather even the slightest reason to doubt that they meant everything to me. For as long as I lived, I'd take care of them.

Avery laid the puppy on her shoulder, not minding that it was licking all over her ear. She had something on her mind.

"Is there something you want to tell me, Avery? You can ask me anything."

She glanced up at me for a beat before pulling the puppy to her chest. What was going on?

"Do you want to be my dad?" she whispered.

I gripped the edge of the step I was sitting on tight. "Yes, I *f—*do." I'd almost said *fucking do*. Jesus. "Yes. But you didn't want that before. Are *you* sure?"

She looked up, nodding energetically. "Yes. You buy me everything I want, and you love us. I think you will be a good dad."

"I promise I will."

She got up from the stairs and threw one little arm around me, holding the puppy in the other one. Laughing, I rose to my feet, hoisting them both up. She trusted me enough to tell me her fears. She wanted me to be her *dad*. I couldn't wrap my mind around that yet.

"I'm going to tell Mom you're here," she said.

"Actually, I'd like to talk to her first. And when she asks about what we talked about, maybe don't tell her everything."

"Why?" she asked suspiciously.

"I have a few surprises for her."

Avery frowned for a split second, but then her expression lit up and she bounced up and down in my arms.

"Can we take her with us to New York?" she asked, pointing her chin to the golden retriever. Remembering what Heather said about Mrs. Prescott bribing her with animals to come here, I put two and two together. She wanted a dog to keep quiet? Talk about being an excellent negotiator.

"Sure, we can see what your mom thinks about it too," I said. Avery frowned again, putting the puppy down on the porch. I wondered if she was reconsidering her decision about me being her dad.

"Ready to go to the fair? Jill is already waiting for us," Mrs. Prescott told Avery the second we returned inside the house.

"Yes." Avery climbed down from my arms, heading to her grandparents. "I want to tell Mom that Ryker is here, but he says he wants to do it."

The corner of Mr. Prescott's mouth tugged upward. His wife chuckled.

"I think that's a great idea," Mrs. Prescott said. "Ryker, see you and Heather later. Keys to the house are on the kitchen counter." Then she added with a wink, "We'll be gone for about two hours."

They headed to the front door, explaining to Avery in hushed voices why it was a good thing for me to talk to Heather alone.

I waited until they left before heading out to find my woman.

Chapter Thirty
Heather

The pool was exactly as I remembered it, only it wasn't as popular as in my childhood. A newer pool with a slide had been built downtown. As a result, this one was empty.

I removed my cutoff shorts and tank top. I laid them on one of lounge chairs before entering the water.

I swam energetically, bringing one arm in front of the other as fast as possible. I was out of practice though. I turned on my back, moving at a slower pace. I'd always been able to just half float, half swim like this for hours.

Being in the pool brought back memories of long, lazy summers, where my biggest worries were whether the town's only movie theater would run the newest movie early enough that I could return home before my curfew. But then thoughts of Ryker entered my mind, and I became jittery again. Holy shit! Why had he called Mom?

Right... change of plans. Swimming wasn't helping. If anything, I was even more worked up than before. I needed to know what they'd talked about and was determined to find out no matter what. Mom was even more stubborn than I was when she wanted to be, but I just had to be more creative, that was all.

Goose bumps broke out on my skin as I got out of the pool. I headed to the lounge chair where I'd put my clothes.

Wait a second, where were they?

I could have sworn I'd placed them here. I inspected the tiles around the chair... maybe a gust of strong wind blew them away. No such luck, there was barely any wind today. But my clothes were nowhere to be found. Had someone stolen them? Impossible. I mean, as a kid we'd played this prank on each other from time to time, but there were no thieves around here. Or, well, shit. Maybe there were. And I was supposed to walk like this to Mom's house? I groaned. My ass was hanging out. My boobs were practically on display through the soaked bra.

A low chuckle sounded behind me. A bolt of heat danced along my nerve endings, because it was very familiar. Ryker was here? I turned around slowly, heart beating at a million miles an hour. He stood there, in the flesh, gaze trained on me... and holding my shorts and top.

"Oh my God," I exclaimed. "You're here. When did you fly in?"

I didn't give the man a chance to speak though, because I practically jumped his bones. I nearly slid on the wet tiles in my haste to get to him. Wrapping my arms around his shoulders, I soaked my clothes and Ryker's shirt. I stepped back, blushing. "I can't believe you're here. When did you arrive?"

"Just now." Ryker smiled widely, looking me up and down slowly. I felt as if I was wearing absolutely nothing.

"I should probably get dressed," I murmured.

"I disagree."

"Ryker!"

"If you insist...."

"I do."

He stepped closer, handing me the clothes. I tried to ignore the current of awareness that jolted through me when our fingertips touched. He'd only been here for a few seconds, and yet I was already overwhelmed by the intense feeling of longing.

"Where's your towel?" Ryker asked.

"Don't have one."

"You're just going to put clothes on over your wet bathing suit? You'll get sick."

"I've done this my whole childhood, no worries." I quickly dressed while asking him, "How did you know the address?"

"I spoke to your mom."

"Ah, so that's what you called her for."

"Yes... among other things."

"What things?"

Ryker shook his head. "Can't tell you yet."

My jaw dropped. "What do you mean? Of course you can."

"I will," he assured me. "Just not yet."

I laughed nervously, feeling completely off-kilter. What did that mean?

He took another step toward me, until there were just a few inches between us. Oh, why did he do that? I could barely think when he was this close. I could put some distance between us, of course, but I just didn't want to. He'd called Mom *and* had flown over half the country just to see me. No one has ever done something like that for me, and I almost couldn't believe he did, but then here he was. Ryker beamed widely, cupping my face with both hands, and his warmth spread through me. I loved his touch, just having him here with me.

"I love you, Heather."

"I can't believe you're actually here," I repeated for what felt like the millionth time. But I really couldn't believe it. It was so romantic.

"Of course I'm here. Came to take care of my girls."

"Oh my God, I just realized today is Friday. What are you doing here? How could you take time off with everything going on?"

"You and Avery are here. Everything else is just background noise. Of course I came."

Oh, wow.

"How did Owen react to you taking today off?"

"Don't particularly care what he thinks. Owen is an ass. He doesn't have any right to an opinion about my personal life, and I told him that. I'm so sorry Avery heard Owen's bullshit."

"I felt so guilty when Avery got upset," I

whispered.

"Don't. You have no reason to feel guilty." Tilting his head, he added, "I spoke to her."

"When?" I asked, loving this man even more.

"Before coming down here. She was still at the house."

"Oh my, I bet she was surprised to see you. What did you talk about?"

"Let's just say we're good. But I can't tell you more."

"Ryker! Come on."

He shrugged, but I could tell he wouldn't relent. What was going on? I felt like something was being kept from me.

"Fine, you won't tell me what you and Avery spoke about. But I at least want to know what you told Mom to win her over that fast."

"That you and Avery are everything to me."

I was itching to touch him again. Grabbing his T-shirt with both hands, I pulled him toward me while at the same time rising on my tiptoes. I caught Ryker's smile right before he claimed my mouth. Wow. I'd prepared myself for a chaste kiss, not *this*. Ryker's kiss was so deep, so possessive that it completely consumed me. My entire body lit up.

I went back and forth from my toes to my heels, then back up because I just had so much heat and energy coursing through me that I couldn't stand still.

He bit my tongue teasingly before doing the same with my lower lip. I shivered lightly.

"Ryker, what if someone sees us?"

"We're in the middle of nowhere," he countered. His eyes were dark and determined. He traced his thumb lazily up and down the strap of my tank top, as if he was just moments from pushing it away.

"You New Yorker, you! The neighbors here are very nosy."

"The houses are far enough away."

"Sort of... but they'll know who it was."

"How?" He kissed my cheek, tracing his mouth all the way to my ear, as if he needed at least this much contact.

"Well, you're the hottest man around here, and you're mine. They'll put two and two together."

He pressed his fingers against my lower back, smiling against my cheek.

"Hottest guy in town, huh?"

"That's the only piece of information that registered?" I taunted.

Instead of answering, he brought his mouth to mine again. He'd stoked a fire in me before, but this... this was a downright inferno. I placed my palms on his arms for support *only* at first, but then I drew them down his torso, lingering on his chest before making my way down that six-pack I loved so much. When I reached just below his belly button, he groaned, capturing my wrist, stopping my descent.

"Heather... don't."

"Oh, I see. So you can kiss me until my panties are on fire, but I can't fondle you? This is a two-way street, you know."

His eyes flashed. Oh, wow. I'd meant that as a warning, but I had a hunch Ryker saw it as a green light to push his previous shameless agenda.

"Heather...." His voice was almost a growl, and experience taught me that when he reached this point, I had two, maybe three minutes until he unleashed his full power of seduction on me.

"Why don't we go inside the house?" I suggested.

"Excellent idea."

I laughed, lightly pinching his ribs. He caught my hand, holding it for a brief second before surprising the hell out of me and twirling me around, hugging me from behind, kissing the side of my neck. I laughed, just melting against him, touching his arms, every part of him I could reach. At this rate, we'll never make it to the house. But I was completely okay with that.

***

Ryker

"How long are we staying?" I asked as we approached the house.

"Well, Avery will be here until Monday evening, but you and I should probably go back on Sunday."

"Yeah... I'll use Monday to catch up on everything."

The second we were inside, I curled an arm

around her waist, pressing her against me, wanting as much contact as possible.

"Looks like we have the house all to ourselves," I said.

Heather narrowed her eyes. "Is that code for something?"

I grinned, pressing her even tighter to me. "What do you think it's code for?"

"Something dirty. You're very creative in that department."

"You think?" I moved my fingers in a slow, circular motion on her lower back. I wanted to hold her for a beat. The last twenty-four hours had taken a toll on me too. When I'd listened to Heather's voicemail, for a few excruciating seconds I'd thought I'd lost them both. I kissed her until she hummed, curling her fingers onto my arms, but I needed her closer—I needed to know that I owned every part of her. Her lips were a little swollen when I pulled back. I traced the contour with my thumb, smiling.

Heather poked my chest with a finger. "You look a little too full of yourself."

"So?"

"So that means you're going to try and seduce me."

"Not just try. I *will*."

She rolled her eyes. I pinched her ass, enjoying immensely the way she pressed herself into me.

"Okay, okay," she answered quickly. "Want to see my room?"

"Gladly."

Heather smiled shyly before taking a step back. I intertwined our fingers as she led me up the stairs, bringing the back of her hand to my mouth, kissing it. A small shiver ran through her. I smiled against her skin. Heather chuckled, looking at me over her shoulder.

"Here you go again, being pleased with yourself."

"Can't help it. You're giving me too many reasons."

"I see. So it's *my* doing. Since you're in such a great mood, I'll try again; what did you and Avery talk about? Just saying, if you don't tell me, she will."

"No, she won't. I asked her not to."

She jerked her head back. "And she agreed, just like that?"

The corners of my mouth twitched. "We might have to get a dog."

Heather burst out laughing. "Serves you right for thinking you can negotiate with Avery."

"Hey, it got her on my side."

"Still conspiring, I see," she said as we climbed the last step. I whirled her around so we were face-to-face. Her eyes widened a little.

"Don't knock it before you try it. It's a survival strategy in the Winchester family. Get as many members on your side as possible, or you're never going to win any fights."

"But we're on the same team," she said, obviously confused.

"Only on certain topics." I smiled, kissing one corner of her mouth, then the other I walked her backward toward the bedroom, already slipping my thumbs under her tank top, caressing her soft skin until I felt goose bumps.

"So you're continuing to conspire behind my back?" she asked once we were inside.

I grinned, closing the door. "Always."

She took off my shirt and jeans, stopping every few seconds, looking at me.

"I don't think I'll ever get enough of the view."

"Music to my ears."

I dragged my fingers up her arm, drawing circles over her shoulders and neck. Her breath was already shaky with anticipation. I kissed one corner of her mouth, moving my hands up to her breasts, where her skin was still a bit damp from her swimming session. I couldn't wait to sink inside her, to indulge in her. She was here. She was mine.

I took off her top, running my mouth along the rim of her bra, hooking my thumb in the elastic band underneath, following it all the way to the clasp at the back. After getting the bra out of the way, I teased her breasts with my fingers and my tongue until she had goose bumps everywhere. I moved my mouth down her body until I was on my knees. She guessed my intention before I went for the button of her shorts and undid it for me. I tugged the pants down, holding her to step out of them. I got rid of her panties next, then gripped her hips, but instead of seating her on the bed, I guided her to the wall.

"Oooh, right. You don't even need a bed. A wall is enough. You…."

The rest of her words faded. I parted her legs, placing one thigh on my shoulder, kissing the inside of it, sliding two fingers toward her opening, slowly, teasing, tempting. I loved feeling her come apart so fast, feeling her want me.

When I slid a finger inside her, she bucked her hips, nearly slamming into me. I nipped at her clit, working her up slowly, savoring every second.

She came spectacularly, arching her back and gritting her teeth. She pressed her fingers against the wall so hard that I knew she was going to leave marks on it.

Pulling back, I rested on my haunches, one elbow on the bed, patting the mattress. She blushed furiously, drawing in deep breaths. I watched her intently as she lay down.

Her chest was moving up and down rapidly. I drew a finger from one nipple to the other, then back, teasing her. I wanted to bury myself inside her, but I also wanted to indulge in foreplay, explore every part of her.

I rose to my feet and kicked off my boxers before focusing on Heather again. Lying on the bed too, I kissed up her legs, alternating between biting and licking all that smooth skin.

Aligning our hips, I drew my cock from her clit all the way down to her entrance. She gasped, rolling her hips. I slid inside her the next second, and nearly came.

"Fuck, fuck, fuck," I groaned. Her inner muscles still pulsed from her last orgasm; her nerve endings were still sensitive.

I moved in and out, pushing up on my elbows so I could watch her, drink in the way her expression changed—from chasing pleasure to being overwhelmed by it.

The second she surrendered to her second orgasm, every muscle in my body burned and tightened, but I didn't want to let go just yet.

Straightening up, I hooked my forearms under her knees, pulling her toward me. I wanted her at this angle, where I had a perfect view of her breasts bouncing with every thrust. She rode out her wave of pleasure until she was spent, barely able to meet my movements. Smiling, she clenched her inner muscles.

Fuck.

My hips shot forward. Pleasure blindsided me, licking up my spine, spreading to my limbs. I wasn't in control of my body anymore. I'd never felt anything like it.

"Fuuuck, Heather."

I stopped midthrust, the breath knocked out of me, and fought for a lungful of air. When she clenched her inner muscles again, I gave in to my orgasm, losing myself in this woman completely.

I wanted to stay entwined like this, but knew I was crushing her with the weight of my body, so I shifted a few inches to the right.

She rolled on her side, making room for me. I

lay down on my side too, facing her.

She grinned. "Watch it. Don't scoot too far back, or you'll fall out of bed."

I laughed, moving closer until our fronts were touching. I hooked her upper thigh on top of me.

"Speechless, are you?" she teased, running one finger from the corner of my mouth down my neck. Her skin was damp, her hair clung to the back of her neck and temples, but she was right, I was even more out of sorts than she was. Time to change that.

I rolled her on top of me, chuckling when she yelped.

"What's this for?" she asked, bracing her palms on my chest.

She was grinning. I wiggled my eyebrows. "I'll show you speechless."

Chapter Thirty-One
Heather

On Sunday evening, Ryker and I returned to New York. Avery was coming tomorrow with Mom, who'd decided to spend the whole week here.

"I have an idea," Ryker said as he pulled out his phone to order an Uber.

I grinned. "Oh, yeah?"

"Spend the night at my apartment."

"Why did I know you were going to ask me that?" I teased.

By way of answering, he just wiggled his eyebrows. I was still racking my brain for ways to make him tell me what he and Avery had talked about. They'd exchanged secret glances in Arizona , but I couldn't get anything out of her, hard as I tried.

As soon as we stepped inside his apartment, all my worries slammed back into me. I hadn't told him yet about my issue with the landlord, because he honestly had enough on his plate and I didn't want to add to that. I could still stay in my apartment until the end of the month, but that was it. I just had to figure something out. I always managed to come out ahead.

Aside from the office issues, there was a new

gala coming up in three weeks, and he had plenty to do.

"How's the gala coming along?"

"I'm going there tomorrow evening, meeting with the moderator." A few seconds later, he added, "Want to come with me?"

"When? Mom and Avery arrive at seven."

"Before that."

I grinned. "Sure. That would be fun."

Ryker grinned back. "You're looking for any excuse to be at the ballroom."

"Just like you use every trick in the book to get me here. We all have our weaknesses."

"True," he said, sitting on the couch, already opening his laptop. I curled up next to him, yawning. I had no idea how he still had energy to prepare for tomorrow. All I wanted to do was go to sleep. The weekend had been great, but I didn't really get a chance to rest. Despite tomorrow being Memorial Day, Ryker still had to go to the office.

"Holy fuck. Owen was fired."

I straightened up. "What? On what grounds?"

"Apparently senior management considered him reaching out to Dawson a bad idea, just like we did."

Ryker was silent then as he started reading his emails. I wondered if that would have any implications for him and what they could be. I kept watching him, admiring the calm and collected way in which he dealt with difficult situations.

"I can feel you watching me," he said

playfully.

"What? You're smoking hot when you're all focused like this."

Chuckling, he shut off his laptop, placing it to the side, turning to me. Before I realized what he intended, he awkwardly pulled me toward him and I climbed onto his lap.

"Stay here tomorrow too?" he asked.

"Yes, sir. On second thought... why were you and Avery exchanging all those secret glances in Arizona?"

Ryker laughed, feathering his fingers around my ankles. "Are you trying to negotiate, love?"

"Yes. Is it working?"

Smiling devilishly, he moved both hands all the way up under my skirt.

"No, but you have all night to keep trying."

***

The next morning, Ryker left the apartment early, but I slept in until eight. I had two articles to work on but had more than enough time to finish them.

I was making myself a coffee at Ryker's fancy machine when Danielle called.

"Morning," I greeted.

"Hey! So, I have some news for you. I don't know if you're aware, but Owen was fired from Pearman. Apparently there was some disagreement there with management, I don't know the details, but that changed *our* management's perspective."

"I've heard." I didn't want to share anything else, since Ryker told me everything in confidence.

"Anyway, I spoke with our higher-ups again, and they've decided to publish your article after all, but they want you to rework it a little, include Owen's departure and emphasize how Dawson's article played a role in it."

Holy shit. I was suddenly bursting with energy and hadn't even touched my coffee.

"Sure! I'll get on with that right away."

"You're also getting your bonus. Finally made them sign that. It's there, in black and white."

"Thank you, thank you, thank you."

My mind was already spinning with ways to weave the recent developments in the existing piece I'd written.

As soon as I ended the call, I texted Ryker to tell him the good news.

Ryker: Sounds like we have a lot to celebrate tonight.

My fingertips tingled as I typed back. Something was telling me that my man had a plan... and it went beyond just finalizing the gala preparations.

Heather: I'm all yours.
Ryker: Music to my ears.

A huge weight had lifted off my shoulders, because this meant I could finally persuade my landlord not to evict me.

I got to work right away, rewriting sections of the article, not even bothering to take a shower until I realized it was four o'clock. Holy shit! Ryker was going to arrive any second now. We were going to the ballroom together.

I showered quickly, putting on the clothes I'd traveled in yesterday.

I heard the front door open just as I finished my makeup.

"I'm ready, I'm ready!" I exclaimed, running to the foyer.

"I'm a little late, so you'd better be ready."

I checked the time on the wall clock. "Holy shit, you're a lot late."

"Had an errand to run," he said vaguely. "I see you're in a great mood."

"Well, yes I am. I'm super happy with the way the article is coming along. Danielle also said I'm getting my bonus earlier as well." And since things had settled for him at the office and I was handling things with my landlord, I decided to share that with him too. "I was a little stressed out when they'd told me they weren't going to publish the piece, because I knew I'd be evicted without that additional money. But now I can send him confirmation of my income so that should put his mind at ease. Anyway, I'm sure it'll all work out."

Ryker looked at me with a confused and dark expression.

"Why didn't you tell me this before?" He actually sounded a bit hurt that I didn't share it with him, and it made me feel a little uneasy. I should have told him before now, it was silly of me really, but I hadn't wanted to burden him with everything else he had going on.

"Well, I thought you had enough to deal with already, and anyway, now it's all cleared up."

If I thought this was going to appease him, damn was I wrong. If anything, his expression turned even darker. He stalked toward me until he was right in front of me, nearly pressing me into the shelves.

"Heather, we need to talk."

"Okay."

"I don't want you to do this. Doesn't matter if I have a deadline, shit hits the fan in the family, or anything else. You still tell me, okay? We're in this together. I want to be there for you to help you whenever I can."

"O-okay."

"You and Avery are... you're family. But I can't be there for you if I don't know what's happening."

I nodded, because he made perfect sense, of course.

"Move in with me. Cancel the lease."

"Oh!"

I swallowed hard, trying to find the right words. I'd clung so much to the idea of providing a stable home to my girl in our apartment, that I hadn't even dared to dream about what it would be like living with Ryker as a family.

"Trust me, Heather. To make you and Avery

happy. Make this a home with me."

My heart swelled; I swear I could feel it expanding in my chest. I couldn't find any words at all, let alone the right ones, so I simply nodded.

Ryker's smile widened even more. I calmed down just from feeling the warmth of his body, the possessive way he touched my face. I felt centered again. *He* was my center.

"I'll call my whole family to help with packing... and we'll bring your stuff to my place."

Oh my God. I fought the silly impulse to press my palms against my chest, but I really felt as if I might just burst from so much joy.

I couldn't believe that he wanted to intertwine our lives so deeply, that he wanted both of us to be such an integral part of his life.

"Between you and me, I think Avery's going to be psyched. She loves my place."

I scoffed, playfully rolling my eyes. *Duh*, of course Avery loved it. *I* was psyched too.

"Shouldn't we go to the ballroom? Otherwise we'll miss the moderator," I said.

"Yes, you're right." He straightened up, as if he'd suddenly remembered something. Dropping his hand from my face, he took a step back. "Let's go."

"I don't think I'll ever have enough of these events," I said once we arrived at the venue, looking around with a smile. A wedding had taken place over the weekend, and a group of men were rearranging the tables. The moderator of the next event, a woman in her forties, waved to Ryker. After he introduced me to her, they started talking about the order of speeches. I volunteered to guide the men setting things up according to the chart lying on one of the tables, since every gala had its own seating arrangement.

I felt Ryker throw me sizzling looks every now and then but kept my composure, even though I was blushing madly. But when he surprised me by appearing behind me and kissing the side of my neck, my entire body turned to goose bumps. Hot damn.

"The moderator just left. I'll help with the table coordination," he said just as he let me go. Something tugged at the pocket of my dress. When I touched it, I realized there was a note half-stuffed inside.

Had Ryker just put it there?

"Ryker!" I called out after him. He looked at me over his shoulder, but merely mouthed "*Later.*" What?

I felt giddy, and instead of finishing assisting with the table placement, I slipped behind a partition in one corner, where the audio equipment was hidden. My stomach was full of butterflies as I opened the note.

Meet me in the room upstairs, behind the red curtain, after everyone's gone.

My pulse quickened, thumping in my ears. I remembered the last time he'd given me a note like this. I'd gone there expecting a kiss, perhaps, and I hadn't come out the same. What should I expect this time?

What could he possibly tell me that couldn't wait until we were home?

That question bounced in my mind for the remaining hour. I became more nervous with every passing minute, especially once everyone left.

If I didn't know Ryker was meeting me behind the curtain, I would have thought I was completely alone.

I crossed the empty ballroom with quick strides, barely keeping myself from breaking into a run. I was smiling from ear to ear. My heartbeat was so erratic that I felt light-headed.

When I entered the changing room, Ryker was already there, leaning against a wall, smiling widely.

"Hi! What are we doing here?" Oh God, why was my voice so throaty?

"Come closer." His tone was playful, but his gaze was so intense that I instantly felt the air between us charge.

"Tell me, first."

He said nothing, but he walked toward me until we were close enough to touch. He brought a hand to my face, caressing my cheek.

"Remember the first time I asked you here?" he asked softly.

I nodded.

"What did you think I wanted?"

"Something you couldn't do with everyone watching," I teased. Ryker laughed, sounding so happy that it warmed me on the inside. "What do you think I have in mind now?"

"Better not be sexy times," I warned. Ryker grinned.

"No, not quite."

He skimmed his fingers down my arm, taking both my hands in his.

"I'll be honest. When I asked you to come here last time, I didn't have a plan. I just knew that I wanted to be near you any way I could, for as long as I could. But now... now I have a plan."

"You do?"

He nodded, tightening his grip on my hands.

"I've thought about where to do this for weeks. First I thought about taking you to a restaurant, or on a trip, but then I figured... why not do it here? It's where I first realized that I wanted to do whatever it took to win you over. This place means something to both of us." He interlaced our fingers, squeezing them lightly before letting go of my left hand. He reached inside his jacket. I didn't see what he took out, because he was holding it in his closed fist. What was going on?

He opened his hand slowly, and my heart all but exploded. He was holding an engagement ring! The most beautiful one I'd ever seen. It had a round diamond in the center with tiny green gemstones around it.

"Marry me, Heather Prescott. Be my wife.

You, Avery, and I are already a family, but I want to make it official. I want everyone to know that both of you are mine."

I had never felt overwhelmed by so many emotions in a matter of seconds.

I put my arms around his neck, going up on my tiptoes and kissing him. I'd intended a light smooch only, but the second I touched my lips to his, I became ravenous... and so was he.

Ryker kissed me so deliciously well that I just wanted to melt against him. I felt him put one palm at the small of my back, pressing me into him until I was flat against his chest... and still he kept pressing. I loved the possessive touch, the nearly desperate way he was claiming my mouth. I'd been on edge this past hour, but it was nothing compared to how I felt now—completely wrapped up in Ryker. When I ran a hand through his hair, lightly tugging at it, I felt him smile against my mouth.

"That counts as yes?" he asked, pulling back, smiling from ear to ear.

"What do you think?"

I looked between us when he took my left hand in his. He slid the ring on before interlacing our hands again, just holding them tight. This felt surreal. I wanted to find the right words to tell him how happy I was, but I couldn't form any words at all. Ryker didn't seem to share my predicament.

"I love you, Heather. I can't wait for us to be a team. A family. Every day, when you wake up, I want you to look at our life together and smile. I'll make sure of that."

Oh goodness, why was he saying all these sweet things? I'd just discovered they were my kryptonite.

"And how?" I asked playfully, determined *not* to become misty eyed.

Ryker let go of my hands, cupping my face.

"You'll see. You don't have to know everything right away."

"Ah, so one of your tactics is to always keep me guessing?" I was grinning now.

"One of my *many* tactics."

"In that case, I'm promising the same in return. Not the guessing part. The smiling part."

He kept cradling my face, and something told me he wasn't done making me swoon.

"Whatever you want, you name it, I'll get it for you. Do it for you. I'll be there for everything. The busy days, late nights. Shopping trips for which I still have to sharpen my negotiation skills. When you have a deadline, I'll be there pushing you toward the finish line... celebrating after it. When you're too stressed, I'll help you relax."

"I think I know how you plan to do that."

He gripped my waist possessively before skimming one hand down to my hip, pressing his fingers on my skin. I licked my lower lip. His eyes flashed.

I traced my hand over his chest slowly, loving the way his grip on me tightened, as if he was barely hanging in there. The passion was always there, simmering just under the surface.

"I promise that I'll give in every time," I said with a wiggle of my eyebrows. "And *pretend* to be surprised."

He pinched my ass. I yelped, in turn pinching *his* arm. When I realized he was about to retaliate, I took a huge step back.

"Okay, okay, I didn't really mean that. You're quite good at surprises. And promises." On a sigh, I added, "How can I keep up? Oh, I know! I promise I'll always be up for anything from getting down and dirty to generally just taking care of you," I finished.

Ryker's eyes were full of happiness. I'd had no idea that you could feel joy like a physical force inside you. Only now, I felt as if there was so much of it that it couldn't possibly fit inside me.

"Define up for anything," he said playfully. "Does it include naughty trips to my office or sneaking behind the red curtain during galas?"

"That's a *no* on both counts," I said seriously.

"We'll see about that."

I laughed, stepping closer again, touching his jaw, tracing his lips with my fingers, because apparently I couldn't keep my hands off him for even one full minute. I just loved feeling him against me. Bringing a hand to the back of my head, he pulled me into a kiss. It was different than the one before. Hotter, even more urgent. As if in a haze, I realized we were moving through the room. I almost stumbled, and blindly reached a hand backward—there was a wall here somewhere—but Ryker was ahead of me. He'd braced one hand against the wall, pushing me against it with his hips. He needed a hard surface for leverage so he could kiss and touch me the way he wanted to. The realization sent a wave of heat through me. I rose on my toes, needing leverage of my own.

"What are you thinking about?" I asked.

"How to seduce my fiancée tonight."

"And what are the options? Your fiancée would like to weigh in."

"Does she now?"

"Oh, yeah."

"Well, then. Can't deny my fiancée's first wish, can I?"

***

"This is an engagement ring," I told Avery later that evening, after we picked up her and Mom from the airport. I was a little nervous but a lot excited to tell my little girl about our plans. We were at our apartment, and Mom had slipped out of the living room to give Ryker and me some privacy with Avery. I'd told her on the phone about the engagement, because I just couldn't hold back, but asked her to keep it a secret from Avery.

"What's an *engagement*?" Avery asked, wide-eyed.

"It's like a promise," Ryker explained. "Your mom and I are promising to each other that we're going to always be together."

"We're getting married," I said. Her mouth formed that adorable O, where her cheeks also went hollow from the effort.

"You're going to be a bride, Mommy?"

"Yes. And we're also going to move in with Ryker."

"Ohh, so I can always play in my big room." She turned to look at Ryker, speaking in a loud whisper. "Can we tell her now?"

Ryker grinned. "Yes, we can."

"Tell me what?" These two. I'd known something was up ever since we'd left Phoenix.

Avery straightened up. "I asked Ryker to be my dad. And he said yes."

I blinked, sure I'd misheard her, then quickly looked away so she couldn't see that I had misty eyes.

"And you will not just be my dad, but also Mom's *hubband*?"

"Yes," Ryker said.

"Can I get a ring too? So we can also promise to always be together?" Avery asked.

Ryker smiled warmly at her. I reached for his hand behind Avery's back, squeezing it lightly.

"Sure. We can go buy a ring whenever you want. Or a necklace if you want. Or a bracelet."

Oh, damn. They were going to buy half the store; I was sure of that. But they both already looked so excited that I promised myself I would just let them have their fun this time.

When Avery yawned, I pointed a finger at her. "Bedtime, Avery."

Avery's expression was mutinous, but then she yawned again.

"Come on, off we go," I insisted.

After taking care of Avery's bedtime routine, Ryker and I snuck to my tiny room.

"I can't wait to move to your apartment. It's so big, and I love that it's on two floors," I said when we were almost at my bed. Ryker laughed, putting an arm around my waist, walking in tandem with me.

"You just pointed out my two favorite things about it."

Chapter Thirty-Two
Heather

The following Saturday, I woke up before Ryker and just stared at my ring for a few minutes. The past week had been a bit of a whirlwind.

I gave notice to my landlord and started packing. Mom helped until she returned to Phoenix yesterday. Moving day was in two weeks. Ryker being Ryker had decided to pay the rent for another month so I wouldn't have to pack in a hurry.

Ryker stirred soon after, blindly putting his hand over my shoulder. I loved that his first instinct was to reach for my side of the bed, check to see if I was still here. I pulled back a little, teasing him. He stretched toward me even further, only stopping when his fingers grazed my thigh. Then he blinked both eyes open. Groggy with sleep as he was, he smiled at me.

"Morning," he said. "Is it late?"

"Nah, I just woke up early."

He turned on one side, watching me intently. "You're smiling. Why?"

"You were cute, trying to fondle me even in your sleep."

"Hey, I'm an honest man. I want what I want."

Yawning, I got out of bed. In a fraction of a second, Ryker was up too and trapped me between his body and the door. Damn, he was fast.

"What are you doing?"

"Not letting you go until you admit that you were teasing me on purpose."

"You just woke up two minutes ago. How are you so good at blackmailing me already?"

He kissed the side of my neck, laughing. "You inspire me."

"Oh, I see. So I brought this upon myself?"

He pulled back, cocking a brow. "You say that like it's a hardship."

I wiggled my ass, parting my thighs so I could accommodate him more easily.

"It can be."

"You did *not* say that."

"I did. Whatcha gonna do about it?"

His eyes flashed, before he whirled me around, putting my palms up against the door above my head, holding them tight.

I swallowed, exhaling sharply. I was *not* expecting that. Where my instincts were slow and groggy in the morning, he was already quick and alert.

He kissed along the back of my neck, first only skimming his lips, then teasing me with the tip of his tongue. My whole body reacted to his attentions. Letting go of my hands, he moved his mouth lower, tracing a straight line of kisses down my back. At the same time, he skimmed his hands over the sides of my breasts, down to my hips.

Oh, wow. There had to be a rule against

getting me so hot and bothered this early in the morning. How was I supposed to resist his charm for the rest of the day? Oh wait, I didn't want to do that.

One hour later, the two of us and Avery walked into Tiffany's.

"We're looking for a ring for this little lady," Ryker told the sales assistant. I was in heaven, admiring the sparkly displays... right until I saw the price tags. Wow! Everything had one digit more than I imagined even in my wildest dreams. How much had Ryker spent on my ring? And now on another one for Avery?

"Yes, an *ekagenment* ring, like Mommy's. That means we will all be together for all times. Until Mommy and Daddy are really old."

"We can even put it on a necklace," I said. "That way you can also wear it after you outgrow it." I actually had a more practical reason in mind, minimizing Avery's risk of losing the ring.

"I have a better idea," the woman said, clearly able to read my panicked expression. She reached for a drawer under the counter, pulling out a selection that was clearly for children. The price tags were also more reasonable.

"Would you like a necklace with a pendant in the form of an infinity knot?" she asked Avery.

"It looks like a bow," Avery said skeptically.

"Yes, exactly. You know what infinity means? For all times."

Ryker and I were content to watch them go

back and forth over several options. He put a hand on the back of my neck, keeping me so close that my breast squished against his chest. I barely kept from grinning when he moved that hand a little lower.

"Why are you smiling like that?" he asked. Ah, I'd kept my grin at bay, but not a smile.

"I was wondering how long it would take you until your hand started... wandering." I spoke in a low voice, even though there was so much commotion in the store that there were zero chances of being overheard.

"And?"

"You lasted seven minutes since we came in," I informed him.

"That's five more minutes than I expected."

"Love that you're not even pretending."

"Should I?"

"Nah, I quite like knowing that you can't resist me."

He laughed, just as Avery turned around, proudly pointing to the infinity pendant the sales assistant had hung around her neck. Her smile was so huge, it was obvious she'd fallen head over heels for it.

"We're taking it," Ryker said to the sales assistant. Avery squealed when he paid.

"Thanks for doing this," I whispered as we left the store.

"I love making our girl happy." *Our girl*. Oh, heavens. I didn't think I'd ever swooned *quite* this much. And when he kissed my forehead, taking my hand as we walked out of the store, I knew that he wasn't anywhere near done.

Epilogue
Heather
Two weeks later

"I'll have refreshments ready right away," I announced, just as I filled the last glass with lemonade. Tess, Skye, Cole, Hunter, and Josie were here, helping me move. Josie's siblings, Ian, Dylan, and Isabelle were also here. They'd come in to see their sister and attended the Ballroom Gala on Friday. When they got wind of the fact that I was moving today, they offered to give up their Sunday to help too, so we made a party out of it.

The three of them were arriving in a different Uber with the last few boxes, but everyone else was sitting in the living room, exhausted though still chatty as usual. Amelia had taken Avery out for ice cream, something my little girl couldn't refuse.

I put the tray with glasses on the coffee table in front of the couch before sitting next to Ryker. Or well... *on* Ryker too, at least with one butt cheek. But hey, I had a great excuse, as we all sat close together on the couch. Ryker's playful gaze clued me in that he was on to me, but I wasn't going to make any apologies for my behavior. Not that he seemed to mind. In fact, he was taking advantage of the crammed sitting situation too, touching me *a lot*.

"This was a very productive day," Tess exclaimed.

"I never thought we'd get everything done so quickly. Thank you so much for helping. How can I make it up to all of you?" I beamed, looking around. I loved this loft so much. It was just *so* bright. No matter where you were in the room, you had plenty of light and an amazing view. I couldn't believe my life had changed so much since March. It was mid-June now, but I felt as if a lifetime had passed since I met Ryker.

"Don't mention it," Cole said. "On second thought... I'm going to cash in on that later. Never know when I'm going to need an ally."

"Against whom?" I asked. I was slowly starting to understand what Ryker meant with getting as many members on your side as possible being a survival strategy in the group.

"Don't know yet, hence why I'm cashing in later."

I raised my glass of orange juice in a mock toast. "Got it."

"Tess and I are less demanding than our little brother," Skye said. "We just want more of this amazing lemonade."

"Perfect."

"A word of warning," Ryker said. "Don't say yes so quickly every time... it's a surefire way to get into trouble with this group."

That hand on my lower back slid *even lower*.

"I think I can handle this lot." I looked him straight in the eye, trying to convey that I could handle *him* too, only I couldn't, really. All it took was for him to be this close, and I was already done for. I was pretty sure it was written all over my face, because Ryker smiled brilliantly. I loved being surrounded by this group. Watching Skye and Tess work so tirelessly for their store had rubbed off on me. Between that and Ryker's encouragements, I'd started working on that book I'd always wanted to write. I could tinker with it whenever I had some time in between assignments.

My Pearman article had been published at the start of the week, and let's just say, it hit the mark.

"We need to go back to the store," Skye said, yawning. "Our sales assistant's shift ends in one hour."

I shifted in my spot, looking at her and Tess. This was the right moment for me to put *the plan* in motion. We'd started brainstorming ways to help Skye and Tess while they were going through this rough period. They were no longer looking for an investor, because they'd decided to postpone their expansion projects. But they had their hands full trying to put out the fires that had escalated because their last investor pulled out at the last minute.

"I've had an idea," I said. "Since I'm now living a stone's throw away from your store... I could help out sometimes. Say, Saturday afternoons? Your mom said she'd love to spend that time with Avery."

Tess tilted her head, assessing me. "And let

me guess, since you and Ryker are inseparable, he'll join you too?"

Damn, they caught on fast. Ryker had warned me they would, but I'd thought that if *I* was the one who voiced the idea, we stood a better chance.

"Why not?" I said. "It's something fun for us to do, a change from our regular jobs."

Skye tapped her chin. "I'm trying to picture Ryker in the store. He'll scare the clientele away."

I held up a finger. "Already thought of that. He'll be in the back office most of the time, doing whatever you girls don't get to do during the week. Something you can delegate, obviously."

"Well, Tess... this is the chance we've waited for—we can boss him around again like when we were kids," Skye said.

Ryker's eyes bulged. "Talk about an unexpected angle."

Tess focused on Hunter, Josie, and Cole, who'd been silent during this whole exchange.

"And let me guess... the three of you would alternate on Sundays?" Tess asked.

Damn! This was scarily accurate. How was this even possible?

Cole shook his head. "Told you they'd catch on to the plan, Heather."

Eh... it was more a conspiracy than a plan, but I was getting the hang of this conspiring thing and absolutely *loved* it.

Hunter cleared his throat. "This might be a good time to mention that Amelia's in on this too."

Skye elbowed her sister. "If everyone's telling us the same thing, it's a sign, sis."

"That's what I always say," Josie piped up. "If more people tell you the same thing... it's time to listen."

Tess shook her head, but she was smiling. Finally, she threw her hands up. "Okay, let's do this. Thank you. But we'll alternate weekends. I'm not negotiating that."

I clapped my hands once. "That's a great start."

"When did you get so good at this?" Tess asked me.

"I learned the art of charming from a certain someone." I nudged Ryker's arm with mine playfully. "You should have seen him winning my mom over. I mean... I didn't actually see it happen, only the end result. Very impressive." Feeling feisty, I turned to Cole. "Careful, or Ryker might steal away your thunder as the *Charmer*."

"Charming is a basic skill. *Flirting* is the extra," Ryker said in such a serious tone, you'd think he was explaining a scientific discovery.

Cole smirked. "Keep telling yourself that, bro. If it makes you feel better."

I felt compelled to take Ryker's side.

"Well, I didn't think Mom could be charmed *that* fast, so he's definitely a pro."

Cole groaned. "I see this ally thing won't work when it comes to Ryker."

Before I had a chance to answer, Ryker said,

"Of course not." Then he brought a hand to my neck, possibly intending to push my hair to one side, but he touched a ticklish spot. I covered my mouth with one hand, but my half laugh, half shriek still echoed in the living room. Everyone burst out laughing. Just then, Dylan, Ian, and Isabelle arrived, placing the small boxes they'd brought by the entrance door.

"By the way, have the raffle tickets been counted?" Ian asked. "Just saying, but I think I raked in the most."

Dylan smirked. "No, you didn't."

"What would your lovely girlfriend say about your evening?" Ian asked.

Dylan's girlfriend hadn't been able to attend.

"I was dancing, not flirting. She's proud that I was by far the most popular."

Isabelle rolled her eyes. "Stop being so full of yourselves. Cole was by far more popular."

Cole looked very pleased that Isabelle was taking his side. As did Ryker, happy that someone was giving Cole a run for his money.

"Even if you did rake in the most tickets, it's beginner's luck," Cole said. Ah, someone loved to have the last word. However, I loved that they brought up last night. Tess and I exchanged a glance.

Yeah, I was on a double mission today. I'd teamed up with Tess this time. Our goal? Check if Skye was out of the funk she'd been in since her breakup.

"Skye, I'm surprised you're not tired from

dancing," I said.

"Nah, I had a great partner."

"Yeah, he did seem to know what he was doing," Tess said. "You seemed to be having fun with him."

"He asked for my number, but I politely declined," she said.

Well, crap. So she was still in a funk. Tess and I had to up our game and cheer her up.

We chatted for a few more minutes, but then Tess and Skye had to leave for the store or they'd be late. They promised to make a list of tasks they could delegate as soon as possible.

Hunter, Josie, and her siblings left with Tess and Skye. Cole stayed for a while longer, helping us move some boxes we'd left askew at the front door.

"Thank God, Skye was on our side on the store issue," I said afterward, as Cole was preparing to leave. He winked, throwing his jacket over one shoulder. Ryker opened the door for him.

"I might have softened her up a bit before," Cole said.

"Oh, wow," I exclaimed.

"What did I tell you about getting others on your team *before* making the actual move?" Ryker asked.

Ohhh... *now* I understood what he'd meant. Seemed I still had a lot to learn in the fine art of conspiring.

"Well, I take back what I said about Ryker stealing your thunder. You definitely deserve your nickname, Cole."

Ryker cocked a brow.

"What? It's harder to win Skye over than my mom," I reasoned. Cole laughed, giving me a thumbs-up before leaving.

As soon as Ryker closed the door, the air between us charged.

"So!" he said.

"So," I replied, grinning. A smile played on his lips. His eyes glinted.

"You're gonna give me shit about what I just said?"

"I have a better idea, now that we're finally alone."

"Oh, okay."

He stalked toward me with strong, determined strides. On instinct, I walked back... but didn't make it very far. I bumped into the huge dresser in the hallway. Ryker came closer still, until he practically pinned me against the furniture. He touched my lips with two fingers, slowly, as if trying to decide what to do next.

Damn. Feeling his hips pressing against mine and his fingers on my mouth was already messing with my senses. A light shiver coursed through me. I was expecting him to kiss me... instead, he lifted me up, throwing me over his shoulder.

I covered my mouth with one hand again, trying to stifle my yelp.

"What are you doing?" I whispered, first patting his back, then realizing his ass was within reach too.

"Taking you to the couch. We need to set a few things straight."

"And we have to be on the couch for that?"

"Damn right we do."

I kept silent while he carried me to the living room, laying me on the couch. I grinned, stretching out as much as possible.

"Oh, you wanted to lie next to me?" I teased. "I don't think you'll fit."

Ryker's gaze smoldered. He pressed one knee on the edge of the couch, leaning forward, bracing his palms on either side of my head.

"No, actually. I planned to be on top all along." His grin was devilish. I squirmed as heat curled through me, and he wasn't even touching me.

"Of course you did." I placed my palms at either side of his face, lifting my head and touching my lips to his lightly. I just needed the contact. I couldn't even explain why.

Ryker's eyes widened, but he didn't attempt to take over the kiss. I bit his lower lip playfully before pushing myself up on one elbow and deepening the kiss. I loved having him so close, being able to just touch him as much as I wanted. I ran my hand from his shoulder down across his chest in a straight line, enjoying the way his breathing changed, becoming quicker the lower I went.

When I reached his belt buckle, I dropped my hand completely to the side, laying my head back on the couch. There was *so* much heat in his eyes. Ryker cupped my breasts over the fabric, but even so, my nipples hardened. On reflex, I rolled my hips forward. He positioned himself on the couch so that his mouth hovered over my belly before pushing my shirt up, tracing a circle with his mouth around my navel. Then he moved up my belly in a slow motion. I swear, the nerve endings in my entire body were wired to the spot he was kissing. He stopped right before reaching my bra, shifting his position until we were face-to-face.

I smiled. His eyes flashed.

"So... about those things you wanted to clear up?" I reminded him. "Those things you needed a couch for?"

"I forgot."

"What? How is that possible?"

"You distracted me."

"Do you at least remember where the couch came into play?"

He didn't miss a beat. "Yeah. You're more agreeable when you're underneath me."

I burst out laughing, placing my palms on his shoulder blades, pulling him even closer.

"Points for figuring that out."

"Thanks for helping out with my sisters. I love that you care about my family so much," he murmured.

"You're a great group." And I planned to help out every chance I got. I knew how important it was to him, and it was to me too, because I just adored his family.

"I'm happy you think so."

"Now that we have the apartment to ourselves, what shall we do?" I asked.

"How about a tour of the place?"

"Why?"

He dropped his gaze to my mouth before snapping it back up.

"Oooh... a sexy tour. I'm on board with that," I said.

Ryker climbed off of the couch, holding his hand out for me, helping me to my feet as well. Then he whirled me around, hugging me from behind, walking in tandem with me. It was a bit ridiculous, but I loved it anyway.

Was it just a few weeks ago that we'd brought in things for Avery so she could have a room here? I'd still had some fears back then, but now, I looked forward to our life together. I mean, I couldn't imagine *not loving* anything coming from Ryker.

On one hand, things happened so fast, but on the other, things could never be more right. Ryker and his family accepted Avery and me like we were already part of it.

"What are you thinking about?" he asked.

"Sorry, can't tell you."

"What do you mean, you can't tell me?"

"Well, let's put it this way, if I do, you'll forever have too much power over me." If he realized that I was more agreeable when he held me captive underneath him, I couldn't even imagine what he'd do with this information.

"It's a good thing we have the whole day to ourselves," he said. "I'll get it out of you eventually."

"I have no doubt, but I love to see you try your best."

As he led me upstairs, my phone vibrated in my pocket. Taking it out, I discovered a message from Tess.

Tess: Skye and I are going to the Guggenheim this evening. Want to join us?

Heather: Is this part of the get-Skye-out-of-her-funk operation?

Tess: Hell, yes.

Heather: I'm in.

I slipped the phone right back in my pocket, focusing on Ryker. I loved my new life, and was excited for everything it had in store, from sexy times with this gorgeous man right down to conspiring with his family.

***

The end

***

Other Books by Layla Hagen

The Bennett Family Series

Book 1: Your Irresistible Love
Book 2: Your Captivating Love
Book 3: Your Forever Love
Book 4: Your Inescapable Love
Book 5: Your Tempting Love
Book 6: Your Alluring Love
Book 7: Your Fierce Love
Book 8: Your One True Love
Book 9: Your Endless Love

The Connor Family Series

Book 1: Anything For You
Book 2: Wild With You
Book 3: Meant For You
Book 4: Only With You
Book 5: Fighting For You
Book 6: Always With You

The Lost Series

Book 1: Lost in Us
Book 2: Found in Us
Book 3: Caught in Us

Standalone

Withering Hope

JUST ONE KISS

Made in the USA
Monee, IL
26 April 2020